# Hate

# Like You

# Mean It

Gabe and Renée – Summer Lake Book Seven

SJ McCoy

A Sweet n Steamy Romance

Published by Xenion, Inc

Copyright © 2015 SJ McCoy

Smile Like You Mean It Copyright © SJ McCoy 2015

All rights reserved. Except as permitted under the U.S. Copyright Act of 1976, no part of this publication may be reproduced, distributed, or transmitted in any form, or by any means, or stored in a database or retrieval system without prior written consent of the author.

Published by Xenion, Inc.
First Paperback edition 2017
www.sjmccoy.com

This book is a work of fiction. Names, characters, places, and events are figments of the author's imagination, fictitious, or are used fictitiously. Any resemblance to actual events, locales or persons living or dead is coincidental.

Cover Design by Dana Lamothe of Designs by Dana
Editor: Mitzi Pummer Carroll
Proofreader: Aileen Blomberg

ISBN 978-1-946220-15-8

# *Dedication*

*For Sam. Sometimes life really is too short. Few xxx*

# Chapter One

Gabe shut down his computer and stared at the blank screen for a few moments, wondering why he felt nothing. In the early days he used to feel a huge sense of elation when a case settled before going to trial. Admittedly, it meant he missed out on a showdown with the defense in court, but a settlement meant he'd beaten them before ever getting into the arena. He hadn't felt elated about anything in a long time though—it seemed he rarely felt anything at all. He pressed his fingers into his temple. Perhaps that wasn't true, he felt impatient to get out of here. Impatient to get to JFK and onto the plane that would take him back to California.

He'd been spending as many weekends as he could back in Summer Lake recently. He couldn't explain why, but the little town where he'd grown up was drawing him back like a magnet. As soon as he was certain that the Carradon case was going to settle, he'd changed his flight so he could stay the whole week. Rosemary, his assistant, had stared at him in disbelief when he'd told her to change the reservation. He hadn't taken a whole week off in years. Well, things were changing. He didn't know why, but for weeks now he'd felt out of sorts. There was nothing wrong—nothing wrong with him, nothing wrong with the firm, with his life—but nothing was right either. Everything was running perfectly, yet none of it meant anything to him anymore. He'd told his brother, Michael, that he might be having an early midlife crisis. At the time he'd been joking, but he was starting to wonder whether it might be true.

He stood up and stretched. Whatever was going on with him, he had a whole week to figure it out. He looked around his office and stared out at the view of the river. It was time to trade Manhattan for his hometown. Perhaps going back to his roots would help him figure out where he wanted to go next.

He popped his head around Rosemary's door on his way to the elevator. "I'll see you a week from Monday then."

She smiled. "And I'll no doubt talk to you later."

Gabe nodded. He'd no doubt talk to her several times a day.

She held his gaze for a moment. "I'm quite capable of handling everything, you know. If you want a real break."

"I know you're capable. But we both know I'm not capable of taking a real break."

She smiled. "I have to say I'm impressed that you're taking a week. I hope you manage to relax. You never know, you might even enjoy yourself, have some fun."

He stared at her for a moment. Wouldn't that be something?

She shrugged. "You could start by trying out a smile."

He pursed his lips and shook his head at her.

She laughed. "Almost! I saw your lips twitch, that's a start. Your facial muscles may need some practice, but I'm sure you can get there."

He did smile at that.

"See! I knew you could do it!"

He laughed. "I'm not that bad, am I?"

Rosemary raised her eyebrows sternly. "No comment."

"In that case, I'll be on my way."

Her face softened. "Take care, Gabe. Please try to have a good time."

"Thanks. Take care of you, too."

It was going on midnight when he pulled into the driveway at his parents' house. He sat in the car a moment. Thirty-six years old and he was spending all his weekends staying with his parents—some success he was! Perhaps he should buy himself a place here. He pulled his bag from the back seat of the rental car and let himself in through the back door to the kitchen. He smiled when he saw his nephew sitting at the big table with a glass of milk and a packet of cookies in front of him.

"Hey, Uncle Gabe! Grandma said I wouldn't get to see you till morning."

Gabe plucked him from his chair and hugged him. "But Grandma didn't know that you'd be sneaking around raiding her cookies in the middle of night, did she?"

Ethan grinned and wrapped his arms around Gabe's neck. "Nope, and I know you're not going to tell her. My secret's safe with you, right?"

Gabe nodded. "It is."

Ethan looked at Gabe's bag. "Are you here to stay for a while? Are you going to start working in San Francisco like you said?"

"I'm staying for the week. I'm not sure what I'm going to do yet."

"I think you should just stay here. Did you know Auntie Kenzie's going to stay?"

"That's good news."

"It is, and if you stay, then I'll have all my family right here. I'd like that."

Gabe ruffled his hair. "I don't think I could move here if I wanted to."

"Why not? I told you Taylor's dad is a lawyer, he might give you a job."

"And I told you, I'm too much of a big-head to work for someone else. Besides, Taylor's dad practices family law. I'm a trial attorney."

"What difference does that make?"

Gabe thought for a moment how to explain it. Ethan was a smart kid, but he was only ten. "Family law is all about..."

"Yeah, I know divorces and people dying and stuff. You could do that, it would be easy for you after making big companies pay for hurting people."

Gabe stared at him. It really was that simple, wasn't it?

Ethan stared back. "Well, it would, wouldn't it?"

Gabe nodded. "Yeah, but I don't like easy. I get bored with easy. Easy is no fun."

"Grandma said she's worried that you never have any fun, so that wouldn't be any different, would it? And if you came here you could see me more, and we always have fun together."

Gabe considered that. It was true.

Ethan downed the last of his milk and wiped the cookie crumbs from around his mouth with the back of his pajama sleeve. "You look tired. You should go to bed."

Gabe laughed. "So should you."

Ethan grinned. "Come on then, but watch the second stair, it creaks. If you wake Grandma up you'll get us in trouble."

"You mean I'll get you in trouble."

"No, I mean us. Grandma won't be very pleased that you let me eat cookies in the middle of the night, will she?"

Gabe shook his head and pursed his lips.

Ethan grinned back at him. "I'll see you in the morning. Grandma said we can go to the bakery for doughnuts. Do you want me to bring you one back?"

Gabe was surprised to feel his pulse quicken. He wouldn't mind visiting the bakery himself, and Ethan would be the perfect excuse. "How about I take you and we give Grandma a break?"

"Awesome! You let me have more than she does."

"Just don't tell her that, okay?"

"Don't worry, your secret is safe with me, too."

~ ~ ~

Renée pushed her hair out of her eyes then grabbed for the handlebar again as the bicycle started to wobble. All she needed was to fall off the damned thing. Riding to work had seemed to be a better idea than walking, but then ideas and reality rarely matched up anymore—at least not in her world. She rounded the corner and applied the brakes; no way was she going to freewheel all the way down the hill to Main Street. Once upon a time she would have, but these days she felt as though she'd used up all her luck by relying on it too much. She needed to save any she had left for the big stuff, not trust it and use it up on dumb stuff like hoping she wouldn't break her neck hurtling down a hill on a dodgy old bike at four o'clock in the morning.

She dismounted and walked the bike down, remembering as she did all the times she'd gone flying down here as a kid. It would never have occurred to her then that she might fall and hurt herself. Even just a few months ago she wouldn't have thought twice about it. She hated that Eric's lies and deception had changed her. Stolen a part of her spirit it seemed. He'd taken so much—all their money, their home, their business, even her good name. She knew she'd come back from all of that with time. But that part of her, the girl who feared nothing, who found fun in everything? Renée shook her head. She couldn't let him kill that. That part of her lived on. That part of her had survived much worse, had survived the loss of her sister. How could she let Eric's betrayal be more important than Chloe's death? She wouldn't. Reaching the bottom of the hill she climbed back onto the bike and wobbled off down Main toward the resort. She was just recovering from the shock—that was all. She'd come back to Summer Lake because she hadn't known where else to go or what to do. At least here she was able to work, thanks to Ben, and she had a place to live. Her childhood home wasn't exactly a palace, it never had been. After standing empty for so many years it was barely livable, but it was all she had and she was making the most of it.

She let herself in through the back door of the bakery and breathed a sigh of relief. This place put her at ease—even though she had to get here so early and she worked her butt off the whole time she was here. The smells and sounds reminded her of her childhood and of her mom. It brought her a sense of comfort she hadn't felt in many years.

By five o'clock she had the first breads, muffins, and doughnuts laid out, and more in the ovens. She unlocked the front door and turned the sign. It was tough going, running the place by herself. Shelley had called in sick two weeks ago and yesterday she'd stopped by to say she wouldn't be coming back. Renée hoped that Ben would be able to find a replacement soon. Though even if he didn't she'd still rather be working here by herself than in the bar. She shuddered at the memory of her short lived career as a bar tender. She'd taken the job because it was the only one available, but having made a career out of educating about the dangers of alcohol, it hadn't sat well with her to make a living serving the stuff.

She looked up as the bell on the door tinkled.

"Emma!" She grinned as Emma Douglas came in looking half asleep. Emma Benson, Renée corrected herself at the sight of the gorgeous dark haired guy at Emma's side, her husband Jack.

Emma came around the counter to give her a hug. "Hey Renée. How do you do it? I didn't even know there were two five o'clocks in a day." She rubbed her eyes. "I won't be awake for at least two hours yet."

Renée laughed. "What I want to know is why you did it? What on earth are you doing here at this hour when you can bake any of this stuff yourself?"

"Em doesn't make doughnuts," said Jack.

Emma hung her head with a sheepish grin.

"So why didn't you just send your lovely hubby to get them for you?"

Renée didn't understand the look the two of them exchanged. She could see it was full of love and understanding though.

Jack wrapped an arm around Emma's shoulders. "It's a long story. Let's just say we made a deal a long time ago. When Em wants doughnuts, we both need to go."

"Fair enough, what can I get you?" Renée didn't need to know the story. What surprised her as she filled the box with a dozen doughnuts for them, was that she didn't even want to. It was so obvious that Emma and Jack were deeply in love. They understood each other, they had their little story and their knowledge and acceptance of one another. They had their own little world and were very happy in it. In the early days with Eric she'd hoped they would build that kind of relationship over time. They never had.

The doorbell brought her thoughts back to the bakery. She almost dropped the box when she saw him. Her heart leapt in her chest and she watched the box shake visibly as she handed it over to Emma. Gabe Morgan!

Green eyes met her own and held them for a moment. She felt like a deer in the headlights, confused, mesmerized. Fight and flight were both forgotten as she froze.

Emma tugged on the box which Renée hadn't let go of. "We need to get going." She put a twenty dollar bill on top of the counter and gave Renée a knowing smile. "Call me. We need to catch up."

Renée looked down at the money then up at Emma. "But that's…"

Emma winked and took Jack's hand as she turned away. "Just call me, okay?" She turned to Gabe. "Hi Gabe, bye Gabe."

Gabe nodded and watched them leave.

Renée tried to smooth her hair down with her hands. She knew it would be frizzing everywhere. Then she tugged at her apron, feeling self-conscious for some reason. Gabe turned his gaze back on her. How was it that he'd gotten sexier since high school? She'd been convinced he was the sexiest guy on earth then, now he was… She took a deep breath. Now he was a successful lawyer and even more serious and uptight than he'd been as a kid. Just because she hadn't had sex in forever didn't mean she should go lusting after her old high school crush. He was the success story, back here visiting family. She was the utter failure, back here trying to scrape together some semblance of a life.

"Good morning." She made herself sound bright, breezy, and businesslike. "What can I get you?"

For a moment his eyes turned a deep emerald green. If she let her imagination come up with an explanation, it would say that he knew she was shutting him out and it hurt him. But then she knew better than to let her imagination run wild!

He opened his mouth to reply, but didn't get the chance.

"Good morning, Miss Renée!" A small dark-haired head peered around from behind Gabe's butt. No. She couldn't let herself think about that butt.

Instead she smiled. "Hey Ethan. How are you today? I see you talked your uncle into bringing you this time."

Ethan shot Gabe a cheeky grin. "Actually, I think Uncle Gabe talked me into bringing him."

Renée was surprised to see a hint of red appear on Gabe's neck and ears. What was he embarrassed about? Looking him over, the answer was fairly obvious. With a body like that he probably considered cakes and pastries to be a sign of weakness or worse! She gave him a conspiratorial smile. "Don't worry. I won't tell a soul you were here."

Ethan cocked his head to one side with a puzzled look. Gabe stared at her, looking equally puzzled and possibly…hurt? She had no idea what his deal was. Good looking guys tended to be a mystery to her though. She needed to sell him some goodies and send them on their way—so she could get her heart rate and her temperature back down. And stop that overactive imagination of hers from getting carried away!

~ ~ ~

Gabe was relieved when Ethan started pointing out doughnuts, picking out a dozen of the gooeyest creations he could find. He watched Renée smile as she filled up the box for the little guy. What was it about her? Whenever he got around her he felt like a kid again. A kid who couldn't help blushing, couldn't find the right words—he adjusted his pants—and couldn't control his urges!

She'd grown into a beautiful woman. Her long red hair refused to be restrained by that silly looking cap, and her green eyes danced as she laughed with Ethan. She wasn't as well rounded as she used to be, but she still had curves in all the right places. She had the look of someone who was going through a stressful time, and, from what he'd heard, she was. But she was still so cheerful. She had Ethan giggling away with her as they loaded up the box.

She met Gabe's eye as she straightened up. "And what about you? What can I do to put a smile on your face?"

"Hang out with me this afternoon? I'll pick you up when you get done here." The words surprised him as they came out, though at least he hadn't spoken some of the other things she could do to put a smile on his face.

Evidently, they surprised Renée, too. Her eyes widened, as did Ethan's. She wasn't going to say no though. He knew it. He prided himself on being able to read people. It served him well in court, and he applied it to the rest of his life. He could tell that Renée needed someone to talk to, Gabe wanted to spend some time with her—two birds, one stone. His confidence wavered a little as she continued to stare at him. He held his breath as the silence lengthened.

He felt himself smile when she said. "Sure. I close up at two thirty. See you then."

Ethan grinned and tugged at Gabe's sleeve. "Come on. We need to get these doughnuts home."

Once they were outside the kid put his hands on his hips and scowled up at him. "You got lucky there Uncle Gabe, but you almost blew it! You'd better let me teach you about girls if you want Miss Renée to be your girlfriend."

Gabe had to laugh. "What do you mean I got lucky?"

Ethan shook his head and let out an exasperated sigh. "You don't even know? You're supposed to ask girls out. Not tell them. You're supposed to let them think they're in charge or they don't like it. You can't be bossy like that!"

Gabe grinned down at him. "That's one way to go about it, but the worst thing you can do with a woman is pretend to be something you're not. I'm a take-charge kind of guy."

Ethan looked puzzled. "And you still get girlfriends?"

"I do. In fact it's what some women like best."

Ethan cocked his head to one side. "Why?"

He laughed. "Someday I'll teach you about girls, but you stick with what you know for now, okay?"

Ethan nodded and climbed into the car, his attention returning to the box of doughnuts on his lap. "Okay."

As Gabe settled behind the steering wheel he couldn't help but think Ethan might be right. Perhaps he should dial it back a bit. While it was true that some women enjoyed his no-nonsense approach—to everything—Renée might not be one of them. He shrugged as he drove his nephew and his doughnuts back down Main Street. What did it matter? She was just an old friend who was going through a hard time. They were going to catch up. That was all.

# Chapter Two

Once Renée had everything cleaned up and laid out ready for tomorrow morning she closed herself in the little bathroom in the back of the bakery. She needed to get a grip! She'd had butterflies in her stomach ever since Gabe left. He'd be here to pick her up in a few minutes, and they were going to…hang out? Why? She dragged the little cap off her head and stared at herself in the mirror. Because that's the kind of guy he is, she told herself. He probably wants to give me some free legal advice! Gabe had always been the kind to look out for the underdog, to champion the cause of the needy. He was no doubt just being the same stand-up guy he'd always been and looking to help out an old classmate. She grinned as she pulled a comb through her hair. She was a mess, just as she always had been. Her hair refused to be tamed. Her freckles refused to be covered. Her eyes were nice though, and with this extra lick of mascara they looked great. She stood back to get a better look at herself. Yep, definitely a mess, but she was her own kind of mess, and that's all she ever had been. Gabe probably wouldn't even notice what she looked like anyway, he'd be too busy assessing the merits of her case and deciding what he could do to be of service.

She turned up the tail of her shirt and tied it around her waist. It was warm out there, that was all. She started at the sound of the bell tinkling as the door opened. She'd turned the sign to Closed so it could only be Gabe.

She sucked in a deep breath at the sight of him. A polo shirt and chinos wouldn't normally grab her attention—too neat and pressed—but stretched over his body they held her gaze all right and set her heart racing. Damn, he was amazing. Realizing she'd been looking a little too long, she slowly lifted her gaze. She didn't meet his though, as he was still looking her over. So much for him not noticing what she looked like. She could almost feel the way his gaze traveled over her, lingering on her exposed midriff before traveling up to linger even longer on her breasts. Her heart hammered in her chest. Oh yeah, he was noticing her and looking as though he liked what he saw.

He finally met her gaze. He didn't smile, just raised an eyebrow. "Are you ready?"

She had to bite back a laugh. After being ravaged by just a look like that? Yeah, she was ready. Ready and willing. She nodded, not trusting herself to speak. She needed to get her imagination back under control or she'd end up making a fool of herself.

He held the door open for her and waited while she locked it behind them.

"Any ideas what you'd like to do?" she asked.

"I brought a picnic. I figured you probably didn't get a chance to eat today since you're by yourself in there."

Wow! She was starving, but had been happy to forego food until afterward. She hadn't thought they'd be hanging out for too long. It wasn't as though they'd ever been really close friends or anything.

He opened the door of a green Avalon and gestured for her to get in. Apparently he didn't need her agreement. She obeyed, who was she to argue? She was hardly going to say no to an afternoon with Gabe Morgan and a picnic basket!

She fiddled with her hair as he drove out onto West Shore Road. Now that she was here in the car with him, she didn't know what to say. They'd chatted a couple of times when she'd been working at the bar in the resort, but other than that they hadn't seen or spoken to each other in, what, fifteen years or so? Maybe this was a stupid idea.

"So, how have you been?"

Oh, God. Maybe this was a really stupid idea. An afternoon of small talk with a condescending stranger wasn't going to be any fun. No matter how good looking he was. "You really want to know?"

Gabe shot her a quick look. "I really want to know." Something about the way he said it, the way his face softened when he did, made her decide to tell him.

"It's been a living hell, Gabe. I've been awful. I've been in shock, I've been in denial, I've been hurt, and I've been angry. I've hated the man I spent ten years of my life with, and, worse still, I've hated myself. That's how I've been. How about you?"

He said nothing as the car bumped down a rutted dirt road that led to the river. He cut the engine before he finally turned to look at her. Renée swallowed. Why on earth had she just blurted all that out? He'd probably want to head straight back to town and get away from the crazy redhead as soon as he could.

Instead, his words stole the breath from her lungs. "I've been worried about you."

"What?" That didn't make any sense at all.

"Renée, I always admired you when we were kids."

Huh? What kind of BS was that? She didn't have time to wonder as he continued.

"After what happened and we all went our separate ways, I used to think about you a lot. I admired the way you handled it, handled yourself. When I heard what you were doing with the charity and everything I wasn't at all surprised. You've been an inspiration to so many."

Renée watched his lips move, not quite sure she was correctly hearing the words coming out of them.

He met her gaze. "Since the first time I saw you back here, working behind the bar, and Ben told me what you were going through, I've been worried about you. I've wanted to talk to you. Tell you I'll do whatever I can to help. Tell you you've got a friend if you want one."

She screwed her eyes up as she tried to process his words. "But why? We were never really friends."

That seemed to surprise him. "I thought we were. You didn't?"

She shook her head. "We were in the same group of friends, but, come on, Gabe. You were the golden boy, the town doctor's son. I was the town drunk's daughter."

"I never saw it like that."

"Well, I did. And so did everyone else."

He stared at her for a long time, long enough that she started to feel uncomfortable. She had no idea what was going on behind that intense gaze. "What?" She had to break the tension.

"You say we were never friends. Would you like to be my friend now?"

"Are you serious?" What on earth was he playing at? She didn't get it.

"I'm deadly serious. You'll get to know that about me. I don't say anything unless I mean it. I don't do anything unless I mean it."

"Then would you do me a favor?"

"What's that?"

"Smile."

The corners of his mouth turned up, but his eyes were still concerned.

"You just proved yourself a liar, Gabe."

"How?"

"Smile like you mean it, or don't smile at all!"

He smiled. It spread all over his face and touched his eyes. If she wanted to let her imagination get involved she might have thought it touched her heart, too. But no. She had to keep her imagination and Gabe Morgan as far away from each other as possible!

"I mean it. So what do you say? Want to be my friend?"

She pondered it for a minute. "I could certainly use one. How about you, do you want to be my friend?"

"I do." He held her gaze for a moment and then looked away. When he looked back he reached over and touched her cheek. "For now."

What did that mean? Probably that he wanted to be her friend in her time of need and he'd be on his way once he'd done what he saw as his duty. Although part of her wanted to say no thanks—she was used to running a charity, not receiving it—she didn't. He meant well, and she hadn't lied, she really could use a friend right now. "Okay then, well I never had a friendship with a time limit on it before, but you just say the word and there'll be no hard feelings when you've had enough."

Gabe opened his mouth to speak then seemed to think better of it. He got out of the car and pulled a huge picnic basket from the trunk. Renée scrambled out and followed him down the path that led to the riverbank. She watched as he spread the blanket out in the shade under the trees and opened up the basket. She laughed when he pulled out a bottle of champagne and two flutes.

"Who the hell drinks champagne on a picnic?"

Gabe patted the blanket beside him for her to sit while he poured. "We do," he said, and smiled—a smile that looked an awful lot like he meant it.

~ ~ ~

The look on her face as he handed her champagne made Gabe close his eyes for a second. It was such a strange reaction, he had to wonder why he did it. She was so beautiful, so brave, and so honest. He knew, as he saw the image of her imprinted on his memory, why he'd done it. It was to capture the moment so he could keep it. When he was a kid he used to believe his mind was a camera and his eyelids were the shutter. When he closed them he created a photographic memory he could keep forever. He hadn't done that for years and yet now he thought about it as a rush of happy childhood picture memories flashed through his mind. It made him smile.

Renée gave him a puzzled look. "That looked like another genuine smile. Two in the space of a minute. What is it with you? Are you trying to live by the politicians' motto?"

"The politicians' motto?"

"Once you learn to fake sincerity, you can achieve anything."

He laughed. "Not me. I'm usually accused of being too sincere."

"I didn't know there was such a thing."

"Okay, maybe too honest. Too ruthless in my quest for the truth and too blunt in my use of it."

She shook her head. "I didn't know that was a thing either. How can the truth ever be a bad thing?" He watched her stop and think, knowing that she'd recently learned some truths that had hurt her, that had destroyed her life. She seemed to understand what he was thinking. "I mean, the truth about

Eric wouldn't have been so bad if I'd known it at the time. It's when the truth is hidden for so long and you build your life on a foundation of lies, that's when everything goes to hell. Not because of the truth itself, but because everything crumbles around it when it comes out."

Gabe nodded. He hadn't thought of it like that before, but it was true. She'd given him the opportunity to ask what was going on with Eric and the case, and he wasn't going to pass it up. "So how are things going with all that?"

She took a gulp of her champagne and met his eye. "Didn't you promise me food? You're right, I didn't get a chance to eat today and I'm starving. If you don't feed me, this champagne will go straight to my head, and I will not be accountable for my actions."

"What actions might they be?" The way she was looking at him told him the champagne was already going to her head, and he was very interested in the kind of action that look suggested. He didn't wait for her answer though. He turned away to unpack the picnic basket so she could eat. However interested he might be, she was still married. She was in a very precarious situation, and he wasn't in a position to do anything more than be a long-distance friend. He laid out the sandwiches he'd made and she grinned.

"Wow. Thank you. Homemade. I'm impressed. I was expecting store-bought."

He laughed. "Why? Is that what usually happens when guys take you out for a picnic?"

"I've never been on a picnic with a guy before."

"Never?"

She shook her head and grabbed a sandwich, busying herself with removing the wrapper.

"Were you happy with him, before you knew?"

She took a bite of the sandwich without looking up. As he watched her eat he wondered whether she would answer, if she'd even heard.

"We were never happy." She met his gaze. "I'm not just saying that. I'm not revising history because of everything that's happened. We got along okay in the beginning. I thought we would get better with time. It turned out I was just a useful idiot to him. The marriage, the charity—they were the perfect front. He got to syphon off so much money, live his seedy life, and still seem respectable."

"You didn't notice all that money disappearing?" Gabe knew the moment the words were out that they sounded like an accusation. He was cross-examining her out of habit. He could have kicked himself.

"I'm sorry, I…"

She held a hand up. "No. Don't be. I've asked myself the same question a thousand times. Whatever the outcome of this court case, I already know I'm guilty."

Gabe couldn't believe she meant that.

She shook her head sadly. "Not like that. I didn't know. Didn't have a clue. So surely that makes me guilty by ignorance, doesn't it?"

"No. It doesn't. Not in a court of law, but, more importantly, you can't let it make you feel guilty. What are you guilty of? Trusting your husband?"

"I'm guilty of allowing my husband to steal thousands of dollars. I'm guilty of violating the trust that people placed in me when they donated their hard-earned money. I'm guilty of trying to keep a marriage going…of trying to make myself a better person for a man who was stealing from me, lying to me, and cheating on me." She took a deep breath and pushed her hair out of her eyes. "I guess all of that makes me guilty of being pretty damned stupid, huh?" She drained the last of her champagne before smiling and holding her glass out for more.

"You're not stupid, Renée. As I remember, you're one of the smartest people I've ever known."

She laughed. "I thought you only said things you really meant."

"I do."

"Well sorry, Mr. Harvard Law-educated trial attorney of the year, but I don't believe you."

He could see there was no point arguing with her. It was true, though. She'd been his only competition in high school when it came to academics. It wasn't only that kind of smart he'd been talking about though. She'd been smart about people, too. The way she'd handled herself after Chloe died. The way she'd dealt with her father and his drinking. She'd met everything head on, dealt with things in a calm and efficient manner. She was capable and in control and yet she'd always seemed...what? What was the word? It wasn't happy—not when her sister died, not when she was dealing with her father and his drinking. It wasn't fun either, although he'd always envied her that. In their group of friends they'd both been considered the smart ones, but she was the creative one, too—the adventurous one, the one who thought outside of the box.

She was watching him. "What? You can't argue because you know I'm right?"

He smiled. "No. I'm not arguing, because you're a worthy opponent. I'm biding my time, building a case, and when I hit you with my evidence, I'll take you down. You won't have a leg to stand on."

"Oh." She looked surprised. "So you're planning on being my friend long enough to build a case then?"

He nodded. "I am. Though I may need to interview you repeatedly. Can you stand that?"

She smiled. "I can. Next time you're back in town I'll treat you to lunch. How about that?"

That was good. She was at least open to the friendship, though he wasn't sure how long he would be able to keep it to just that. "No, sorry."

He felt bad about it, but he was thrilled to see the disappointment in her eyes before she started apologizing. "I'm sorry. I guess I was getting carried away…"

"No, you weren't. I'm staying here the whole week this time. So saying we can have lunch next time I'm in town isn't as much or as soon as I wanted."

She grinned. "So how much do you want? And how soon do you want it?"

Despite his earlier insistence that he always told the truth, he decided this was one of the rare moments when it was best left unspoken. The way she looked sitting there on the blanket, her wild red hair framing her beautiful face, the way her shirt showed off just enough bare skin to make him want to taste it. He wanted all of her—naked—and right now. "I can't tell you yet, but I'll be able to give you a better idea if you'll have lunch with me tomorrow."

"You've got yourself a deal, counselor."

# Chapter Three

It was almost six by the time Gabe pulled up in front of the bakery. He looked over at Renée. It had been a great afternoon and he didn't want to say goodbye yet. At the same time, she'd agreed to have lunch with him tomorrow, and he didn't want to overdo it either. "Where's your car?" he asked.

She gave him a funny look. "My trusty steed is around back."

"I'll take you around there."

She started to open the door. "That's okay. I can walk. Thanks for this afternoon."

Gabe pulled her back before she could get out. "Your car isn't back there, is it?"

She shrugged. "I never said it was. You assumed."

He shook his head at her. "You walk down here at four in the morning?"

"I told you. I have my trusty steed, thank you."

Gabe pulled into the alley behind the bakery and saw an old bicycle leaning against the wall. "You trust that thing?"

Renée laughed. "I have to. It's all I've got."

That bothered him. She must be worse off than he'd thought. "Well, how about we put it in the trunk and I'll give you a ride home."

22

"I'm fine…honestly."

That did it. The speed with which she replied made it damned sure he wouldn't take no for an answer. If she hadn't wanted him to see her bike, it was pretty obvious she didn't want him to see her house. Well tough. "I'm taking you home, Renée. No arguments. We can bring the bike or leave it here, but, either way, I'm driving you home."

She glared at him, looking as though she were about to explode. He glared right back; no way was he backing down. After a few moments she started to laugh; it was such an infectious sound, he had to join her.

"You're used to getting your own way, aren't you?"

He shrugged. "Yes, but only when it matters." Even as he said it, he wondered why this mattered so much.

The look on her face told him she had the same question, but she didn't voice it. "Well, if you insist on taking me, you'd better bring the bike, too. I don't want to have to walk down here tomorrow morning.'

As they rounded the last corner to the old Nichols place, Renée looked uncomfortable. "You can drop me here; this is fine."

Gabe looked over at her. "Come on. You should have noticed by now that you can't bullshit me. We both know you don't want me to see the place. We also both know that I'm going to. I've already told you I'm worried about you. I need to know how you're living."

Renée sighed. "Okay then…"

"Is it really that bad?"

She let out a little laugh. "No. It's worse. But it's the only option I have right now, and I'm making the best of it. Just don't be too shocked or too critical, or this friendship of ours might be very short lived."

Gabe said nothing as the car bumped along the rutted driveway. As the house came into view, he was grateful for the warning. The place looked derelict. The roof was sagging badly in one corner, and one window was boarded up. Yet, there were planters full of colorful flowers brightening the dilapidated front porch.

He brought the car to a halt, and Renée jumped out. He followed her to the trunk where she was tugging at the bicycle to get it out.

"Here, let me."

He was surprised when she stood back and let him get it out for her, and, even more surprised, when she gave him a bright smile. "We may as well get this over with then, huh? I can tell you're not going to give up, so come on in. I'll give you the grand tour, and you can feel justified in your pity."

"Ouch! I don't want to pity you, Renée."

Her smile was less brittle when she replied. "Then don't. That's not what friends do, is it?"

He shook his head. "No, friends want to help and…"

"And friends don't judge or interfere!" She cut him off with a laugh. "Come on in. It's not as bad as all that."

As Gabe followed her inside he wondered how bad all that might be, because this was pretty awful. The place was falling down. Bare floorboards were rotted through in places. A couple of the windows were covered with clear plastic instead of glass. It was hard, but he said nothing until she brought him to the kitchen and turned to face him. It was hard to believe this room was in the same house. It was clean and neat and bright. The window frames were in no better shape than any of the others, but they'd had a lick of white paint. The cabinets and table were old but clean. There were more flowers and plants in here, and the walls were painted bright blue. It felt like a real home.

She waved her arm out. "Welcome to my humble abode. It's not much, but it's all I've got. And please don't criticize, because it sure beats sleeping under a bridge."

Gabe pursed his lips. He knew she wasn't joking. During the investigation of an embezzlement case, all joint assets would be frozen. "Didn't you have anything in your name alone? A checking account? Anything?"

She shook her head. "I told you. I was a useful idiot. I thought it was sweet that he wanted us to share everything."

"So you have nothing at all?"

She turned to the fridge. "I have cold beers. Would you like one?"

Gabe took it, wondering as he did what her opinion on alcohol was these days.

She seemed to pick up on his thoughts as she popped the top of her own bottle. "I've never had anything against drinking responsibly. It's alcohol abuse that ruins lives." She took a long gulp of her beer and stared out of the window before adding, "And ends them. Anyway…" She turned back to him and met his eye. "I'm kind of screwed financially while this whole investigation is going on. I don't even know that I will be charged with anything. But, in the meantime, everything Eric had a financial interest in is considered part of the investigation. Basically, that means everything—our home, our business, all our finances, the cars, everything. So as bad as this place may seem to you, I consider myself very lucky to have it. I won't deny that it's barely fit for human habitation, but barely is a lot better than I would have otherwise. So I'm grateful. I'm grateful, too, that the community has welcomed me back. Ben gave me a job when no one else in the world would, and people have been kind. I'm a lot better off than I could be, and I choose to look at it that way. So don't go putting a downer on it, or I'll have to ask you to leave."

Gabe nodded. He admired that she was determined to look at the positives and make the best of what most would consider to be an unlivable situation. He didn't like that she was simply choosing to ignore the negatives, though. Not when he felt he could maybe help her with them.

She narrowed her eyes at him. "I can tell whatever you're about to say is going to start with a 'yes, but...,' so do me a favor and don't even say it? I deal with as much as I can every day, and today's quota has already been filled. Maybe I'll listen to whatever you have to say tomorrow." She gave him a sassy smile. "Maybe. But for today, if you want to stick around, let's just catch up on other things. We can sit out front, you can tell me about your life, about any of our classmates you know of, and leave it at that. How does that sound?"

It sounded doable to Gabe. It wouldn't have been his first choice, but he didn't need to push her. "Okay, but I want a shot at tomorrow's quota of things you have to deal with. I know you think I'm being an interfering shit, but..."

She laughed. "I don't see where the but comes in—you are!"

He smiled. "But, only because I care."

Her smile faded. "Why, though?"

It was a fair question. He didn't really know the answer himself. He shrugged. "Because I'm a nice guy?"

"If you say so."

"You don't think so?" That hurt.

She met his gaze. "You're a great guy. I just don't want to be a charity case; the recipient of Gabe's good deeds."

"What do you want?" The way she was looking at him made him wonder if she was feeling the same attraction to him that he was to her. He held her gaze, silently asking that question. He was pretty sure the answer was yes.

She looked away. "To be friends, like you said. So how about we do what old friends do? Let's sit awhile on the porch and you can tell me all about your life in New York and your fancy law firm, huh?

Gabe nodded. The moment was gone. He wasn't sure what he should have done with it, but he wished he'd done something.

~ ~ ~

When they were settled on the rickety old rockers on the front porch, Renée took another swig of her beer and wondered why on earth she was drinking the stuff. She'd bought them last week when Ben had come out for dinner. He was the only person she'd allowed to visit till now. He'd been so good to her—giving her a job, helping her out wherever he could. Ben was a real friend. She looked over at Gabe. Was he? She wanted to blame her imagination and the beer on top of the champagne they'd had this afternoon, but she kept getting the feeling that he was attracted to her. That he wanted to be more than a friend, or, at least, a friend with benefits. She almost choked on her beer at the thought. What she wouldn't give for benefits with Gabe! But she shouldn't even be thinking like that. She was a married woman! Kind of. Did it still count if your husband had slept with who knew how many other women and hadn't had sex with you in over a year? Did it still count if he was currently locked up for lying to you and deceiving you for years in the course of committing fraud and embezzling huge amounts of money that you helped to raise? She chewed her bottom lip. Did it still count if you were currently slightly tipsy and sitting out on a warm spring evening with the guy who'd starred in all your high-school fantasies?

"Dare I ask what you're thinking?"

She laughed. "Maybe, but I daren't tell you."

Gabe smiled and let his eyes travel over her, sending her temperature and her heart rate soaring yet again. Her imagination insisted he was doing it on purpose. The little voice of reason kept trying to remind her that he was a guy, and guys did that all the time without even knowing they were doing it. When his gaze met hers, even the little voice couldn't deny that he knew damn well what he was doing and was checking for her reaction.

She ran her fingers through her hair, instinctively trying to tame it. "We've talked enough about me today. Why don't you tell me about you?" As she started speaking something occurred to her that should have been obvious all along. "Tell me about your life, your work." She swallowed. "Your wife? Kids? A girlfriend?"

His low, deep chuckle resonated through her. "That won't take too long. My life is my work. No wife, kids, or girlfriend."

She stared at him. "Doesn't sound like much of a life. Aren't you supposed to be the big success story who got it all right?"

He laughed. "You know, I've been thinking the same thing lately. Don't get me wrong, I love my work, but as for the rest of my life—I don't really have one."

Renée raised her bottle to him. "I guess we're not that smart after all, are we? I mean, we were the ones who went off out in the world to build something, to contribute to the greater good, and look at us."

Gabe frowned at her. "Hey, we've both achieved an awful lot more than most."

Renée let out a bitter little laugh. "Yeah, it's just a pity neither of us achieved any of what really matters."

"How can you say that after the work you've done, the lives you've no doubt saved? What is it that really matters?"

"I'm not dismissing the importance of my work—or yours. But aren't love and family and happiness the things that matter most in life? I know I don't have any of those, and, from what you're saying, neither do you."

Gabe stared at her for a long time, but said nothing.

She twirled a strand of hair around her finger and left him to his thoughts. What had she been thinking? She'd felt that way for the last several years; she'd loved her work, but had yearned for more personal fulfilment. She'd never given voice to those feelings before, though. She'd felt kind of guilty for even feeling them. Wasn't it selfish to want more for herself when she was doing so much for others?

She realized Gabe was watching her and untangled her fingers from her hair. "Sorry. I think I'm just a woman of a certain age, you know?" She made a face and tried to laugh it off.

"Do you wish you'd had kids?"

She took a deep breath. "Every single day. Don't you?"

Gabe nodded. "I thought my brother, Michael, was crazy when he got divorced and Ethan stayed with him. I had no idea how a guy could raise a kid by himself. I still don't think I could, not by myself. But I'd love to be a dad. What you said, about not having achieved what really matters? Thank you."

Renée raised her eyebrows at him. Was he being sarcastic? "I didn't mean to offend you."

He shook his head rapidly. "No, I mean it. I've been in a weird place lately. My work used to be so important, but lately it feels hollow. I haven't known why. I kept wondering how I could feel so empty when I've achieved so much. You just made it all so clear. I haven't achieved any of the things that really matter. I gave Michael shit about settling down here because I worried it might not be enough for him. Yet, I see him so happy with Megan and Ethan and his medical practice. I was worried about him, yet he's the one who's got it all figured out. He got it all right; I got it all wrong."

He looked so lost. She reached over and patted his hand. "You didn't get it all wrong. You've done so much good. It's not an either or situation. You can have both. You've achieved the career success, so now that you've figured out what's missing, you can go out and find the personal success, too."

He squeezed her hand and met her gaze. "Can I?"

She really had to curb her imagination. She'd swear he was asking her personally, as if she could help him find it. But that was plain ridiculous. She needed to lighten the moment. "Of course you can. You're Gabe Morgan, the mighty angel, Gabriel. You can do whatever in the world you want to."

He smiled. "It's going on the record that you said that."

She smiled. "Well, we both know it's true. You can make anything happen when you set your mind to it."

"That is true." He stood up abruptly. "I'd better go."

Oh! She hadn't been expecting that. Maybe she had offended him and he just wasn't saying. She stood, too. "Okay. Thanks again for today."

"No, thank you." He held her gaze for a moment, and then turned and strode back toward the rental car.

She trotted after him feeling confused. Was this it? Was he leaving because she'd said too much? Were they still going to have lunch tomorrow? She had no clue.

When he reached the car, he turned and looked her over. He was giving off waves of...what? Strong emotion of some kind, she knew that much. Was he angry? She'd hate that. "Still friends?" she asked.

He stepped toward her, making her senses reel. His eyes were that deep emerald color as he lowered his head to hers. Was he going to kiss her??

He reached out and tucked a strand of hair behind her ear. "For now." With that he got in the car and was bouncing away down the drive before she could gather her senses.

Wow! She didn't know if that was good or bad. What she did know was that she would be awake most of the night thinking about it!

# Chapter Four

"Where the hell have you been, mate?"
Gabe gave Michael a puzzled look as he let himself in through the kitchen door. "Greetings, little brother. It's good to see you, too. I didn't realize I had to report all my movements."
Michael laughed. "Defensive, huh? Now you've got me real curious. Mom said you were coming this weekend, so I reckoned you'd either be moping around here or down at the resort in the bar. No one's seen you all day, except Em and Jack at five o'clock this morning. So spill. Where've you been? What are you up to?"
Gabe thought about it. Did he want to talk to Michael about Renée? They had fairly well-defined roles. Michael was the younger brother—the joker and the flirt. Gabe was the elder brother...hmm, what was he? He was the go-getter, the take-charge one. What else? He didn't even know anymore. Whatever he was, he wasn't sure he wanted to be that guy anymore. He didn't know who he did want to be either.
Michael's grin faded. "Are you all right?"
Gabe shrugged. "Yeah. I think so."
"There you are, angel. I was starting to worry about you."
Michael rolled his eyes at Gabe. "He's okay, mom. The angel Gabriel is all grown up and quite capable of taking care of

himself, you know." He made a face at Gabe. "Even if he is coming home to Mommy and Daddy every weekend."

Gabe laughed, but it rattled him, too. He'd been thinking the same thing last night. "It's just that I'm the good son and always have been." He put an arm around his mom's shoulders and planted a kiss on top of her head. "Isn't that right, mom?"

She laughed. "I'm not getting caught in the middle. You're both my angels and always will be. Now, are either of you here for dinner?"

"I am," they both replied at once.

"You are?" Gabe had assumed Michael would be heading home.

"Yeah, Meggie's taken Ethan over to see Missy and Scot tonight. In fact, all the girls are getting together over there. I think the wedding planning is getting pretty intense."

"Not intense enough for my liking," said their mom. "When are you and Megan going to name the date? I can't wait, and neither can Ethan."

Michael laughed. "That's not fair, mom. Ethan's fine with waiting. He understands. I just wish you would. I don't want to rush Meggie. We'll get there when she's ready. You know she's still got a lot to work through."

"Sorry, I do know. I just get so impatient, and I don't think your brother is ever going to give me a chance to be mother of the groom." Her eyes were laughing as she looked at Gabe. "Are you?"

He didn't have an answer. Normally he would have laughed it off, talked about how he was married to his work, but after his conversation with Renée this afternoon, that didn't feel too funny. He shrugged. "Never say never, mom."

Her hand flew up to cover her mouth. Michael swung around to stare at him. "What the…"

"Michael!"

He laughed. "Heck, Mom! I was going to say what the heck. What did you think I was going to say?"

She shook her head at him. "Never mind. Gabriel, talk to me! Tell me what's going on. "

Gabe chuckled to himself. This was business as usual in the Morgan household. "There's nothing to talk about. I just said never say never, that's all."

"But darling, you've always said never. At least when it comes to getting married. You're married to your work and there are too many beautiful women in New York. That's what you always say. What's changed?"

He shrugged. "I don't know. Maybe I'm changing. He looked at her, then at Michael. Maybe it's all your fault, little brother. I felt like a huge success until you came back and showed me what success really looks like."

Michael's mouth fell open. "What the fuck?"

Gabe had to smile that his mom let that one slide as she too stared at him openmouthed. Maybe shaking things up like this could be fun. He'd created the box that he lived in, the parameters that defined him. He could break out of it if he wanted to, and watching his family's shock was fun. How about that? Fun! "You heard me. Seeing you with Ethan and with Megan. Seeing you going into the family practice, taking over the reins from Dad so he can retire. You're doing all the important stuff, and you're doing a fantastic job of it. I thought I had it all figured out. Now I'm realizing I don't. In fact, if anything, I've been a long way off the mark." He was enjoying the shock on their faces so much he couldn't resist adding. "And I'm starting to think it's time to make some changes, get on the right track before I end up a miserable, lonely old man."

Michael was recovering quickly. "A very rich lonely old man," he said with a laugh.

"Money doesn't mean a thing compared to love and family."

His mom came and wrapped her arms around him. "You have no idea how happy I am to hear you say that, Gabe."

He hugged her back, surprised how happy he was to understand it finally.

She stepped back and winked at him. "You're scaring me a little bit, too. Are you sure you're feeling okay?"

He laughed. "Thanks Mom, but there's no need to worry. I feel fine. In fact, I feel better than I have in years."

She hugged him again.

"Given Gabriel's revelation," said Michael, "would you mind if I take him out to dinner, Mom? I can dig for the dirt that he won't tell you and report back later."

She laughed. "Of course. You two take each other out. I'll see you later."

The bar at the resort was busy; they were sitting in a booth Ben had managed to find them. He kept the place going pretty well through the winter, but now that spring was here, the weekends were really buzzing. Gabe wondered what it would be like once tourist season was in full swing. He smiled at the thought that he'd like to be around to see for himself. Michael peered over his menu at him. "What are you smirking about over there?"

"Just enjoying myself, little brother. That's all."

Michael lowered his menu. "Are you going to tell me what the fuck is going on? You're smiling without anyone having to tell you to. And what you said back there, about me showing you what success looks like, was that some kind of joke?"

Gabe shook his head. "Never been more serious in my life. It's true, and I want to apologize. I worried about you, thinking that you might miss out on the important stuff, might make your life too small by coming back here. I couldn't have been more wrong, and you couldn't have been more right. All the important stuff is right here, and you're living it well."

"Wow! Just wow. I don't know what else to say. I guess, thank you? But I also kind of want to say I'm sorry."

Gabe smiled. He loved his brother, and the one thing he knew Michael would never say was, 'I told you so.' Even though he had every right to. "Thanks, Michael. Don't be sorry for me, though. Just keep an eye on me as I pick my way through this? I'm bound to fuck up as I figure it out, and I'd appreciate a kick in the ass when you think I need it."

Michael laughed. "Now that I can help you with. It'll be my pleasure. You want to tell me what's brought this on?" He raised an eyebrow. "Or not?"

Gabe had decided that he did. The server came to take their order, and once she'd left, he nodded slowly. "I'm not sure I fully understand it myself yet, but I'll try. You know how I've been these last couple of months?"

"Out of sorts, grumpy, and coming home every weekend? I know that much."

"Yes. All of that and feeling like nothing means anything. I don't get excited about work anymore. I just settled a big case yesterday, and it was just kind of ho-hum, you know?"

Michael cocked his head to one side. "What was the case?"

"Carradon. What does it matter?"

"It matters because you get so invested when there's a cause or some kind of injustice involved. I can see you feeling ho-hum when it's simply a matter of money, but when there is a wrong to be righted you're all over it."

Gabe considered that. "Well, going by that I should be over the moon about getting Carradon to settle. They've offered a huge payout to the families involved, and they're overhauling their whole manufacturing process. To be honest, the terms of the settlement are even better than I realistically could have hoped for in court. Turns out a few of their executives were uncomfortable with the direction they were taking. The suit we filed gave them the opportunity to step up and make some major changes that shareholders would never have agreed to otherwise because of the costs involved." He shrugged. "Now I put it like that, I really should be elated. It's a great result. But it doesn't rock my world the way it would have not so long ago."

"Do you know why?"

He nodded. "I think I'm starting to understand, yeah."

"Care to share?"

Gabe let out a big sigh. "Someone pointed out to me today that love and family and happiness are the things that matter most in life." He closed his eyes and pressed his fingers into his temples then looked back at Michael. "And I don't have any of them. They've never even been on my priority list. Hell, I don't even know how to have fun anymore."

Michael waggled his eyebrow. "Those paralegals you date sound like a lot of fun."

Gabe shook his head. "I don't date them. I just screw them. And they're mostly lawyers, if you don't mind. I don't remember the last time I ever shared anything more than dinner and a quick fuck with a woman."

"And you say that like it's a bad thing?"

"It feels like a bad thing. It never did before. But now I don't want it anymore, I want…" What did he want?

"More?" asked Michael. "Love and family and happiness perhaps?"

Gabe nodded. Apparently he did.

The server came back with their food. Michael smothered his burger with ketchup as he asked, "And can I ask who helped you on your way to this epiphany?"

This was the part Gabe was less sure about sharing. He picked at his fries before looking up to meet Michael's gaze.

Michael grinned. "Sorry, big brother, but your hesitation and the look on your face tell me this is where it gets interesting."

Gabe had to laugh. "You got me. I'm struggling to catch up with myself here, so go easy on me, will you?"

"Tell you what. How about I make it real easy for you? I won't even make you tell. I'll tell you that it was Renée Nichols. And although you think you've only realized all this stuff today, Renée has been on your mind for weeks now. Thinking about her has made you re-evaluate everything else in a different light."

It was Gabe's turn to stare openmouthed at his brother. "How the hell do you know that, when I wasn't fully aware of it?"

Michael grinned. "I'm not just a pretty face, you know. That first night you came to the resort with me, when Meggie and I still hadn't quite got it together, you spent most of the night sitting at the bar watching Renée. You didn't talk to her much, didn't even interrogate her like you do everyone else. You just sat and watched her. You've been back pretty much every weekend since then, and you've spent most of your time in the bar." He laughed. "Until she started working in the bakery and then all of a sudden Mr. My-Body-is-a-Temple Gabe, becomes a frigging doughnut lover!"

Gabe had to laugh. It was so true. But if Michael hadn't pointed it out, he would never have figured it out for himself.

"What I want to know is what you're going to do about it."

Gabe shook his head. That was the question he'd been avoiding since he and Renée had left the river this afternoon. He'd known he was attracted to her, not just physically, but in so many ways. That didn't mean he had to do anything about it though. When he'd taken her home and seen her place—seen how she was living—his mind had screamed the question.

What could he do about it? When she'd told him that he could find personal success, told him that he could do anything in the world he wanted, he'd had to leave. He had to leave, because, in that moment, he'd wanted nothing in the world more than to kiss her and see where it went. There were so many reasons he couldn't do that.

He looked at Michael. "I can't do anything about it. She's married."

"To a guy who cheated on her, stole from her, and is now locked up. I don't see that as a major obstacle."

"Even if it wasn't. She lives here; I live in New York. I want to help her out; she doesn't want to feel like a charity case. There are so many reasons not to even think about it."

"But you can't stop thinking about it anyway, can you?"

Gabe shook his head. "And I'm having lunch with her again tomorrow."

"You'll work it out."

"Maybe." Gabe was starting to wonder whether he was just getting carried away. Maybe he was just thinking from his pants? No. He knew that wasn't true, though he wouldn't deny there was definitely a large influence down there. He'd had enough of talking about it for now. He'd made some major shifts today, and he needed time to process it all. "Anyway. I've opened up enough for one day. Can we move on?"

Michael nodded. "'Course we can, mate. There's something I've been meaning to ask you. When Meggie and I finally do get around to tying the knot, would you be my best man?"

Gabe cleared his throat before he replied. What was with all these emotions today? He hadn't felt this much in one day in as long as he could remember. He didn't even want to deny the swell of love and pride in his chest as he said, "I'd be honored to."

~ ~ ~

Renée checked the clock again. Sunday mornings were usually so busy in here that they flew by. Today was dragging though, and she didn't want to admit that it was because she was counting the minutes till closing. After the way he'd left her place last night, she wasn't sure if Gabe was still coming for lunch. She kept telling herself it would be better if he didn't. She found him far too attractive; he made her imagination run wild. She'd do well to remember that she was still married, and Gabe was only a visitor here. He didn't live here, and she didn't know that she would once the whole mess with Eric and the court case was resolved. There was no point daydreaming about Gabe; her life was too much of a mess, and he was out of her reach anyway.

She smiled when she saw Kenzie outside the bakery. As different as the two of them were, they'd become quite close since they'd traded jobs. Kenzie was now the bar manager at the resort and was engaged to Chase, the lead singer of the band. Renée couldn't help envying her as she watched her kiss her fiancé and pat his backside before he carried on walking down to the Boathouse. The two of them were made for each other, it was so obvious. Wouldn't it be wonderful to be with someone who was perfect for you? And no, she was not thinking about Gabe again. Not at all.

"Hey, girlfriend." Kenzie smiled as she came in. "Since you hardly ever come into the bar, I'm here to visit you again."

"Then we both win," said Renée. "When I come to see you, you try to fill me with booze, which I don't like. When you come to see me, I try to fill you with cookies which you love!"

Kenzie laughed. "You've got a point there." She was eyeing the batch of double chocolate fudge brownies Renée had just pulled from the oven. "I need at least two of those."

"I'd love to know where you put them," said Renée as she handed one over. Kenzie had been nothing but skin and bones when Renée first met her. She was still tiny, but she at least looked healthy now. Renée knew that was mostly down to Chase who seemed to do most of the cooking at their house and often came in here to buy Kenzie goodies.

Kenzie shrugged and moaned as she bit into the brownie. "God, this is amazing! I guess it'll all catch up with me one day. I'm still getting the hang of eating every single day. It seems weird to me, but Chase insists. I know I shouldn't be eating these things all the time, but, until I wake up twenty pounds heavier one morning, I'm going to enjoy it while I can!"

"It's so not fair," said Renée. "You can eat whatever you like and you're so svelte, while I'm a big girl no matter what I do." She had lost a lot of weight these last few months due to all the stress, but she was never going to be slim. She just wasn't made that way and it didn't really bother her. Her attitude had always been that she was what she was; take it or leave it.

Kenzie frowned at her. "Why do we women always bitch about what we're not instead of celebrating what we are? I'm naturally skinny; you're naturally rounded. What does it really matter?"

"It really doesn't. I was just envying you that brownie." Renée picked out a large one for herself. "So instead of wishing and whining, I'll just have one." She stuck her tongue out at Kenzie before taking a bite of the delicious gooey chocolate. She moaned as she savored the taste.

"I know! Isn't it? It's just about orgasmic."

Renée sputtered chocolate crumbs as she laughed. "I can't say I fully remember. It's been so long, but I'm pretty sure this is better than any orgasm I ever had!"

Kenzie stopped munching and stared at her. "That may be the saddest thing I've ever heard."

Renée laughed, feeling a little embarrassed that she'd admitted that.

Kenzie's grin returned. "So why aren't you getting it on with the sexy Gabe yet? I'd have thought he'd be giving you all the orgasms you could handle by now."

Renée felt all the color drain from her face. "What...what do you mean?"

Kenzie gave her a sly look. "Don't play the innocent with me. The guy is gorgeous, and he's got the hots for you big time. Who do you think gave him your number?"

"You gave him my number? When?"

Kenzie looked worried now. "I shouldn't have? I thought you two were old friends. I'm sorry."

"No, no need. It's fine." It was, wasn't it?

Kenzie gave her a puzzled look. "You mean he hasn't called you?"

Renée shook her head, feeling as puzzled as Kenzie looked.

"Maybe he's just building up the nerve?"

Renée made a face; they both knew Gabe Morgan had all the nerve he needed.

"Well, I heard he's here again this weekend. Maybe he'll call and take you out?"

"No, you're right. He's just an old friend."

Now it was Kenzie's turn to make a face. "Whatever you say, but, if he doesn't get his act together soon, let me know. There are lots of guys around here who'd love to make you feel better than a brownie ever could."

"McKenzie Reid! You're the only person I know who can make me blush!"

Kenzie laughed. "Then Gabe had better hurry up and get his act together, or I'll introduce you to a guy who will turn you beetroot from head to toe with the things he'll say to you. And that's before he gets started on the things he'll do to you."

Renée had no interest in a guy like that, but she did wish Gabe would at least let her know what was going on. The fact that he'd asked Kenzie for her number was only fueling her overactive imagination that perhaps he really was attracted to her. And all this talk about orgasms had her wondering again about the possibility of adding some benefits to their friendship—if they still had one after the way he'd left last night.

# Chapter Five

Gabe had to park a block away from the bakery. As he got out of the rental car he looked up at the sound of his name being called. He grinned when he saw Kenzie waving at him. He had to admit that he wouldn't normally give a woman like her the time of day. She was brazen—hell, trashy was the word he would have used to describe his soon-to-be sister-in-law's sister. But she was good people. Maybe he was changing in more ways than one. A woman he would normally have judged and dismissed on sight, was about to become part of his family, and more than that, he realized, she was becoming a friend.

"How's it going? Ethan tells me that you're staying."

Her whole demeanor softened when she smiled. "I am. It seems my running days are over. Chase asked me to marry him."

"Wow!" Gabe tried to hide his surprise. He had no clue what to say. "Erm. Congratulations!"

Kenzie laughed. "Yeah, I'm pretty shocked too. Even I didn't have me down as the marrying kind."

Gabe felt bad. He wouldn't have said it, but she must have sensed his surprise.

Kenzie put a hand on his arm. "Don't sweat it, sugar. I know what I am, or, at least what I was, until I met Chase. That man and this place have worked their magic on me. I've got everything I never thought I wanted, and I'm happier than I ever thought I could be." She gave him a shrewd look. "It seems life does that to people sometimes."

Gabe met her gaze.

She laughed. "And I'm guessing you might be about to find that out for yourself."

He frowned at her.

"The intimidating stare isn't going to work on me, Gabe. You might have everyone else fooled, but I can see right through the tough shell to the softie underneath. It takes one to know one, right?"

Gabe had to laugh. "Apparently, but I think I'm more surprised than you were to discover I even have an inner softie!"

Kenzie nodded. "Take your time. I'll be honest, it's scary as shit! But it's worth it. Now get your ass into that bakery, and take my girl out. Just treat her nice, okay? She doesn't have the same self-preservation instincts that you and I do. You could break her without even knowing it."

That took him by surprise. He thought of Renée as strong, smart, and capable.

Kenzie shook her head at his expression. "I'm talking about her heart, stupid. She's tough as old boots and will come through this court case and everything just fine. But she'll put her heart and soul on the line, and a guy like you could trample all over them without ever knowing."

Gabe didn't know what to say to that. It was already difficult enough trying to figure out what he could or should do. Here was Kenzie adding a whole new angle. The possibility that he could hurt Renée? Was that a risk he even wanted to take? She was already going through so much; he wouldn't want to add to her troubles in any way.

Kenzie patted his arm. "Don't over-think it. Take her out, go have fun, just treat her nice."

Gabe nodded. "I will."

"I know. Anyways, I need to stop running my mouth and get to work. I'll see you around."

"Yeah. See you."

Gabe hesitated before he pushed the bakery door open. Should he just turn around and walk away now? He didn't know where this was going. Didn't know where it could go. The thought of hurting Renée was almost enough to make him stop before he started. Almost. He took a deep breath and went inside. The smile on her face when she saw him confirmed it was the right move. Knowing that he was responsible for how happy she looked did strange things to his insides.

"You came."

He raised an eyebrow. "I said I would."

"I know, but the way you left... I thought maybe..." She looked uncomfortable now.

Gabe went around the counter and stood before her. "I told you. I don't say things I don't mean."

She smiled up at him. "You did. Sorry. I guess it's just going to take me some time to get used to that."

He smiled. "Take all the time you need."

Her eyes widened, but she didn't reply. He didn't know what to do. He knew what he wanted to do, what he would have done with any other woman in the world—he wanted to back her up to the wall and kiss her. But he needed to stick with what he'd just said, and let her take all the time she needed to let him know that was what she wanted, too. He was pretty sure she did, and Kenzie wouldn't have talked the way she did if she didn't think Renée was interested in him.

"And while you take your time, I'll just keep being me and proving it to you. I said I'd take you out to lunch. So. Are you ready to go?"

She visibly pulled herself together. "I am. Where are we going?"

Gabe smiled. "It's not like there are too many choices around here. I thought you might like to sit out on the deck at the Boathouse?" He saw her hesitate, and he knew why. Having lunch together at the restaurant at the resort would be very public. It would get people talking. It was why he'd suggested it. In part he wanted people to see them together. More than that, though, he wanted to know if she would mind people seeing them together.

She pushed her hair out of her eyes and looked up at him. "So you want to take this friendship public, huh?"

He nodded and waited.

She mulled it over as she stared back at him. "Well, all righty then. As long as you're not worried about your reputation?"

"No. I was thinking more along the lines that you might be worried about yours?"

She gave him a quizzical look. "You're going to be seen out and about with the town drunk's daughter who is now under a cloud of suspicion because of her husband's fraud and embezzlement. I'm going to be seen out with golden boy Gabe, the town's beloved son and most eligible bachelor. Why would I be the one to worry?"

He shrugged. "Perhaps there's someone who wouldn't be happy to see you with an eligible bachelor?" He was pretty sure there wasn't another guy in the picture, but he wanted to be certain.

Renée laughed out loud. "The only someone I can think of would be Candy."

Gabe groaned at the mention of one of his high school girlfriends. "If we run into her, don't be surprised if I take hold of your hand or put an arm around you." He smiled, warming to the idea. "If it looks like she's going to come over and talk to us I may even have to pull you in and kiss you." He met her gaze and held it as he asked, "Would you have a problem with that?"

She slowly shook her head, then smiled. "Only because I know what she's like. It'll take extreme measures to get her off your back. I'll do it to help my friend out. That's the kind of girl I am."

Gabe smiled. "Good to know." He was getting a good vibe from her. He wanted to know more. "And what if I hugged you?"

She tilted her head to one side with a little smile that said she knew this wasn't about running into Candy at all. "That would depend. What kind of hugger are you?"

"I hadn't realized there were different kinds."

She laughed. "You're such a guy! Men don't read body language at all!"

"Hey! I'll have you know I'm trained in reading body language; it's important to know how a jury is perceiving what's going on in the courtroom."

"Yet you're not aware there are different kinds of hugs?"

He shrugged. "By the time you see anyone hugging in court, the decisions are all made. But do tell, since you're so expert. What kinds of hugs are there?" He raised an eyebrow at her and decided to throw down the challenge. "Better yet, why don't you show me?"

There went that little smile again. She knew what he was doing, and she was willing to play along. She stepped toward him. "Okay." She placed her hands on the outside of his arms and leaned against him briefly, then stepped back. "That's the awkward, I don't want to hug you really, or I'm-not-a-hugger-but-I-will type hug.

"Hmm, that's a non-hug. Show me another."

She grinned and slid her arms around his middle, briefly resting her head against his chest. He started to close his arms around her, but she stepped back again before he could.

"I like that one better, what was that?"

"That was the genuine, it's good to see you hug. It's affectionate, but not intimate."

"I see, well in that case I don't think it would be enough to keep Candy away. What kind would be the don't-even-try-it-girlfriend-he's-mine hug?"

She raised her eyebrows. "Well…Since I'm such a good friend and I'm only doing this to protect you from a rampant man-eater, I'll show you." She stepped toward him again and looped her arms up around his neck. He slid his arms around her middle pulling her closer and enjoying the feel of the length of her body pressing against his. He'd have to be careful though, a certain length of his body was waking up and wanting to do more than press. She went to step back, but he held her to him. There was a slight flush on her cheeks as she met his gaze.

"This one is affectionate, too."

She nodded.

"And more intimate."

She nodded again as she searched his face.

"What do you think it is that creates such intimacy in this one?" He tightened his arms around her as she looked up into his eyes. She melted against him as he lowered his head.

The doorbell tinkled.

Renée stepped quickly away from him and turned toward the door. Gabe smiled at Max Douglas; Gramps, as everyone still called him. Gabe liked the old guy and would normally be happy to run into him. His timing couldn't have been worse today, though.

Gramps seemed to know it. He gave them an apologetic smile. "I know I'm late, Renée, but you wouldn't have any of them cheesy bacon rolls left, would you?"

Renée nodded and hurried into the back. Gabe was a little disappointed that she seemed embarrassed to have been seen in an embrace with him. Gramps met his gaze and mouthed sorry. Gabe shrugged and gave him a rueful smile. He didn't want the old guy to feel bad. "It's okay."

Gramps nodded, then smiled at Renée as she came back out. "Here you go, Gramps. There were a half dozen of the rolls left, and I slipped in the last of the brownies for you, too." She smiled at him now, apparently having regained her composure. "I know how much you love those."

"Aw, thanks Renée." He reached for his wallet, but she put a hand on his arm. "Those are from me."

"Well, in that case, I owe you one." He turned and winked at Gabe on his way to the door. "And I owe you one too, son. You kids enjoy your afternoon. For what it's worth, I think you're onto a good thing."

As the door closed behind him, Gabe looked at Renée. They both burst out laughing.

"He is the best!" said Renée. "I adore him."

Gabe nodded. "He's about as cool as they get, and he's pretty smart, too. If he thinks we're onto a good thing…" She met his gaze, but didn't seem prepared to go there, so he changed direction. "Then maybe we should carry on where we left off. Any other hugs I need to know about?"

She still looked a little uncomfortable, but quickly pulled herself together. "Not for now, and besides you never did tell me what kind of hugger you are."

He walked toward her and slid one arm around her waist. He slid his other hand under her ear, cupped her neck, and tilted her head back so she was looking into his eyes as he pulled her against him. "I'm not a hugger."

"Never?" she whispered.

He held her gaze as he shook his head. "I only hug if I know I don't want to let go."

"Or as a demonstration, right?"

He looked into her eyes for a long moment. Holding her like this, he already knew he didn't want to let go. But it wasn't that easy for her. Kenzie's warning about not hurting her still echoed in his mind. "Right," he said and reluctantly let her go. "So, let's go get some lunch, shall we? Now we know you can rescue me if we do run into Candy."

"Okay. I'll get my things."

As she went into the back, Gabe wanted to think that she looked disappointed. But he wasn't sure he dared to.

~ ~ ~

Sitting on the deck of the restaurant, Renée stared out at the lake. In the years she'd been gone she'd forgotten just how beautiful this place was. Spring was her favorite time of year here; it felt like a new beginning, new hope. She looked across the table at Gabe who was talking on his cell phone. She must not let her imagination run wild! Back there in the bakery when he'd held her so close like that, her ridiculous imagination had been envisioning new hope and a new beginning…with Gabe! For a moment there, everything had felt possible. Well, for two moments. She'd thought he was going to kiss her right before Gramps came in. Bless him! She loved that old guy, but would have given anything not to have seen him today. Then, after Gramps had left, when Gabe said he only hugged if he didn't want to let go? She'd thought—

hoped—that he meant he didn't want to let go of her! She'd so wanted to believe it she'd had to check. And of course he'd agreed with her that it was just a demonstration. Oh well. That'd teach her not to get carried away. She mustn't go hoping. Gabe wasn't a new beginning for her. He was just a good guy who wanted to help her through a tough time, to be a friend to her. She had to smile. He was definitely a guy; she'd felt that when he held her to him. From what she understood, sex was much more straightforward for guys. Maybe they could add some benefits to their friendship. She shouldn't be thinking like that, but, whenever she got around him, it was hard not to. If she had to be realistic about the possibility of a relationship with him, then she could also be realistic about the fact that he was a guy—guys liked sex and didn't necessarily need a relationship to go with it.

"Okay. I'll talk to you tomorrow." Gabe ended his call. "I'm sorry, I had to deal with that."

Renée smiled. "No problem. I was enjoying the view."

"You looked as though you were enjoying something. What was going through that mind of yours?"

She had to bite back a laugh. She couldn't exactly tell him she'd been wondering how she could get him into bed! That was so not like her. She smirked and bit her lip.

Gabe gave her a hard stare. "That looks like too much fun not to share! You have to tell me."

She shook her head, unable to stop herself from laughing. She couldn't tell him she was thinking about sex with him and how much fun that would be!

"I'll get it out of you."

She was giggling uncontrollably now. What she wanted was for him to get it into her! She had to get a grip or he'd think she'd lost it completely.

He pursed his lips and narrowed his eyes at her. "Correct me if I'm wrong, but that sounds like a dirty laugh to me."

She nodded through her giggles and brought her hand up to cover her mouth. People were turning to look at them now, but she couldn't make herself stop.

He grinned at her. "Tell me!"

She shook her head again.

"After we've eaten, we're going to get out of here, and you're going to tell me. I'm not taking no for an answer."

That caused another fit of giggles. He had no idea what he was saying. If only he wanted to get her out of here for the same reason she did. How would it feel for him to want her so much he wouldn't take no for an answer? She needed to stop this. She was aching to find out, but she was just being ridiculous. She managed to catch her breath. "I'm sorry. Sometimes I just get the giggles. I'll be good."

He gave her that look again, the one she couldn't figure out. It looked a lot like desire, but that was just her pesky imagination. Or was it?

The way he said, "I believe you will," made her wonder. She didn't have time to wonder too long though as Ben appeared with their food.

"Hey guys. How are you?" He smiled at Renée, his eyes asking so much more than his words.

"I'm hanging in there, Ben. How about you?"

"Oh, you know me. Keeping busy."

Ben was always busy. She wished he'd find himself a good woman and learn to have some fun instead of working all the time. "Why don't you take a break?" she asked.

Ben laughed. "I wouldn't know what to do with myself if I did. My work is my life."

Gabe nodded. "I know that feeling."

"The pair of you should get a life, then," said Renée. "You know what they say about all work and no play."

Ben looked at her. "And when was the last time you played?"

She pushed her hair out of her eyes. "I'm out for lunch, aren't I?" She looked at Gabe. "We're having a mini class reunion. And if you can find a replacement for Shelly any time soon, I might have enough energy after work to start horseback riding again. I've been thinking about it."

Ben looked uncomfortable.

She immediately felt bad. "I'm only messing with you. I'm perfectly capable of running the place by myself. I appreciate the job and you know it."

Ben nodded. "I know. No worries. It's just... Well, I think I'll have someone working with you by the end of the week."

"But?"

"But getting her here will mean adding another face to your little class reunion."

Gabe raised an eyebrow. "Someone else is coming back to the lake and you're giving them a job, too?"

Ben shook his head. "No. April is from Montana, but she's coming to live here." He looked from Gabe to Renée and held her gaze as he said, "Chance is bringing her."

Renée's heart jumped into her mouth. Was she ready to come face-to-face with Chance Malone? Her hand shook as she reached for her water and took a long drink. The possibility of

running into Chance had almost stopped her from coming back to the lake. She'd had no choice though. She had nowhere else to go, and Ben had reassured her that Chance hardly ever came back anyway.
Both guys looked concerned.
"I'm sorry," said Ben.
She smiled brightly at him. "No problem."
Gabe held her gaze. She didn't know what to say, so she picked up her fork and started to tackle the salad she now had no appetite for.

# Chapter Six

Gabe pulled up and looked across at Renée. She'd hardly spoken through the rest of their lunch and hadn't said a word on the drive back to her house.

She gave him that brittle, bright smile. "Thanks for lunch, my friend. Sorry I put a damper on it. I'll see you around." She let herself out and was halfway up the path before Gabe caught up to her.

He put a hand on her shoulder. She stopped, but didn't turn around. "I'm not leaving you like this, Renée."

"I'm fine."

"No, you're not." He could feel the tension in her. He wanted to take it away, make it better for her, but he knew he couldn't. He wrapped an arm around her waist and pulled her back against him. For a moment she resisted, but he held her there until he felt her start to relax. "You're so stubborn…"

"Thanks!" She tried to pull away, but he didn't let her.

"Let me finish. And that's a quality I admire. However, you are not as stubborn as I am. I'm not about to let you go back in that house and spend the rest of the day stressing out."

"It's not up to you. And, besides, I'm not stressing. It just took me by surprise. I need time to process it. To mentally prepare to see him."

"Do you know the best way to process something like that?"

She shook her head. "That's what I'm hoping to figure out."
"Well then, let me tell you. The best way is to talk it through. With a friend."
She leaned back against him and he had to shift his hips. He was concerned about her. He wanted to help her, but he couldn't help the way his body reacted every time he got around her. Today had been torture. He'd held her in his arms three times now, felt her gorgeous curves pressed against him, and a part of him was getting very impatient. He wasn't used to denying himself. Not when it came to women. He took what he wanted, when he wanted.
"You really want to stick around and talk about it?"
He wanted to stick around, and he knew she needed to talk about it. "I do."
Slowly, she turned around. He loosened his arm so she could move, but not enough so that she could step away. She looped her arms up around his neck. The pain and sadness in her eyes before she rested her head on his shoulder made him forget all his less chivalrous desires. He hugged her to him. "I want to be here for you."
"Thank you."
They stood that way for a long time before she lifted her head. "Come on in then. I hate to say it, but I need a drink."
Gabe nodded and followed her inside.

~ ~ ~

Renée opened the fridge door and enjoyed the feel of the cool air against her warm skin for a moment. Chance or no Chance, Gabe and the way he kept putting his arms around her was causing her to overheat! She passed him a beer and took one for herself. "Want to sit out front?"
He followed her back out and they made themselves comfortable in the old rockers. Gabe sipped on his beer, but said nothing. She knew he was waiting for her to talk. Part of

her didn't want to. She'd kept it all to herself all these years; she had some pride in the fact that she'd never leaned on anyone. She also had some fear about finally talking about what had happened, finally sharing her guilt. She stared out at the old orchard where she and Chloe had played as kids. Where she knew Chloe and Chance had spent so many good times together. She had to blink away the tears. The guilt was laying heavy on her heart. She looked over at Gabe. Did she want to tell him?

He replied as if she'd asked the question out loud. "You don't have to if you don't want to."

"I think I do want to. I just don't know where to start."

"Do you want me to ask questions? I'm pretty good at that."

She nodded slowly. She didn't know how to unjumble everything that was rolling around in her mind. Maybe Gabe's laser focus would help. Maybe. "Okay, but don't expect quick answers."

"I won't. I don't need any answers at all. This is all about you and what you need."

She shot him a grateful smile, "Thanks."

"So let's start with the big question. Why don't you want to see Chance?"

"That's easy. I don't want to see him because I feel guilty as hell. He might have saved Chloe if I hadn't stopped him. He reminds me that my sister might still be alive if it weren't for me." She stared out at the lake for a moment, surprised at the wave of relief her confession brought. She turned back to Gabe. "And saying that brings me some relief. To finally admit that…" She shook her head. "But then the relief just brings more guilt. It's so selfish of me. I should have to live with what I did." She swallowed back the tears that were threatening to fall. "Chance shouldn't. I don't want to see him because I ruined his life."

Gabe stared at her for a long moment, but said nothing. What was he thinking? Was he silently agreeing with her? Maybe he was the wrong person to talk to. Chance had been his friend.

She rushed on before he could pass judgment. She didn't want to hear it, and now she'd started, she wanted to talk. "If it weren't for me, his life would have been completely different. He and Chloe were going to go away to school together. They'd probably have come back here and have a great life and a bunch of kids by now. Instead, Chloe's dead and Chance spent all those years in prison. He couldn't come back here. He doesn't even have a life. He lives in the wilderness in Montana."

"You have no idea what his life would have been like, Renée. Tempting as it is, we can never claim that something we did changed the course of someone else's life."

"That's not true. I know full well that if I hadn't stopped him, Chance would have gone after Kyle that night."

Gabe nodded. "I won't argue with that, but you have no idea what would have happened if he did. Chloe might still have died. Chance might have died, too. You just don't know. And besides, you didn't forcibly stop him from going. Chance made a choice. He listened to what you had to say and chose not to go. If he had been determined to go, there's no way you would have stopped him, and we both know it."

"I know, but if I hadn't said anything he would have gone. If I hadn't convinced him that it was best to wait until he'd calmed down. That Chloe was just being stubborn. Gabe, I thought I was so smart! I made him promise me. And I promised him that I would get Chloe to talk to him the next morning. Chance kept his promise…" A sob escaped from her lips, but she forced herself to finish. "I couldn't keep mine. I couldn't make Chloe talk to him, because she was dead." She couldn't help it. The tears came.

Gabe took hold of her hand and pulled her toward him. She rose from her own chair and let him pull her into his lap. He closed his arms around her as she buried her face in his chest and sobbed. She felt as though she'd killed Chloe herself. Chloe and Chance had been together since sixth grade. They were made for each other; everyone knew it. They were going to get married as soon as they graduated and go off to college together. That fateful night they'd had a fight. Chloe had been jealous over another girl flirting with Chance. Kyle Hutchens had always had a thing for her and he'd made the most of their argument. He'd invited her to go out on the lake with him on his dad's boat, and, angry at Chance, she'd gone with him. Chance had come out here looking for her, angry that she'd gone off with Kyle. He'd wanted to know where they were, wanted to go after them. Renée knew Chance had a temper. She knew he'd never hurt Chloe, but she was worried what he might do to Kyle. She'd made him promise that he'd go home, calm down. And she'd promised she'd get Chloe to talk to him the next morning. But Chloe never came home. The next morning Kyle had rowed into the resort, hungover and scared. He said they'd been drinking and swimming. Chloe had drowned. He'd claimed he'd tried to save her. Chance never believed his story.

Chance had never spoken to Renée again. He'd hardly spoken to anyone. He changed, from the popular life and soul of the party guy he'd been, into someone else completely. He was angry and withdrawn. He'd left town straight after graduation. Renée had carried the guilt over destroying his family, too. His little sister Missy had been devastated. She'd been left alone with her dad, just as Renée was left alone with hers. Her own father had been an alcoholic for as long as she could remember. He'd raised his girls as best he could, taking whatever work he could find and holding each job as long as the bottle would allow. Chloe's death had been the end of him. He'd hit the bottle hard. Two months after Chloe's death her dad had followed her. Renée had come home one afternoon to find him sprawled in the orchard, a picture of Chloe grasped tight in one hand, an empty bottle of cheap whiskey lying beside him.

Chance had surprised everyone by returning to Summer Lake to attend the funeral. In the two months that had passed, he'd changed. His hair was longer, he rode a Harley and had a threatening air about him that made most folk get out of his way. Renée had tried to talk to him, but he wouldn't even look at her. She'd put a hand on his arm, and he'd angrily shaken her off.

She remembered calling after him. "I'm so sorry, Chance."

He'd stopped in his tracks and turned around. The pain and anger etched on his face had made her catch her breath. He'd held her gaze for a long moment. She'd thought he was about to speak, but he just shook his head and walked away.

The next day, Kyle Hutchens had been found badly beaten. He was rushed to the hospital where he remained for several weeks. Chance had been arrested and taken into custody where he'd remained—in one form or another—for several years. By the time he was released, Renée was living in San Francisco. She'd kept in touch with Missy periodically and knew that Chance had gone to live in Montana. That he rarely came home. She'd thought she'd made her peace with herself, until Ben had told her Chance was coming to Summer Lake. Now she realized that she hadn't, and that she never would until she made her peace with him.

She lifted her head and looked up at Gabe.

He stroked her wet hair away from her face. "It's not your fault, Renée. It never was."

"Part of me knows that. Part of me doesn't want to believe it. Part of me needs someone to blame, you know?"

Gabe nodded. "I can see that, but why not Kyle? If you have to blame someone, why not blame him?"

She shrugged. "Because realistically I know that blame doesn't change anything. It's easier to turn it on myself."

"Well, maybe it's time to let it go? Maybe you and Chance will finally be able to talk to each other and you'll both be able to find some peace?"

"Maybe. I don't think it's too likely though. I've tried to contact him; I used to send him letters. He never once replied."

"It took years before he would reply to anyone."

"But eventually he did, didn't he?"

"Yeah, but he's never let anyone back in. I tried for years myself. He agreed to meet me once, and that was only because I was right there on his doorstep in Montana."

"And you were one of his best friends. So why do you think he would open up to me?"

"Maybe he won't. Maybe it's just wishful thinking on my part. I want him to, because I think it's what you both need before you can really move on in life."

Renée nodded. "You're probably right, but that doesn't mean it's going to happen."

"No, it doesn't, but if you two are going to run into one another, I'd like to think that you'll at least be open to the possibility. You blame yourself; you don't know that Chance does."

"I think it's a fair assumption given the fact that he's never spoken to me."

"All I'm saying is try again."

She let out a big sigh. "I will, but I won't expect anything good to come of it."

"Maybe it won't; maybe it will. You won't know unless you try."

"True. Can we leave it now though? I've tried not to think about it all for years, let alone talk about it. This is kind of exhausting."

She was relieved when he smiled. "Okay. I shall drop this line of inquiry." He hugged her tight for a moment then dislodged her from his lap so he could stand. She was a little disappointed. She'd been enjoying the comfort of snuggling against him like that, but she had to remember that he was just being nice. She was even more disappointed when he said, "In fact, I should probably get going."

Well, damn! Here she was thinking he was going to stick around. She was surprised how much she wanted him to. "Okay." She didn't know what else to say. The green eyes looking down at her had that strange intense look in them again. She'd be damned if she could figure him out. "Thanks for your time, then. Sorry to have kept you." She knew it sounded petulant, but she couldn't help it. She'd thought he was going to stay a while. Once again, he was abruptly leaving, and it made her feel bad about having taken up his time when he didn't really want to be here.

He shook his head slowly. "You don't understand."

She smiled at him, trying to pull herself together. "I'm sorry. I do. You have better things to be doing and I shouldn't be leaning on you so much. I apologize. It's just that for a minute there, I stupidly believed that you gave a shit. Don't worry, I won't be making that mistake again."

He moved so fast she was crushed against his chest before she knew what was happening. He held her close and slid his free hand into her hair as he glared down at her. "Don't, Renée. You have no idea how much I care. How much I want to help you."

Her breath was coming fast as she stared up at him in disbelief. She clung to him as his hard body pressed against hers. There could no longer be doubts about whether or not he desired her—not with the bulge in his pants that was pushing against her belly.

"Unfortunately, what I want most right now is to lay you down and show you. I don't think that's what you need at the moment, so I'm leaving while I still can."

Her heart hammered in her chest as he lowered his mouth to hers. It wasn't a gentle kiss. He crushed her lips and invaded her mouth. She had no defenses as she opened up to him and kissed him back hungrily. She'd never been kissed like that in her life—he was demanding she let him in, taking possession of her—and she loved it!

When he finally lifted his head, they were both breathing hard. She searched his face.

"I'm sorry."

"Why?" The only thing she was sorry about was that he'd stopped. She could kiss him like that forever!

"It's not what you need right now, is it? You need a friend."

"You're being a friend."

He shook his head, he looked frustrated. "I'm taking advantage of you, that's what I'm doing."

She had to laugh at that. "Don't be ridiculous, Gabe."

He raised an eyebrow. "Ridiculous?"

She nodded. "How is giving me what I want taking advantage of me?"

He narrowed his eyes at her. "You wanted me to kiss you?"

She smiled. "And the rest."

"The rest?"

"Well, a friendship between a man and a woman usually has some benefits, doesn't it? That's what I'd like. I mean you're trying to help me through a tough time, and there's no better way a man can comfort a woman." She couldn't believe she'd said it, but why not? While he was kissing her, his body had told her how much he wanted her. She was aching for him right now, and, wrong as it may be, she knew she'd forget all her troubles for a little while if he would use his body to comfort her!

He stared down at her, his eyes boring into her. "What are you saying?"

She'd already made a fool of herself, she may as well spell it out. "That if you want me, I want you. I think you've already noticed that I'm more than a little attracted to you. You feel bad because you want to have sex with me. I'm saying there's no need to feel bad, because I would like that, too. It doesn't have to get weird; we can just do the friends-with-benefits thing." She met his gaze. "If you'd like?"

# Chapter Seven

Gabe pulled up a seat at the bar. He still couldn't quite believe he was here, that he'd left Renée's place. What was that woman doing to him? She'd asked him for exactly the kind of arrangement he normally preferred with a woman and he'd refused. Why? Because he wanted more than that. Because his ego had taken a hit because he wanted her to want more than that. But that was some crazy mixed up shit! There was no way there could be anything more than that between them. He lived in New York and she was in a mess and was still married anyway. He scowled to himself. Why couldn't he have at least given her what she claimed she wanted—just once?

"Hey, Gabe." Ben gave him a puzzled look. "I didn't expect to see you this evening. What can I get you?"

"I'll take a bourbon on the rocks." He glared at Ben. "And why didn't you expect to see me?"

Ben raised an eyebrow. "Renée?"

"What about her?" he snapped. Had Ben thought that he'd be screwing her by now, too?

Ben held a hand up. "Whoa. I thought she might want a friend around after hearing that Chance is coming. And I thought you were her friend."

Gabe blew out an exasperated sigh. Apparently he was overreacting. "Sorry. She did. She does, but at the moment I'm not the right friend."

"You're not? Why not?"

"Because I have an agenda of my own."

"Ah, and it doesn't match hers?"

Gabe didn't know. Apparently she wanted to sleep with him, but his agenda went a whole lot deeper than that.

"Sorry. None of my business."

At that moment, Pete Hemming came in through the bar and pulled up the seat next to Gabe. He looked like hell.

Ben gave him a worried look. "Hey bud. Are you okay?"

"Yeah. Just great." He loosened his tie; he was still in full business suit. "I just need a strong one before I head home."

That surprised Gabe. He thought Pete had a hot little fiancée waiting at home for him, but if that was the case, he wouldn't be in here.

"S'up Gabe? What's going on in your world?"

Gabe shrugged. "Not much. I'm just taking a bit of a break."

Pete nodded. "And then you'll head back to the Big Apple, right? Back to reality."

"I don't know… I'm starting to think that reality is here, that this is where I need to get back to."

Pete snorted. "I'd think long and hard about that one if I were you. It sounds like a great idea until you try to make it work. Then it gets a lot more complicated."

Ben slid Pete his drink. "You're just burned out on everything right now, bud." He looked at Gabe. "You could make it work back here if you wanted to, I'm sure."

"Yeah, right," said Pete with a laugh. "What would Gabe do here? Are you going to put him to work behind the bar?"

Gabe made a face. Pete had hit on his own big concern. What the hell would he do if he came back to live at the lake? He had no interest in family law, and practicing any other kind of law would have him commuting for more time than he'd be here.

Ben shrugged. "You'd come up with something. I mean who would have thought any of you guys would be able to make it work out here? Jack's doing great; Dan's made the transition from Silicon Valley to small town, no problem." He gave Pete an odd look. "You were doing great for a while there."

"Yeah, sorry. I guess I'm just a little disillusioned at the moment, Gabe. Ignore me. You can make anything work if you set your mind to it."

Gabe was aware of that fact. Renée herself had reminded him of it just the other day. It didn't help that he didn't know what he would want to do here though. And it helped even less that now he wasn't sure if Renée was really looking for the same things he was or whether she was just looking for sex to take her mind off her troubles. He took a slug of his bourbon. Why should he have a problem if she was. Wouldn't that be easier—better—for him, too?

~ ~ ~

Renée climbed into bed. Why on earth had she gone and blown it? She was all over the place, and she knew it. If she wanted to, she could blame the stress over Eric and the court case; she could blame the fact that she would no doubt run into Chance sometime soon, but she knew the real reason. She was all over the place because Gabe Morgan had her head turned right around. He was incredibly sexy and such a smart, genuinely good guy, too. The physical effect he had on her made her stupid. Stupid enough to suggest that they should sleep together! She cringed as she remembered the look on his face. He'd made all the right noises…said he would love to…but told her she needed to think about what she was saying. Then he'd left—in one hell of a hurry! She pulled the pillow over her head and groaned. He was far too nice a guy to just say, no thanks!

He'd even said he'd still stop by tomorrow and help her work on the house. Well, wouldn't that be excruciating?! Still, at least he hadn't withdrawn his friendship altogether. She'd hate that. She'd make up some excuse tomorrow about being stressed or not in her right mind. She'd apologize, and, hopefully, they'd be able to carry on as though she hadn't told him she'd love to screw his brains out!

It took her a long time to get to sleep. When she finally did, she dreamed about Gabe. He was undressing her out in the orchard. It was a beautiful sunny afternoon, and he was going to make love to her. She moaned as he spread her legs; her whole body was tingling in anticipation. She tensed and felt the first waves of her orgasm take her as he thrust his hips and entered her. She was writhing under the sheets, horny as hell. She woke up sweating with tears rolling down her cheeks when Chance's face drifted in the clouds above them. "Promise me! Promise me you won't do it. It'll only end badly, and you know it." The exact words she'd said to him all those years ago.

She lay there staring at the ceiling, wishing she'd had a little longer with Gabe. She'd been right on the edge of what felt like it might have been the best orgasm of her life. She'd been so aroused—hell, she still was! She held the pillow tight, wishing it was him, wishing that he hadn't turned her down, all the while feeling terrible that she was apparently more concerned about sex with Gabe than she was about the possibility of finally getting over the past with Chance.

When she opened her eyes again it was at the sound of the alarm clock. She was a morning person, but these four o'clock starts were starting to get to her. She reluctantly dragged herself out of bed and into the shower. It was going to be a long day and she knew it. Gabe had said he would come by when she got finished and drive her home. He was going to help her board up the upstairs windows. She never went up there and her polyethylene sheets weren't doing a very good job of anything except blowing in the wind.

~ ~ ~

Gabe took a deep breath before getting out of the car. He'd done a lot of thinking since he left Renée's place last night. He'd decided that if she wanted to sleep with him, then—as a friend—the least he could do was oblige. If that was what she wanted or needed from him to help her through a tough time, then he'd be more than happy to give it to her. He'd also decided that he wanted more from her than that. If she was open to it, he was going to start looking for ways they could be together, build a relationship, and see where they could take it.

He pushed open the door to the bakery and smiled when he saw her. She was so beautiful. She was a mess, red hair tousled, and he was pretty certain she had her shirt buttoned wrong since one tail was longer than the other. Her cutoff jeans came down an inch longer on one leg than they did on the other, and, to Gabe, the guy who demanded perfection, she looked absolutely perfect!

She smiled uncertainly. "Hey."

"Hey, are you ready?"

She nodded and followed him out. Once they had her bike in the back of the car and were headed out West Shore she turned to him. "About last night."

He turned and grinned at her. "Let's talk about it later, can we? We've got a lot of work to do."

"Okay."

She looked uncomfortable, so he added, "I mean we can talk about it later if you want to, but there's no need. We're good. Aren't we?"

She nodded.

Gabe couldn't help smiling to himself as he turned onto the dirt road that led up to her house. He was hoping that tonight they'd find out just how good they were.

By eight o'clock that evening they had all the windows in the upstairs of the house boarded up. Gabe would love to just have the whole place torn down and rebuilt, but there was no way she'd let him do that.

She pushed her hair out of her eyes and smiled at him. "Thank you. I haven't got much in, but can I tempt you with a beer and a sandwich?"

He nodded. She was tempting him with so much more than that.

After they'd eaten, they sat in the living room. Gabe hadn't seen this room before it was more like the kitchen than the rest of the house, in that was it was clean and bright and almost livable.

"Do you want to watch a movie?" she asked.

"Sounds good." He wasn't really a movie kind of guy, but it would give him the opportunity to spend a couple of hours on the sofa with her. So, he wasn't lying, that did sound good.

While she sat on the floor in front of the DVD player reading out the names of the movies she had, Gabe sat himself in the middle of the sofa. She'd have to sit next to him wherever she went. When she had the movie running, she turned around and looked at him. The confusion on her face was quite comical. She didn't know where to sit for the best. He smiled to himself as she sat back down on the floor at his feet—even better, although she didn't realize it yet.

He could tell she was no more focused on the movie than he was; the set of her shoulders was a dead giveaway of nervous tension. He leaned forward and stroked her hair. "Do you want a shoulder rub while you're down there?" he asked.

She nodded, but didn't speak.

Gabe grinned to himself. He had her, and they both knew it. He sat forward on the edge of the sofa and positioned her between his legs. He felt her tremble as he swept her hair off her neck and started to gently knead with his thumbs. For a good ten minutes he worked her shoulders, easing away the tension she'd been carrying. He could feel he was building another kind of tension though and not just in his own pants. When he worked a little knot at the base of her neck, the little sighs she'd been making turned to moans, lower more sensual. He worked the flats of his hands down her back and felt her tense when his fingertips dipped inside her jeans. He ran his hands back up her sides, deliberately letting his fingers graze her breasts in passing. He sat back and hooked his hands under her arms lifting her so she sat on the edge of the sofa between his legs. Curling one arm around her waist, he swept the hair off her neck and brushed his lips over her soft skin. The little moan that escaped from her lips urged him on. There was no going back now. He closed his hands around her breasts and was rewarded with another moan. He bit the side of her neck, and she sagged back against him.

"Gabe," she whispered. "Please, stop."

He sucked in a deep breath and lifted his head, but continued caressing her breasts as he spoke. "You really want me to stop?" He didn't think he'd be able to if she said yes. He needn't have worried.

"I really don't want you to stop. But I think that you doing this just because you know it's what I want is way above and beyond the call of friendship. You don't have to do this if you don't really want to."

Even while she was speaking, he slid one hand down and started unfastening her jeans. "When are you going to learn, Renée?"

"Learn what?" she breathed as he slipped his hand inside her damp panties. His own jeans got that much tighter when he felt how badly she wanted him, how hot and wet she was.

He traced his finger over her opening. "I don't do anything I don't want to do. You have no idea how much I've wanted this since the first time I saw you working the bar." He pushed her jeans down over her knees and she kicked out of them. "I want you."

She looked up at him over her shoulder, her eyes darkened with desire. "I want you, Gabe."

Those were the words he'd needed to hear. He soon had them both out of the rest of their clothes and pulled her down to lie face to face with him. She traced her hand over his chest then met his gaze. "Are you sure?"

He caught her wrist as he nodded. "I'm sure," he said as he brought her hand down to touch him through his boxers. "What I need to know is that you're sure." He wanted her to know what she was getting into—better said, what was getting into her.

Her eyes widened as she stroked him. "Oh my!"

He smiled. Much as women joked about how size mattered, when it came down to it some of them couldn't handle the reality. Renée looked anything but scared. Her lips were slightly parted, her skin flushed, and her breath was coming slow and heavy as she touched him. For Gabe, hard lust was replaced by tenderness in an instant when he saw fear flash across her face.

"What is it?"

She met his gaze. "It's been a long time. I might not…What if I can't…"

Gabe slipped his hand inside her panties. She was so wet, he had no doubt it'd be okay. "You can." He closed his other hand around the back of her neck and kissed her deeply. She was so soft, so willing. He got rid of their underwear and drew her under him. He was aching to be inside her. With any other woman, it would have been easy; he would have taken his pleasure, swift and hard. With Renée he was cautious. He spread her legs, kissing her all the while as he positioned himself. She opened herself up to him as he slid his hands under her ass, lifting her to receive him. She screamed as he thrust his hips and entered her. He wanted to scream himself, she felt so damned good! She moved with him, their hips pounding in a frantic rhythm. She was so tight, clenching around him with each thrust of his hips. She was driving him crazy. The pressure began to mount at the base of his spine; it seemed she hit the point of no return in the same moment he did. She tensed and clung to him as he let himself go taking her away with him as the pleasure crashed through them. Gabe gasped as he exploded deep inside her. He was completely at her mercy as her body clenched around him. Her orgasm intensified his own as she moaned her way through it.

When they finally stilled he buried his face in her neck, making her quiver, sending an aftershock through him and back to her.

"Oh my!" she eventually mumbled.

Gabe nodded as he rolled to the side. He didn't have the strength for words yet. He was blown away. He'd had a lot of sex, with a lot of women, and he wouldn't deny that. Over desks, on yachts, under ball gowns, he'd done it all. He liked sex. But this? He hadn't fumbled around on a sofa in front of a TV since he was a teenager and yet this? This was the best ever. She was the best ever. He kissed her neck.

"Thank you."

Her tone made him lift his head and raise an eyebrow. "Thank you?"

She nodded. The passion and pleasure had left her face and had been replaced by…what? Embarrassment? "This really was above and beyond. But Gabe, I don't want to be a charity case, let alone the recipient of a charity fuck!"

"A charity fuck?" Gabe was stunned. "You really think that's what this was?"

She nodded sullenly. "Yesterday I said I wanted to and you went running. Today you gave me what I wanted because you're such a stand-up guy!"

Gabe shook his head. "No guy could stand up for sex if he didn't want it, you stubborn woman! What part of I want you don't you understand? What part of I'm crazy about you don't you get? What part of I don't ever want to cause you to hurt more than you already do isn't getting through to you? I keep telling you I care about you. I didn't keep telling you how much I wanted to fuck you, because I want us to be about more than that. Yesterday when you said you wanted to be friends with benefits, you hurt my feelings because I want you to want more than that. So don't you dare tell me this is a charity fuck!" Gabe ran out of steam and stared at her, not quite believing that he'd just lost it and yelled at her.

She looked totally shocked as she stared back at him. "You mean that?" she asked.

He blew out a frustrated sigh. "What do you think, Renée?"

She smiled. "I think you do."

He smiled back.

"But I think you may need to do it again to prove it."

He laughed and drew her closer. "I'd be happy to."

# Chapter Eight

After dropping Renée at the bakery, Gabe didn't know where to go. He didn't want to roll into his parents' place at four in the morning. He'd rather face that inquisition after coffee. He drove back down Main wondering what time the restaurant opened for breakfast—or even the convenience store—so he could get a caffeine fix. He parked in the square at the resort and decided to take a stroll. A stroll around this place was literally one down memory lane for him. He'd grown up in the big house on Main where Michael now lived with Megan and Ethan. This little town had been his whole life until he was eighteen and went off to college. Unlike many of his friends though, he'd known it wasn't forever, he'd known he'd leave—and thought he'd never come back. Now he was considering it. Seriously considering it. He wandered to the end of Main to the little park where they'd hung out as kids. Who would have guessed then at where they'd all be in life now. He'd thought he was going to follow in his dad's footsteps and become a doctor. He hadn't told Renée, but it was through trying to help his friend Chance that he'd developed an interest in the law. Chance, he'd been just as much a *golden boy* back in those days as Gabe himself. Perhaps more so; he even had the childhood sweetheart. Chloe. Gabe would never have believed that she wouldn't live to see nineteen. She'd been so full of life. And Renée, she'd been bound to do something great, to contribute. That was who she'd always been. Granted her charity work had been shaped by what had happened to Chloe and her dad, but she'd followed a path closer to what anyone would have guessed than the rest of them. Until recently. Until Eric had been discovered for the lying, cheating, fraudulent bastard he was. Gabe had never even met the guy; he didn't want to.

He just wished Renée never had either. He sat on one of the swings and stared out at the lake as the sky turned from dark to gray. He wondered about so many of their other friends, too. Many of them were still here, living the same lives their parents had, raising the next generation to do the same. Some had scattered far and wide. Dex, who had been his and Chance's other best buddy, lived in Seattle. He'd threatened to come back and visit while Gabe was here, but Gabe wasn't going to hold his breath on that one.

He started at the sound of footsteps on the gravel path. Who the hell would be out here at this time in the morning? He relaxed when he recognized Missy's fiancé, Dan.

Dan raised a hand and gave him a shy smile. "Damn, you scared me. I'm used to having this place to myself in the mornings."

Gabe smiled. "Sorry. I'm just killing time until I can get some coffee."

"I can go get you a cup if you like? We live right there."

Gabe looked to where he was pointing. "You bought the old DeWinter place?"

Dan nodded. "Missy loves it. Want me to go make you a cup?"

"Thanks, but I can wait. The store should be open soon."

Dan checked his watch. "Yeah. Another ten minutes is all."

Gabe remembered what Ben had said last night about Dan having made the transition from Silicon Valley to small town. He didn't really know the guy, but he liked him and was intrigued to know how he'd managed to make the move. "Do you mind if I ask you something while I wait?"

"Sure." He looked a little wary. "What do you want to know?"

"How you're finding living here? How you're managing to make it work."

Dan rubbed his hand over the stubble on his cheek. "I love it here. I didn't think it was going to be possible at first. When I met Missy and I knew I wanted to be with her, I thought maybe I could move her to the city." He smiled. "But there was no way *that* was going to happen. She has a great life here, the city could never compare for her or for Scot. I realized that it couldn't compare for me, either." He looked at Gabe. "I know you are, but I wasn't made for city life. This place suits me much better."

Gabe nodded. "I'm starting to think it suits me better, too, but I have no idea how I could make it work. I mean I'm a trial attorney in New York City. How the hell could I make that work here?"

Dan shrugged. "I was a geek in Silicon Valley. How could I make that work here?"

"You did though."

"I did, but I got lucky. A friend of mine needed someone to work remotely, accessing systems from the outside. It didn't matter from where, so here I am."

Gabe wondered what the equivalent situation would be for him. It wasn't as though he could remotely access the courtroom.

Dan cocked his head to one side and stared at him. "What is it that you love about your work?"

Gabe thought about it. "I guess what it boils down to is making a difference. I hate to see people suffer, especially when there's something I can do about it. I hate to see individuals used, taken advantage of, or hurt by corporations or institutions. Especially when it's in the interest of profit."

Dan was quiet for a long time.

It was too long for Gabe. "Are you coming up with any great ideas I'm missing?"

"No, sorry. I'm just trying to boil it down and see how you could translate that into contributing to the life of a small town. You need to be involved." He shot Gabe a smile. "I'm guessing—in charge. You need to feel like you're contributing to the greater good and you need to feel as though you're righting wrongs."

Gabe nodded. "I guess that about sums it up."

"Could you leap straight from the courtroom to Chief of Police or something like that?"

Gabe shook his head. "Nope."

Dan shrugged. "I don't know then. What I do know is that you'll come up with something. It seems as though there's an influx of us, all leaving behind the lives we thought we wanted and coming here to live lives that are so much better than we imagined."

"I hope you're right. I'd like to think I can fit the bill and join the stampede back here, but I have no idea how to make it work."

"You're a smart guy. You'll figure it out." He looked at Gabe for a long moment. "Do you mind if I ask you something?"

"Fire away."

"Has Renée said anything about Chance coming?"

That took Gabe by surprise.

"Sorry. I don't mean to pry. It's just that Miss wants him to stick around for a while, and, for some reason, she doesn't think he's going to because of Renée."

"Do you know Chance?"

"Not very well yet. We got off to a good start. He told me his story, and I know how hard it is for him to come back here. I don't know how Renée fits into it though. Don't get me wrong, I don't need to know. I just don't want to put my foot in it. I'd like him to stay a while, for Missy's sake…and Scot's.. Most of all for his own sake, and I get the feeling Renée is going to either make it a whole lot better or a whole lot worse for him somehow."

Where to start? Gabe liked Dan. He was obviously asking for all the right reasons, but it wasn't Gabe's story to tell. "He told you about Chloe?"

Dan nodded. "Just the bare bones of what happened to her and what he did."

That spoke volumes about what Chance thought of Dan. Gabe wouldn't have expected him to ever tell anyone. "Okay, did he tell you that Chloe was Renée's sister?"

"Ah…no."

"Yeah. They both carry a lot of unresolved guilt about what happened that night. And they haven't spoken to each other since."

"Oh, wow."

Gabe nodded. "That's about right."

Dan checked his watch again. "Do you want to walk over to the store and get that coffee?"

Gabe nodded. He liked Dan and hanging with him for a while was more appealing than roaming the streets trying to figure out what he was going to do with the rest of his life…and how he could make Renée a part of it.

Once they had their coffee, they wandered across the square to the resort. It was getting light now, but the place was still deserted. Gabe followed Dan out onto the deck over the lake, and they sat at one of the big picnic benches.

After a while, Dan asked, "Since I'm asking inappropriate questions about people I don't know, do you mind if I try another?"

Gabe had to smile. "Sure."

"You knew our house was the old DeWinter place. Did you know the family?"

"Not too well. The Dewinters were good people, but their kids were quite a bit older. In fact, their granddaughter, Charlotte, was more our age—just a bit younger than Missy—if I remember correctly. She lived in the UK and came to the lake every summer. She and Missy became good friends."

Dan nodded. "Was she friends with any of the others, too?"

Gabe laughed. "She was pretty good friends with Ben from what I remember. They were inseparable for a couple of summers."

"Do you know what happened?"

"I don't. I know they had some big bust up, and she didn't come back after that. That was the summer I was doing my internship though; I only came home for a couple of weeks. I don't know what went on between them."

Dan nodded.

"Can I ask you a question?"

"Sure, it's only fair."

"You don't strike me as someone who would have much interest in people's personal lives. Why so much interest in Renée and Charlotte?"

Dan smiled. "I couldn't care less about anyone's personal life. For me it's a matter of logistics. We're trying to figure out wedding invites and all that good stuff. Missy wants Charlotte to be there, but doesn't think she should ask her because of Ben. She also wants Renée to be there, but doesn't think she should ask her because of Chance. I want Missy to have everything she wants, so I'm trying to figure it all out." He gave Gabe a sheepish grin. "Though I'm working at a distinct disadvantage because, as you so astutely observed, I don't do *people* very well."

That made Gabe smile. "Sorry I can't give you any answers, but I know enough to tell you to wait a week. I'm pretty sure that by then you'll know whether inviting Renée is going to work or not. As for Charlotte, I can't help you there." He hesitated. "No, I don't think my little brother would be able to either. I'd suggest talking to either Emma or Pete. They'd know more than anyone—apart from Missy."

"Thanks." Dan looked a little uncomfortable as he saw Ben emerge from the back of the restaurant. "I wish I could just ask him," he said in a low voice. "But even I can see that it still hurts him. If it didn't mean so much to Missy to have Charlotte there, I wouldn't give it a second thought."

Gabe shrugged. "You never know, it might give them a chance to finally make their peace."

"From what I understand, that would be quite something."

"It would, wouldn't it?" Gabe was thinking more of Chance and Renée, but he'd be happy for Ben if he, too, could make peace with his past.

Ben grinned when he saw them and made his way out onto the deck to join them. "What's this? Are we starting a morning coffee and motivation meeting?"

"That might not be a bad idea," said Dan. "Although you'd have to start serving coffee a little earlier somewhere."

Ben laughed. "Sorry, but it wouldn't be worth my while. I'd have to pay someone to start work earlier and the profit on two cups of coffee wouldn't justify the outlay."

"Do you calculate everything that way?" asked Gabe.

Ben shook his head. "It's a factor in every decision I make." He shrugged. "But you know me. Profit is *one* consideration, but it's not my main motivator. It's a means to an end, not an end in itself. I like to think the resort contributes to the life of the town, but it can only do that because it *is* profitable."

Gabe nodded. He could see that. He wondered what Summer Lake would be like if the resort weren't here. He also had to wonder what so many of the town's residents' lives would be like. Renée, for example, what would she have done without the job here? And what about this April person that Chance was bringing? He shook his head as he considered all the ways Ben and the resort touched people's lives and made them better.

Ben punched his arm. "Don't look like that. I know the bottom line is what drives you, but there's the bigger picture to consider, too, you know."

That stung. "Hey, I might come across as being purely money driven, but I was just thinking the same thing. I envy you. You've got it figured from all angles, haven't you? You make big money yourself, and you do it while you're enjoying yourself and making other people's lives better. You play a big part in keeping the whole town going to boot. I wish I could do the same."

"You do? I thought you were happy tackling injustice in the big bad corporate world—and raking it in along the way."

"I thought I was, too, but the more I come back here, the more I feel like I'm missing out on what's really important."

Ben gave him a knowing look. "You do, huh? Well, as I said last night, these guys have found a way to work it out. I have no doubt you can do the same if you put your mind to it."

Dan looked at him. "It sounds to me as though you already know what you want. Now you just have to figure out a way to make it work."

Gabe thought about it. Was his decision made already? He had to admit that it was. He wanted to be here. He wanted a life where he could enjoy his morning coffee sitting out here by the lake with these guys, rather than gulping it down as he ran up the steps of the courthouse. He wanted this slower pace; he wanted what to him felt like a bigger life. One where he was personally involved with the people whose lives he touched. He wouldn't deny that he'd spent his whole career touching lives, trying to help people, but he realized now that those people were a concept, not a reality. His purpose had been about upholding an ideal, not about actually caring for real people.

Ben stood up. "It looks like you've got a lot to think about, and I need to get this place rolling for the day. Stop by if you want to bounce any ideas around."

"Thanks." Gabe had so many ideas bouncing around his head, he wasn't sure how to corral them all. He certainly wasn't ready to talk about them yet though.

Dan stood. "I need to get going, too. I was supposed to be heading out for a run, not wandering the streets drinking coffee."

Gabe smiled at him. "I'll see you around. And thanks, Dan."

Dan nodded. "Thank *you*."

~ ~ ~

Renée turned at the sound of the doorbell. It had already been a long morning and she wanted nothing more than to get out of here and go home. She still couldn't quite believe that Gabe had stayed the night with her. She needed some time to herself to think about it all.

She smiled when she saw Missy come in. She'd always liked Missy, admired the way she'd worked so hard as a single mom to raise her son.

"Good morning, hon. How are you doing?"

"I'm fine thanks, Miss. How about you? How's life treating you?"

"Wonderfully! We're finally getting everything pulled together for the wedding, and I'm so excited."

"You're going to Vegas, right?"

"We are." Missy opened her mouth to speak but stopped when the door opened behind her. She waited while Renée served some tourists. Renée had to wonder what Missy was really here to talk about. She wouldn't be hanging around if she just wanted to pick up some pastries. Once the tourists had left with their bag full of goodies she turned back to Missy.

"I'm guessing there's a reason for your visit, other than a sugar fix?"

Missy nodded. "You got me." She wrinkled her nose while she chose her words.

Renée smiled. "If it's about Chance, don't worry. I know he's coming."

"Oh, good. Did Ben tell you?"

"Yeah. Apparently he's bringing someone called April, and she's going to be working here with me."

"Yeah it sounds like she's escaping from a tough time. Chance wanted to get her out of there and thought she might be able to make a new life here. She has a son, too."

"Well good for Chance. I'm glad to hear he's still doing good deeds."

"He's not the ogre people make him out to be." Missy was still so defensive of her brother.

"I know that, Miss. I've never thought of him as an ogre. I just wish he didn't hate me."

"Hate you?!" Missy looked genuinely stunned. "Why would he hate you?"

Renée shrugged. "Why wouldn't he?"

Missy gave her a puzzled frown. "I just wanted to make sure that you knew he's coming. He called last night and said he expects to make it down here sometime tomorrow afternoon."

"Thanks for the warning. Do you think he'd be open to talking to me while he's here?"

"I don't know, hon. I do know better than to try to guess what Chance will think or say or do about anything. I also know better than to get caught in the middle."

Renée nodded. "Sorry, I didn't mean to…"

"No. If I thought there was any way I could do anything to help, you know I would. Normally I'll butt my little ass and my big mouth in anywhere." She smiled. "But when it comes to Chance, I just know better, that's all. Anything I try to make him do will backfire, so I'm keeping my nose out. What I did want to ask you is if you want to come for lunch with the girls on Wednesday? We usually get together on Saturdays, but Holly and Laura won't be around this weekend, and we thought it'd be nice to do it to welcome April."

It was easy enough to turn it down. "Sorry, but I don't get finished here until two thirty."

"We can make it a late lunch. I'd really like you to come."

"Why?"

Missy smiled. "You don't beat about the bush do you? I like that about you; you remind me of me."

Renée smiled back. "I think it's why we've always gotten along so well, despite our circumstances. But I also think our circumstances dictate that we're never going to get all pally, are we?"

"I'd like for us to. Why shouldn't we?"

When she thought about it, Renée didn't really see a reason. She'd just always assumed that though she and Missy shared a connection through their siblings that bound them together, it also dictated that a distance be maintained between them.

"Are you telling me you couldn't use a friend right now?"

Renée had to laugh. Someone else had said that to her recently, and that had just led to more confusion.

Missy raised an eyebrow. "Want to let me in on the joke?"

"Gabe told me I needed a friend, too, and that's getting all kinds of weird."

"Well, I'm talking about a girlfriend. And besides, even if you think *we* shouldn't get too close, Emma's coming, and Kenzie. Then there's Holly and Laura and Megan, too. And even if you want to stay closed off to making friends, don't you think you should come to welcome your new coworker? Get to know her a little before she comes in here?"

"You don't make it easy to say no, do you?"

Missy shook her head with a smile. "So you'll come?"

"You don't leave me much choice."

"That was the plan." Missy gave her a shrewd look. "Do you want to tell me what's going on with Gabe?"

Renée shook her head. "Even if I knew myself, I don't think I'd be ready to talk about it."

"Well, when you do get around to wanting to talk to someone, you know I'm here for you."

"Why though, Miss? What does it matter to you?"

"*You* matter to me. We're bound together, even though it's for a reason we both wish had never happened. I'd love to see you happy; I'd love to see you stay." She shrugged. "So shoot me."

"Hmm. Thanks." Renée didn't know what else to say.

"And while I'm here," Missy seemed to understand and let it go, "do you have any of those brownies? Scotty and Dan both love them."

"There's a batch due out of the oven in seven minutes."

"Okay. I'll just run down to the store then; I'll be back."

As Renée watched her leave, she wondered if she should still wriggle out of this lunch with the girls. She'd told herself she mustn't hope for anything with Gabe. Now it seemed as though they were starting something, but she didn't know where it could go. Why would she start to build friendships with some women she already liked when she didn't know if she was going to be able to stay here, or where her life would go once Eric's court case was finally over?

# Chapter Nine

Renée flopped down on the sofa. She was exhausted. Emotionally as well as physically. She smiled as she remembered lying here last night—with Gabe. He was amazing! She giggled at the thought that Kenzie could keep the brownies. Renée would sooner go for the orgasms with Gabe. Sex with him had been nothing like sex with Eric, and she used to think that Eric was good. She just hadn't known any better; hell, she hadn't known at all for more than a year! She felt a little guilty that since Gabe had shown up, she'd hardly given Eric a thought. She certainly didn't owe him anything, but whatever was going on with him would affect her future. There was still a possibility that she may be charged with something herself. She had no clue how or what with, but the doubt was still there. She felt as though she'd been burying her head in the sand. No, she knew she had. She had been going through the motions of surviving each day since she'd come back to the lake. Working, making the house livable, and facing people; she really had dealt with as much as she had to, to get through the days and left it at that. Then Gabe had walked into the bakery on Saturday morning and everything felt like it had gone into overdrive. She wanted to start thinking about her life and what she would do with the rest of it. She wanted to hope he'd meant all those things he'd said about caring for her last night. But before she could really think about what came next, she had to deal with what already was. She wanted an end to this horrible limbo she was in. She'd been feeling powerless, as though she had no control over her own life, but that wasn't true. She just hadn't been taking control of the things she could change, because she'd been too overwhelmed by the things she couldn't change. She got up and grabbed her cell phone from her purse. It was time for her to take back some control.

She dialed the number and waited.

"Renée, how are you? I've been meaning to call you."

"So why haven't you?" She was tired of that answer. It seemed it was Paul Williams' stock response. He'd been the charity's lawyer for the last seven years, and he was supposed to be helping Renée through while Eric and the charity were being investigated.

"I'm afraid there's nothing new to report. I keep waiting, hoping I'll be able to call you with some good news, but it's just dragging on."

"I'm tired of it dragging on though, Paul. What can I do? I'm as much a victim in this as anyone. I want it to be over."

Paul was quiet for a long moment. "You can do what I've suggested from the beginning. Divorce him."

She thought about it. She'd known all along that was what she'd end up doing, but as with everything else, she hadn't wanted to face it. Until now. Now it seemed it was the one thing she could do to put herself back in the driving seat of her own life.

"Are you still there?"

"Yeah. Sorry, Paul. I am."

"Are you ready?"

She heaved a big sigh. "Yes. I'm ready. What do I need to do?"

"Do you want to come down here so we can go through it in person?"

She really didn't. "Can't you just draw up the papers and send them to me?"

"I could, but we'd need to figure out the details first."

"What details do you need to know, Paul? He lied to me, stole from me and everyone we dealt with, and cheated on me, repeatedly. Can I just divorce him for adultery?"

"Not in the state of California. It's a no-fault state. All that matters are the 'irreconcilable differences.' Exactly what those differences are, is immaterial."

"Oh." His words made Renée realize just how clueless she was about the whole legal side of things. "So what details do I need to figure out then?"

"Well in your case, the division of marital property is going to be the biggie. In fact, given the ongoing investigation, I don't really know how it will work. Let me ask around. You're going to need someone with a lot more experience in divorce law than I have."

"Okay, but get back to me as soon as you can, will you, Paul? I need to feel as though I'm doing something to get my life back under control."

"Will do. I'll talk to you soon."

Renée hung up and looked around. For all she'd tried to make it livable, this place was no more than a shack. She didn't want to live in a shack, and she didn't want to have her life—and what she could do with it—dictated by a man who'd apparently never loved her. The same man who was now behind bars.

She didn't want to wait for Paul. She wanted to do something. Unfortunately she just didn't know what. The sound of a car approaching drew her to the window. Gabe had said he'd stop by tonight, but she hadn't thought he'd come this early. There he was though, climbing out of his rental car and making her heart race. She couldn't help but smile at the sight of him. The way he smiled back when he spotted her certainly looked like he meant it. How she hoped he did!

~ ~ ~

Gabe had to smile at the sight of her. She hadn't changed after work yet, and her hair looked as though she hadn't put a comb through it since they'd gotten up off the sofa last night, even though he knew that wasn't true. She was a mess, and, yet, he'd never seen another woman look as beautiful.

A strange feeling came over him as she appeared on the front porch to meet him. He felt good! He felt comfortable, and he felt as though this was his life, the one he was supposed to be living. Coming home to his beautiful woman, even though this wasn't exactly home, felt a whole lot better than coming home to his own luxurious apartment.

She smiled. "Sorry. I haven't showered or anything yet; I didn't expect you this early."

Gabe ran up the steps and closed his arms around her. "No. I'm sorry. I didn't want to wait any longer and besides, you have to be up early. I want as much time as I can have with you before you have to go to bed."

The way she smiled at him made him want to take her straight to bed.

"You're a sweet talker, Gabe Morgan."

"I'm a straight talker, is what I am." He held her closer to him and landed a kiss on the tip of her nose. "I have to leave at the end of the week, and I want to spend time with you while I'm here." He raised an eyebrow. "If you want me?"

She smiled up at him. "You know I do."

He saw a shadow of doubt cross her face. "But what?"

"But...well. I want to spend as much time as I can with you, but part of me thinks I shouldn't get used to it. I mean, after this week you'll be gone, and then what?"

It made him smile to know that she was also wondering what the future might hold for them. "Then I'll be back the next weekend," he said.

"You will?"

He nodded. "And more than that, I'll be trying to figure out a way I can move here."

"Why?"

He shrugged. "Spending all this time here has made me realize that I want this life more than I want the life I have in New York."

"I see."

"And," he looked down at her, "there's this chick here who's caught my attention. I can't exactly do much about it if she's living here and I'm living in New York."

"And what exactly do you want to do about it?" she asked.

He shrugged. "Spend some time with her." He pressed his hips into hers and grinned. "Have my wicked way with her." He loved the way she clung to him when he did that. He pressed his lips to hers and said, "You know, do all the things a man and a woman do with each other when they're trying to figure out if they can have a life together."

She stepped back. "Seriously?"

He had to laugh at the incredulous look on her face. "Do I say things I don't mean?"

"I'm starting to wonder!"

He drew her back into his arms. "Why?"

"Well, you hardly know me!"

"That's not true. We've known each other since we were kids."

"Yes, but we haven't seen each other in years!"

He shrugged. "Well, if you're not interested."

She slapped his arm. "You know I'm interested. I'm just a little shocked that you are and that you're prepared to go that fast."

"We're not kids, Renée. I know who I am, and it's taken me way too long to figure out what I want. I don't see the point in wasting more time." It was true. He studied her face, trying to figure out what was going on behind those light green eyes of hers. Maybe he was doing it all wrong. "I'm sorry. Is that too honest? Do you need more romance?"

She laughed. "Do you have a romantic bone in your body?"

He gave her a rueful smile. "I don't believe I do, but I'm sure I could get an app or something."

She slapped his arm again. "I don't need romance. I just need honest, and, you're nothing, if not that." She pushed the hair out of her eyes and looked up at him more seriously now. "There's something else I need, too. Don't take this the wrong way, I need a good divorce lawyer. A very good one."

That took him by surprise. It shouldn't. After all, he was the one talking about where this could go between them, but her wanting a divorce lawyer the very minute he talked about them maybe having a future together made him a little leery.

She laughed out loud. "Oh my God, Gabe! You really are such a guy. Don't worry, I'm not planning on marching you down the aisle as soon as the ink dries on my divorce. I was trying to get started with it anyway. I just got off the phone with Paul, and divorcing Eric seemed like one way I could take back a teeny bit of control over my life. Can you see that?"

"Of course I can." Gabe felt bad about his immediate reaction, but, she was right, he was a guy after all! It was okay for him to want to pursue her, but a little creepy to think that she automatically wanted a divorce the moment he did. He felt bad, but he guessed it would take him a while to shake the residual effects of all the women who'd wanted to snag him over the years. He met her gaze and smiled. "I'm sorry."

"No need, and if it's going to creep you out, forget it. But if you can bring yourself to do it, I'd love for you to put me in touch with the best divorce lawyer you know."

The best divorce lawyers he knew were in New York and would be no good to her anyway. He'd have to think about what connections he might have in California and whether she might want or be able to pay for someone like that. He didn't know any of the details of her financial situation, and he wasn't sure he wanted to.

He must have been taking too long to think about it. "Okay, forget I said anything. You're obviously creeped out by it. I'm sorry." She smiled, but it was that brittle smile—the one that didn't fool him at all.

"That's not fair. I just need to figure out who will be any good to you, and I don't know what you can afford. Although I tend to be brutally honest, I didn't want to lead with that because I know your finances are a sore subject right now, okay?"

"Oh. Sorry."

"Not a problem. Just do me a favor and stop jumping to conclusions?"

The smile she gave him this time was genuine and sexy as hell! "I'm going to jump to one more conclusion, and that'll be all for today. How does that sound?"

He liked the sound of this one. He could tell by the way she laughed that it was going somewhere he'd like. "Okay, one last one, so make it a good one?"

"Well, I need to have a shower, and you haven't let go of me since you got here. You're giving me one very big," she touched the front of his pants as she spoke, "indication that dinner isn't your most pressing need. So I'm going to conclude that, for the sake of expediency, you'd like to join me in the shower."

Gabe drew in a deep breath as she closed her fingers around him.

"Or did I get it all wrong again?"

He turned her around and wrapped his arms around her waist as he started walking her toward the bathroom. "No, I'm pleased to say that you jumped to the right conclusion this time." He closed the bathroom door behind them and started to peel the clothes off her. "And I'll be more than happy to prove you right."

~ ~ ~

Renée smiled to herself. She could get used to this. Gabe had more than proved her right in the shower, and then on the bed afterward. When they'd finally gotten up, he'd fetched a cooler from the car and made them a wonderful dinner. Now here she was, lying on the sofa with her head on his lap while he stroked her hair.

One thing was bothering her though. "Gabe?"

"Mm?" He was working his way through his emails and catching up with the office.

"What could you do here?"

"What do you mean?"

"Well, your work has been everything to you until now. You can't leave it alone." She held up a hand at the frown on his face as he looked up from his phone. "I'm observing, not complaining. It's just that your work has been your whole focus, and more than that, it's been your whole purpose. What on earth could you do in Summer Lake that could compare? You need meaning and purpose. How could you find them here?"

He put his phone down and met her gaze. "Honestly, I don't know. I have no clue, but…and this is totally unlike me, I have a good feeling. Something will come up, I know it. I don't do well in a state of limbo, so I'm just going to move forward believing that it will all work out. And if it doesn't," he shrugged, "then at least that will be a challenge, and I do well when I'm challenged."

"But what if nothing does come up? Don't you feel as though you might wither and die here if you can't find something meaningful to do?"

"Is that really a question for me, or is it what you're asking yourself?"

Hmm, he was way too good at this! She was wondering what she could do in Summer Lake if she were to stay for the long term. The job at the bakery was a lifesaver, but she'd go nuts if she thought it was her future. She nodded. "We're cut from the same cloth in that respect. I need meaning and purpose, I need to feel as though I'm making a difference, and I don't see what I could do here that fits the bill."

Gabe mulled it over. "I'm guessing non-profit work is going to be kind of difficult for you to get into now."

Renée let out a bitter laugh. "No one will touch me, and I don't blame them. I'm guilty by association. No matter what I do, I'll have to start from scratch, and I'll have to fund myself."

He raised an eyebrow at her, but said nothing. She didn't know what he meant by that, but for a moment she had a nasty suspicion that he might be implying he'd help fund her. But no. He wasn't that stupid, and neither was she! She decided to change the subject; that was not a path she wanted to go down.

"So, if you're serious about doing all the things a man and woman do together when they're wondering if they can have a life together, what do you have in mind?" She smiled as his hand roved down over her butt. "Yeah, we already know about that. You've had your wicked way with me."

Gabe laughed. "I've done nothing of the sort. You dragged me into the shower, and I think I've been very restrained…" His smile sent tingles down her spine. "So far. I haven't been wicked at all."

"But you plan to?" Her heart beat a little faster at the gleam in his eye.

"I do." He sat up and pulled her with him. "But I don't think that's what you were talking about. One of things I have in mind is taking you out, on a real date."

"Oh my!"

He laughed. "Don't get too excited. I'm only asking if you want to have dinner at the Boathouse. So far all we've done is have lunch and hang out here. What do you say? Want to come out on a date with me? Let the world know we're an item?"

She smiled. She did. "I'd love to. When?"

"Tomorrow?"

"You've got yourself a date, counselor."

He pulled her to him. "I'll look forward to it."

# Chapter Ten

Gabe placed his hand in the small of Renée's back as he walked her through the bar. This felt so strange to him, but strange in a good way. He couldn't remember the last time he'd picked a woman up to take her on a date. He met them at the restaurant or the bar and left them in their bed. Tonight he'd showered and got ready at his parents' place—while dodging his mom's questions and waggling eyebrows—then driven out to pick up Renée. She looked stunning. Her unruly red hair fell around her shoulders. She wore light makeup that set off her eyes beautifully and a dress that had made him want to cancel the date and take her straight to bed. It was a simple, calf length thing, nothing fancy or daring about it, but the way it clung to her curves had him wanting to get her out of it as soon as he could.

Ben called to them from behind the bar. "Hey guys. Your table won't be ready for a few minutes yet. Do you want to come have a drink while you wait?"

Gabe was a little irritated at that. He'd called Ben earlier specifically to request a quiet table for six o'clock. He wouldn't normally eat this early, but Renée's work schedule dictated that they eat early—and get to bed early. He raised an eyebrow at her and she smiled and changed direction.

Once they were settled at the bar, Kenzie popped her head out of the back and grinned at them. "Good evening! What can I get you? I thought you guys had a table booked?"

"So did I," said Gabe, shooting Ben a questioning look.

Ben shrugged. "Sorry." He didn't look very sorry. Gabe had to wonder what he was up to.

While Kenzie fixed their drinks, Gabe was surprised to see Max Douglas emerge from the Men's room and make his way to the bar.

He settled himself on the stool next to Renée and grinned at them. "Good to see you two out having a good time."

Renée grinned at him. "And you, Gramps! I didn't think you came out much these days."

The old guy grinned. "I don't mind telling you it's almost my bedtime, but I was chatting with our Ben here and something he said made me decide to stick around till you arrived. Don't worry. I won't keep you."

Gabe looked at Ben. What were they up to? Ben gave him that weird smile of his and mouthed sorry, though he looked anything but. Gabe turned back to Gramps hoping he'd hurry up and explain why they were sitting here at the bar instead of getting on with their date.

"See, I was telling Ben that he'd be the perfect replacement for Ted Morris when he stands down; but, of course, our Ben's far too busy with this place."

Gabe had no clue what Gramps was talking about or why it had anything to do with him. He waited—impatiently—for the old guy to continue.

Gramps grinned at him. "And besides, it's not exactly Ben's cup of tea. But he was good enough to remind me that there's a far more suitable candidate in town these days. I'd be happy to nominate you if you want to stand, son. What do you think?"

Gabe stared at him blankly. "Ted Morris?" He kept running the name through his memory banks but wasn't finding a match. "Nominate me for what?"

Gramps chuckled. "Summer Lake Development Manager, son!"

"What?"

Gramps laughed and looked at Renée. "I remember him as being a smart kid. Has living in the city made him a bit slow?"

She laughed with him, but met Gabe's gaze and raised her eyebrows. "I don't know, Gramps. I would have thought he'd jump at the chance, but then I don't know him that well."

Both men turned to her with a who are you trying to kid look on their faces .

Gabe was quickly regaining his composure, even as his mind raced. "And what does the Summer Lake Development Manager do?"

Ben laughed. "Pretty much everything that will help the town, attract businesses and manage growth, draw up policies, consult with existing businesses and agencies to make sure we're staying on track and maintaining, hopefully improving quality of life for residents as the town grows."

Gabe liked the sound of that. He looked at Renée. "Didn't I tell you last night that I had a feeling something would come up?"

He loved the way her eyes shone as she nodded back at him. "And, as usual, you were right. It sounds perfect."

Gramps slapped him on the back. "It sounds like it'd suit you, son. And I'm pretty damned sure you'd be perfect for this town. Ted's been good, but he's old school. Town needs new blood, new ideas, a new approach if'n you ask me." He grinned. "Not that anybody did."

Gabe smiled at him. "But what would it take? Is it an elected position?"

Gramps grinned. "Details like that don't count so much back here, son. The town will do what's right for it."

Gabe frowned at him—that sounded dodgy to say the least.

Ben stepped up. "Don't worry, it's overseen by the Economic Development Committee. Everything has to go through the proper channels. It's not just an old boys club." He grinned at Gramps. "I have dragged them into the twentieth century at least. Though I'd think catching them up to the twenty-first may take me a while yet, and it'd be a lot easier with you at the helm."

Gramps just kept grinning at them. "What Ben says. You just let me know what you decide. I need to be getting on home, and you kids need to be getting on with your evening." He slid down from his stool. "Don't take too long to make your mind up though, will you? We need to get you started." He ambled off without waiting for a reply.

Gabe looked at Ben. "What the..?"

Ben grinned. "You were looking for a way to stay here, to contribute..."

"To do something that would have meaning and purpose," added Renée. "This is perfect!"

Gabe pursed his lips. This was going to take some thinking about!

"Anyway, I didn't want to hijack your evening. I just wanted to get you with Gramps while he was here. He's head of the committee and pretty influential. If you've got his backing, it'll be pretty much a foregone conclusion."

Gabe stared at him. "And you're on this committee?"

Ben nodded. "It's kind of necessary in my position."

Gabe could see that.

"Though I won't claim it's easy—or even pleasant a lot of the time. I wasn't joking about having had to drag them into the twentieth century, but we're making progress. Pete has been getting involved these last few weeks since the development over at Four Mile is nearing completion. He's making a difference, and with you at the helm, we could change things for the better in a hurry."

Gabe smiled. He was starting to think of the possibilities. "What's the budget? What's the administrative hierarchy? Who are the key players?"

Ben laughed. "Slow down. You are supposed to be on a date, and I am supposed to be working. How about you meet me for coffee in the morning? Same time, same place?"

Gabe grinned. The suggestion meant that Ben knew he would be spending the night with Renée and would be driving her into work in the morning. It also meant he understood how eager Gabe was to get a handle on what taking the position might actually mean. "That'd be great. Thanks, Ben."

"No worries. Now, let's get you to your table. Sorry I held you up, but I figured you might forgive me once you knew why."

Renée smiled. "Why don't you join us and you can fill Gabe in now? I know all the questions he has will drive him nuts until he can talk to you about it."

Ben gave him a questioning look, but Gabe shook his head. "No, no one is joining us. This is a date…"

"Yes, but…"

He loved her enthusiasm and her desire to support him, but this was a date. Their first real date. "Yes, but nothing, you stubborn woman. I want you all to myself, okay?"

Ben smiled and turned away. Renée flushed a little and nodded as he held her chair out. "Okay."

Once he was seated across the table from her, he reached over and took her hand. "Sorry, I didn't mean to shoot you down. I appreciate what you wanted to do for me, but you…this…us…it's more important.

She nodded and squeezed his hand. "Thank you, but don't ever feel that you have to put off anything like that for me. I, of all people, understand."

He believed she did. At that moment he realized that one of the reasons they worked so well together was because she wasn't like other women in that way either. She got him. Not because she was making some forced effort to understand, but because she worked the same way. Meaning and purpose, as she called them, were what drove her, just as they drove him. He loved that about her. Hmm, that was a strong word, but it felt like it might be true.

~ ~ ~

Renée squeezed Gabe's hand again. She was excited for him. This sounded like something he might really enjoy, something he could really put himself into and get a lot out of. She couldn't help feeling a little pang of jealousy though. How would she ever find something that might be fulfilling for her? She'd tried to steer her mind clear of those kinds of questions. For the time being she had enough on her plate just keeping her head above water and surviving the limbo that Eric's court case left her in.

She realized Gabe was smiling at her and smiled back.

"Weren't you the one who told me to either smile like I mean it or don't smile at all? Why don't you follow your own advice?" he asked.

She heaved a big sigh; she didn't want to be dishonest with him. "I guess I'm so used to taking care of everyone else's needs and problems that my own are secondary. No one really wants to know when you're not happy, so if you cover up your unhappiness with a smile, it just makes life easier."

"Not with me it doesn't. It's going to make your life a lot tougher if you keep giving me false smiles and I have to interrogate you to get to the truth. The easy route would be to tell me what's wrong, and we can seek solutions together. How does that sound?"

It sounded great, maybe even too good to be true! She wasn't used to having someone care about what mattered to her, let alone wanting to help her find solutions. She smiled.

"That's more like it. So come on, what's up?"

She shrugged. "I feel bad even admitting it, but I'm a little jealous. Don't get me wrong. I'm really happy that you've just had what sounds like a wonderful opportunity drop into your lap, but it makes me wonder."

"Wonder what?"

"What the hell I'm going to be able to do!"

Gabe nodded slowly. "What do you want to do?"

"It's not about what I want; it's about what's going to be possible."

"No. That's an excuse. You have to know what you want, then find ways to make it possible."

She couldn't help rolling her eyes at him. "That's easy to say when you're the angel Gabriel, to whom all good things come unbidden."

"That's not fair."

"I know, sorry. I told you, I'm just feeling a little jealous, and that springs from feeling a little hopeless and those two in combination can lead to ugly comments."

"It's okay. I'm not worried what you say about me, I'm worried how you feel about you. You're the upbeat one, at least you are normally."

"It's easier to be upbeat about what might happen for you than what might happen for me. The not knowing, the not being able to do anything, it takes its toll. I guess I must have processed some of the shock and grief, because I'm starting to want to figure out what's going to be possible. Unfortunately, I've reached that point before anything is possible. Seeing things start to come together for you is making me realize that nothing can come together for me yet, and even when the time comes, I don't know what options I'll have because I don't know what money I'll have or if anyone will be willing to work with me given the guilt by association factor." She shrugged. "Anyway. This is supposed to be a date, remember? We weren't allowed to be spending it talking about your new possibilities; I certainly don't want to spend it talking about my lack of them." She picked up her menu and smiled at him over it. "So let's eat, shall we?"

Gabe picked up his own menu. "Fair enough, but we're going to need to revisit this. So if I were you, I'd spend some time thinking about what it is you do want. That's the only place to start." His green gaze held hers for a moment. "Stop making excuses about what you can't and what isn't. Take the time and really think about what you want."

She nodded. He was right, now she thought about it. It was an excuse. She felt guilty about it, but part of her wanted more for herself. She wanted the personal fulfilment that she'd always been so happy to deny herself. She'd made a life out of contributing, of giving what she could to society, to educating kids hoping to help them make wiser choices. She valued what she'd done, but this enforced hiatus had given her the time to question her motivation. Yes, she needed meaning and purpose, but did they need to be the same meaning and purpose that she'd devoted her life to? And the bigger question was whether they had really been her meaning and purpose anyway. "You're right. But can we leave the deep and meaningfuls alone for tonight?"

"Of course we can," Gabe smiled as the server approached to take their order. Once she'd left he took Renée's hand again. "But I don't think you and I will ever really leave them behind, will we?"

There went that imagination of hers again! His words, and the way he looked as he said them, had her thinking that they might have a deep and meaningful future together. She needed to stop that. He was looking forward to coming back here, looking forward to spending some time with her, but that was all. She'd seen his reaction when she'd talked about her divorce. She didn't need to get carried away. He was a catch, and she'd enjoy it while it lasted, but her own future was far from certain. She didn't need to set herself up for heartache by hoping for more than what might be possible. He'd talked about wondering if they might have a future together, but she knew they couldn't. Much as she would love to, it just wasn't going to be possible and she already knew it. She'd go along for the ride while Gabe figured out his new path in life, but she was part of his journey, not his destination. She smiled. "Of course we won't, we're a pair of idealistic do-gooders! We'll never leave them behind!"

He shook his head at her, apparently seeing right through the bravado, but choosing to let it go. "Speak for yourself. I'm no idealist."

That made her laugh. "Oh, no?"

"No," he grinned back at her. "I'm an optimistic realist who likes to uphold ideals."

"Sounds like the same thing to me. What's the difference?"

She was surprised when he didn't reply immediately but stared out over her shoulder. That wasn't like him, he was normally attentive. As she started to turn to follow his gaze, he shook his head and looked back at her. "Chance just walked in."

"Oh." She no longer wanted to turn around. She'd thought she was prepared to see him, but now she felt as though a lead weight had settled in her stomach.

"What do you want to do?"

She made a face. "You keep asking that question."

"Because you have choices; yet, you don't believe you do."

"What I want is to tell him how sorry I am. Sorry that I made him promise not to go after them, sorry for what happened to his life." She swallowed the lump that was forming in her throat. "Sorry that my sister, the girl he loved, is dead."

Gabe reached over to take her hand. "Then do it."

She blew out an exasperated sigh. "What…here? Now? Just call him over and spill my guts?"

"Why not?"

"Why not? Because it would ruin our evening, ruin his evening. And he no doubt wouldn't even listen to me anyway, and I don't blame him! Please drop it, Gabe? I'm going to try to talk with him while he's here, but not tonight, not now."

"Fair enough." Gabe looked up again and smiled.

This time she had to turn, had to see. Chance was standing at the bar. He looked so much older, but then of course he would, because he was. They all were. He'd been good-looking as a kid, and he'd grown into a handsome man. He wore black jeans and a black shirt; he had the rugged look of a man who spent most of his time outside. There was something dangerous about him…wild, untamed. She didn't know what it was, but, at the same time, she did. She finally met his gaze and he held it for a long moment. She wished she could read the expression on his face, but it gave nothing away. After what felt like minutes, he gave the slightest nod and turned back to the bar. Renée let out a breath that she didn't realize she'd been holding.

"And you think he hates you?" asked Gabe.

She shook her head. That hadn't felt like hatred; it had felt more like shared pain. "I think he should."

# Chapter Eleven

Renée locked up the bakery and checked her watch. It was two forty already. She was supposed to meet the girls as soon after two thirty as she could get to the Boathouse. She hated being late and wondered whether she should use it as an excuse to just not go. She liked all the girls, and it might be useful to meet April before she came to work at the bakery, but having lunch with all of them, felt a bit much right now.

"Hey, Renée!" She looked up to see Laura hurrying down the sidewalk toward her. "You're late, too! That makes me feel better. I had to stop at the post office and it took forever. We'd best get going, huh?"

Renée cursed internally. There went her chance to skulk off home.

Laura tucked a strand of her long, dark hair behind her ear and smiled. "Sorry, looks like you were about to blow it off?"

Renée nodded reluctantly. "It's been a long, hard morning. I know I should meet April, but I'd much sooner go home and put my feet up."

Laura tucked her arm through Renée's with a grin. "Well, sorry, but no such luck. You'll enjoy it when you get there, and there'll still be plenty of time to put your feet up when you get home." Laura gave her a sideways glance, "Or do you need all the rest you can get before another date with that hot guy of yours tonight?"

Renée smiled. This was one of the reasons she was hesitant to do a girly lunch. She knew she was going to be bombarded with questions about Gabe.

"Sorry," said Laura. "I'm being nosey. I can't help it though. I mean he is gorgeous. He's been coming up for a while now, all suited and broody. Then when he gets with you he's all smiles and Mr. Laid-back. I can't help but think there must be a lot of great sex going on to make him chill out that much!"

She had to laugh. "I think part of it is just being back here; Summer Lake does tend to have that effect. Everyone's more laid back here, it's like an escape from the pressures and stresses of life in the real world."

"Hmm, I'll give you that, but I'd still put money on the fact that Gabe's transformation is mostly down to you screwing his brains out every chance you get!"

Renée laughed. "Okay! I admit it. Happy now?"

"No way! Now I need all the details!"

"No chance! I'm actually quite a private person."

Laura smiled and let go of her arm as they started up the steps onto the back deck of the Boathouse. She waved when she saw the others all seated around one of the big picnic benches. "Don't worry, I won't embarrass you in front of all of them, but I will get it out of you."

Renée was relieved at that, she'd been worried she might have to turn tail and run if Laura was about to make this a public inquisition into her sex life. The thought of that turned her stomach. Surprisingly though, the thought of talking to Laura about what was going on between her and Gabe didn't scare her at all. In fact, it was quite appealing, but she wasn't about to admit it. "I think I'm safe. Once we get this lunch over with I'll be able to lay low for a while."

Laura stopped and turned back to her. "Then we'll do another lunch, just the two of us."

Renée didn't get chance to reply before Missy was calling them over. "Come on, you two. We've already ordered."

They took their seats at the two empty spaces. This was quite a crowd. Renée looked around as Laura apologized and made everyone laugh with her tales of woe from the post office. There were already six of them; she and Laura made eight.

Emma turned to smile at her. "I'm so glad you came, but I have no idea how you can stay awake in the afternoons after those early starts of yours."

"You get used to it after a while, and I'm a morning person anyway, which helps."

"You're going to have to get used to it too, hon." Missy turned to the woman sitting beside her, who smiled shyly.

"I'll be fine. It's Marcus I'm worried about. He'd definitely not a morning person."

"He'll get used to it," said Missy. "And the bakery is just to get you started."

"Oh, I know, and I'm so grateful for the job."

Kenzie laughed. "It seems as though the bakery is a kind of halfway house doesn't it? I was supposed to start there." She looked at Renée, "Thank you for saving me from the early mornings."

"And how about you?" asked Holly. "It sounds as though the bakery is going from strength to strength now you're running it. Do you plan to stay there?"

"Oh, no." Renée shook her head adamantly. "It's just a stopgap for me." Grateful as she was for the job, no way did she intend to work there for any longer than she had to. She felt as though she had so much more to give than simply baking and selling pastries. "I don't know that I'll ever get back into charity work, but I need to find something a little more fulfilling."

"Well," said Missy, "hopefully the two of you will have some fun in there before you move on to whatever comes next. Oh, and by the way, let me officially introduce you—Renée, this is April Preston. April, meet Renée Nichols.

April smiled warmly, "Nice to meet you."

"You, too." Renée immediately liked her. She seemed a little reserved, but given that Chance had brought her and her son to live down here in order to escape something—Renée didn't know what—that was hardly surprising. April was pretty, but she looked kind of beaten down. Renée wasn't sure if the shadows under her eyes were dark circles or bruises. She'd put her money on the latter, but there'd be plenty of time for April to tell her story if she wanted to.

"How long did it take you to get down here?" asked Emma. "I don't even know how far it is to Montana, but it seems like a million miles away."

"It was about eleven hundred miles. We left on Friday night, but we took our time getting down here. Marcus didn't do too well in the truck, and Chance was so good about stopping for him to get some fresh air and not driving for too many hours each day. We got in late yesterday afternoon."

"You lucky thing," said Emma. "What I wouldn't give to spend a few days in a truck with Chance."

"Emma!" Laura slapped her arm. "You are a happily married woman, and don't forget it's my cousin that you're married to." Laura gave her a saucy grin. "I'd kick you out of the truck…"

"Yeah, but only so you could have a chance at Chance!" said Holly. "You need to remember that smoking hot pilot of yours will be back any day now. And you need to hurry up with the wedding plans, so that you'll be a happily married woman, too."

Missy laughed, "Would you all stop fighting over my brother? You're all spoken for, so none of you can have him."

"What about you?" Megan asked April. "Do you like him?"

April blushed. "No. I mean I do. He's a good-looking guy, what's not to like? But to me he's been a good friend in a time of need. I don't see him like that, and I know he doesn't see me like that."

Missy wrinkled her nose. "Do you know if there's anyone up in Montana who he does see like that?"

April shook her head. "We weren't exactly friends. I didn't get to go out much. My husband…" Renée mentally filled in the blanks as April stopped herself and looked around at them. "I didn't go out much, and I never heard about Chance dating anyone. I'd see him out at Chico sometimes, but he was always with the guys, never a girl."

Missy looked as disappointed as Renée felt. She'd hoped that he'd found himself a good woman—found love again after Chloe—but it didn't sound as though that was the case.

Missy looked over at her. "Oh well, maybe someday."

Kenzie caught the look that passed between them. "You're not telling me you used to date him, Renée?"

She shook her head. All eyes were turned toward her now, but she didn't want to start explaining the history between them.

"Wrong!" cried Emma brightly. "Anyway, we're not here to discuss Chance, fun as it may be. I want to hear about wedding plans! I went first and I would have thought at least one of you would have made it down the aisle by now. I want to hear everyone's plans; I want to make cake!"

The question deflected attention back to Missy and her upcoming wedding in Vegas. Renée gave Emma a grateful smile when she winked at her. She may make out like she was the clueless blonde much of the time, but Renée had noted a few times now how well she managed people and averted potentially awkward situations.

"And you?" Missy was looking at her again. "You are coming, aren't you?"

"To your wedding? In Vegas?" Renée hadn't expected to be invited. Chance would be there after all. It didn't seem right that she should encroach on that day. She wanted him to enjoy his sister's wedding, not have her there to remind of the wedding he never got to have with her sister.

Missy held her gaze. "Please, say you will?"

Renée stared at her, surprised that she would bring it up now in front of all the others.

"Why the hell wouldn't you?" asked Kenzie. "It's Missy's big day, plus a trip to Vegas. What's to think about?"

"Well, I…" Renée had no clue what to say.

"Kenzie!" This time it was Megan who came to the rescue. She was usually really quiet, but never seemed afraid to step up and say something when she noticed someone was uncomfortable. "Leave her alone." She turned red as she smiled around at the others. "Let's put you on the spot instead, shall we? When are you and Chase going to name a date?"

Kenzie shot Renée an apologetic look before turning to her sister. Renée knew she'd meant no harm. She was just used to speaking her mind and didn't always think before she did.

"Me?" asked Kenzie. "You and the good Doctor Michael have had longer to think about it than Chase and I have. What about you?"

Megan gave her a mysterious smile. "We're working on it, and don't worry, you'll be the first to know."

"Ooh, that sounds promising," said Emma. "But I want details, from all of you. If you haven't gotten around to setting dates yet, you must at least know what kind of wedding you want. We all know Miss is off to Vegas. Holly has the grand affair at the Wilshire lined up."

Renée didn't miss the way Holly rolled her eyes and stared out at the lake. Laura hadn't missed it either and exchanged a worried look with Renée.

Emma hurried on. "So what about the rest of you? Laura? I have no doubt that you and Smoke won't be doing anything traditional. Do you have any ideas yet on what you'll do?"

"No announcements yet. It's weird for us, because we have to take his family into account." She grinned around at them, "But I will say, if you're sitting at this table, you're invited and…" she paused for effect, "you'd better make sure your passport is up to date."

"Passport?" asked Kenzie incredulously. "Up to date? I wouldn't even know how to get one!"

Laura laughed. "Well, you'd better get to work on it then, girlfriend. You're going to need it."

"I like the sounds of this," said Missy. "And I'm in." She looked so happy as she added. "Mine had expired but Dan took care of getting me and Scotty new ones."

Despite Laura's announcement that everyone sitting at the table was invited, Renée hoped that didn't include her. She had a passport, but she had to wonder if she'd even be able to use it while Eric's investigation was still ongoing.

"Just give us lots of warning, will you?" asked Emma. "The passport isn't a problem, but I'm working on a release date for my book, and I don't want it to clash with important travel plans."

Laura nodded. "It won't be for a while yet. Between my schedule and Smoke's we're struggling to figure it all out."

"Pft!" Everyone turned to look at Holly. "If you need your schedule fixed or to have your life planned out for every available second, go talk to Pete."

"Is he still on overdrive?" asked Emma, looking very uncomfortable.

Holly nodded her head. "Has he ever not been?"

Emma and Missy exchanged a look. "It's just how he is, hon," said Missy. "You've got to admit he gets things done."

Holly heaved a big sigh. "Oh, he gets things done all right. Whatever he thinks needs doing, whether I agree or not. I thought a wedding was supposed to be about what the bride wants, not what the groom deems appropriate." She looked around at them all. "Sorry. Don't let me put a downer on everything." She looked at Renée. "What about you? You and Gabe seem to be spending a lot of time together. Any wedding bells on your horizon?"

Renée laughed. "No. We're just hanging out. I have this minor detail of still being married anyway. My plans involve a divorce, not a wedding."

Emma smiled. "Yes, but after you're divorced? I think you and Gabe are perfect for each other."

Holly laughed. "Off goes Emma the matchmaker again." She turned to April, "Watch out. Once she gets done with Renée, it'll be your turn next."

April shook her head. "I'm done with men. Marriage wasn't exactly good to me. I've learned my lesson. If I ever manage to get a divorce from Guy, I don't plan on trying it again."

Missy laughed. "Oh dear, I think you may have just become a special project in Emma's eyes. You sound just like she did."

Renée knew Emma had been married for a short time to a Hollywood producer who had cheated on her and made her life miserable.

Emma nodded happily as she looked at April and then Renée. "You both have. I was the world's worst for being scared of men and hating the idea of marriage. It took Jack to make me see things differently, but now I'm like a born-again Christian wanting to spread the word and the joy!"

That had them all laughing. "Calm down, Em," said Laura. "You have to let people get there in their own time."

"I know, I know. I just want you all to be happy. Is that so wrong of me?"

Holly looked at her. "It's not wrong at all, but as I have already told you, it may not work out that way for all of us. Sometimes we don't need pushing, okay?"

As Emma's smile faded, Ben approached the table accompanied by one of the servers. They were both laden down with plates. Renée regretted not having made time to order something when her stomach grumbled at the sight of the food being placed in front of the others. She was surprised when Ben slid a burger and fries in front of her and another in front of Laura. She looked up at him questioningly.

He shrugged. "I'll change them for something else if you prefer, but neither of you made any attempt to order once the girl talk started, and I knew you'd both be hungry."

Laura smiled up at him. "And you know I usually order a burger at lunchtime. You're the best, Ben. Thanks."

He was so handsome when he smiled like that. Renée had to wonder again why he hadn't found a woman of his own and settled down yet.

Once they'd all thanked him, he headed back inside. April watched him go and then looked around at them. "I'm surprised none of you have snagged him. He's gorgeous and such a nice person.

"He's the best," agreed Emma. "We're all lucky to have him in our lives."

Missy nodded sadly. "Unfortunately for him, and for every single woman around here, he gave his heart away years ago. And he never got it back."

Kenzie leaned forward. "Do tell?"

Laura looked puzzled. "Are you talking about that Charlotte who was going to come to the fundraiser last fall? The only time I've ever seen Ben lose his cool was when Dan said that Charlotte was coming. He disappeared for days after that."

Missy and Emma exchanged a glance. Then Missy nodded. "Yep. I'm talking about Charlotte, but I really shouldn't be. Ben doesn't talk about it, so I shouldn't." She wrinkled her nose and looked around at them all. "But... I've been struggling with something and maybe you all can give me some advice?"

They all nodded and murmured their agreement.

"You all have to solemnly swear that you won't say anything to Ben though, okay?" She looked at each of them in turn until they nodded. She held Kenzie's gaze a while longer. "You especially, because you work with him and you don't always know when to zip it."

Kenzie grinned sheepishly. "I can't argue with that, but I promise. Ben's been so good to me. I'd never do—or say—a thing that might hurt him."

"And I hardly even know him, but I feel the same way," said April. "But I can go for a walk if you want me to?"

Missy shook her head. "You stay put, you're here now. You're one of us."

Renée didn't miss the smile that crossed April's face. She understood how good it felt to be accepted, especially after going through a difficult time that made you feel so isolated. She caught April's eye and smiled in encouragement.

"Well," said Missy, "Charlotte and I were really good friends. For those of you who don't know, her family lived in the house that we now own. She used to come over from England every year to spend the summer with her grandparents. We got close when we were little kids and even closer as teenagers.

When she and Ben broke up, she never came back to the lake anymore. She and I kept in touch though. We've met up a few times over the years. I was hoping to see her last fall when she was in LA." She looked at Laura. "Dan didn't know the history between her and Ben when he suggested she should come to the fundraiser."

"Ah," said Laura. "Now I get it. But what do you need advice about, Miss?"

"I would really love to invite Charlotte to the wedding. It was something we promised each other when we were kids. No matter where we were or when it happened, we would each be there for the other's wedding. We," she looked at Emma, "went to England when Charlotte got married."

Emma nodded. "Even though we tried to talk her out of it!"

"Yeah. Even though we didn't want her to marry the asshole, we were there because we're friends. Real friends, friends for life. And friends like that should be at your wedding." She shook her head sadly. "But how can I invite her when I know what her being there would do to Ben?"

"But do you know what it would do to him?" asked Megan.

"He's not over her, if that's what you mean," said Missy.

"That's not what I mean at all. Maybe it would give him the chance to get over her or to make his peace with her. Sometimes seeing what someone has become is all it takes to realize that the person they were doesn't exist anymore. That you can let go of them." She stopped, seeming as surprised as the rest of them that she was speaking up. "I…I…You just don't know. You might be doing him a big favor. The only thing I can suggest is that you ask him. I learned the hard way that thinking you know what people want, but not talking to them about it only leads to trouble." She looked up and blushed as Ben approached the table.

He raised an eyebrow at them. "I just wanted to check everything's okay, but from the looks of it I should exit stage left as quickly as I can? This looks like the kind of girl talk that will have me blushing."

Laura grinned at him. "You're a wise man, Ben. Flee while you can."

He grinned and made his way to the far end of the deck, checking on his customers as he went.

Missy looked at Megan. "Thanks, hon. You just gave me the advice I'd give to anyone else. Isn't it funny how you can't see it when you're the one in a pickle?"

Renée wondered what Megan's story was that she should talk like that. What had she had to learn the hard way? She didn't have time to wonder too long though as she watched Gabe make his way up onto the deck. He raised a hand and smiled when he spotted her. She smiled back and checked her watch. He'd said he'd pick her up at four and she was stunned to realize it was almost that now.

Emma grinned at her. "Looks like it's time for you to head on home." She checked her own watch. "Oh, my goodness. And me, too! Listen ladies, I'll settle the tab with Ben and then I have to run. I'll catch up with you soon." She didn't wait for arguments; she stood up and went inside.

Renée stood, too. She was ready to get out of here. Laura touched her arm as she said her goodbyes. "Don't forget, we need to set a date for our lunch."

Renée nodded, glad she hadn't forgotten or changed her mind. "You know where to find me."

# Chapter Twelve

Sitting out on Renée's front porch, Gabe smiled as he stared out at the rolling hills and the last shimmers of light on the lake. He could get used to this. And after his conversation with Ben this morning, it looked as though he would have the opportunity to do so. He'd been a little surprised how far along the Economic Development Committee was with their plans for the growth of Summer Lake. Surprised…but pleased. The whole area was on an upswing. Companies who could were moving out of the major metropolitan areas and spreading farther and farther into what had been the countryside. Summer Lake was on the periphery of that movement. It was too far out to attract major corporations, and it didn't have the infrastructure to support a large influx, but it was being affected. Gabe was grateful for that. He wanted to see growth, but not major transformation.

The vision that the Committee had was to manage development very selectively. Too many small towns in California had been swallowed up in suburban sprawl. The location of the lake would help it avoid that fate and help steer it toward a different kind of development that was springing forth in Northern California and Oregon. The evolution of the new small town was interesting to Gabe, and he identified with it personally as its path matched his own. Small towns had been abandoned by the younger generations for decades as they went off to seek better lives in the big cities. Now it seemed the tide was turning, just as his own path was turning, as quality of life in the big cities deteriorated and people sought to create something better in small towns. He was excited about the role he might play in the movement as a whole, as well as in the growth of his hometown. He knew that developing a clear vision of what Summer Lake did—and more importantly didn't—want to become would be key in steering a path to the future.

Renée came back out and sat down beside him. "You look very pleased with yourself."

He reached for her hand and squeezed it. "I am. Not so much with myself, but with the possibilities that lay ahead."

"I'm happy for you."

He turned to her. "But what about you? Are you happy for you?"

She gave him a puzzled look. "I don't have much to be happy about right now. I'm grateful, grateful to have a job and to be back here while I live through this limbo, but happy?"

That wasn't what Gabe wanted to hear.

She laughed. "I've told you before, the intimidating stare doesn't work with me, Gabe. Get over yourself!"

He smiled and drew her out of her chair and onto his lap. "I get over myself in a hurry whenever I get around you! You sure as hell know how to put me in my place, don't you?"

She looked genuinely puzzled. "What do you mean? How did I put you in your place? I'm just telling you to quit the bullying tactics."

He wrapped an arm around her waist and used his other hand to sweep the hair away from her neck so he could kiss it. The way she wiggled around in his lap made him shift position to stop the torment. "You." He nibbled on her neck then brought his lips next to her ear. "Put me in my place like no woman ever has, and I would never have believed any woman ever could."

"How?"

She tried to turn to look at him, but he held her in place and nibbled on her earlobe some more. He didn't want her to see the pain her words had caused. "I asked if you were happy for you that I'm going to be coming to live here and taking this Economic Development job. You said you have nothing to be happy about."

"Oh."

"Yeah, that's pretty much how it made me feel. You're not happy. You're grateful to have a job and a place to live and that's it. Right? You're not happy or grateful to have me?"

Now she did wriggle around in his lap. Her green eyes flashed as she looked down at him. "To have you? What does that even mean, Gabe? I have your friendship, for now. We have sex, because you're curious about what two people do when they want to find out if they might have a life together. And when you've satisfied your curiosity, then what? You'll be back to New York after your little interlude? Or you'll be starting out on your new adventure driving Summer Lake into the future, that's all great for you. I, on the other hand, have to think about me. You're not going to want me for the long term. I get that. And I don't even know what I can do in the long term. Can I stay here and make anything of my life? I don't know! Can I leave here and make anything of my life? I don't know that either. I am happy and I am grateful that you want to spend some time with me, but I'm under no illusions that you are my future, and I do have to consider my future."

When she'd finished her outburst Gabe stared at her. "Have we been talking at cross purposes for the last week?"

"What do you mean?"

"As far as I'm concerned, what I said to you the other night, about caring for you, about wanting to do the things that a man and woman do together when they're trying to figure out if they might have a life together? I said those things, because I already know that's what I want."

"What is?"

Damn, she could be so stubborn in her refusal to accept what he was saying! "I want a future with you in it, because I care about you. Why won't you get that into your head?"

She pushed her hair out of her face and stared at him. "You do?"

"For Christ's sake, Renée! What's it going to take? I'm not a romantic. I've never been in love before. I don't know how this is supposed to work. I just wish you'd help me out a little, maybe listen and believe what I say once in a while."

Her eyes widened as she stared down at him.

"What?"

"What did you just say?"

"Which part?"

"You've never been in love before?"

He shook his head. It was hard to admit that he'd made it through thirty-six years of his life and had never experienced this elusive emotion before. That he'd been skeptical as to its existence and more so about his own ability to feel it. She'd made a believer out of him, and she didn't even know it.

"But you are now?"

Oh crap! Her question made him realize that he hadn't shared his discovery with her. He cupped his hands around the back of her head and pulled her down into a kiss. When he let her come up for air, he smiled. "I am. And sorry, it might have helped you a little if I'd actually gotten around to telling you."

She was smiling back at him, her eyes shining.

"I love you, Renée Nichols. I have no idea what you have done to me. All I know is that I don't ever want you to stop, okay?"

"Wow!"

He had to laugh. "That's all I get? I declare my love for you and come as close as I ever will to laying myself at your mercy and all you have to say is wow?"

She laughed. "Sorry. I guess I'm just stunned."

She still wasn't saying it back. He sighed. Why should he expect her to? He might be a catch to women in New York, but Renée wasn't like them. She had a different set of values. He felt foolish, but he didn't regret telling her. "So, anyway… Now I've made a fool of myself, what do we do next?"

"Made a fool of yourself? You think loving me is foolish?"

"I think loving you is the best thing that's ever happened to me. However, my monumental ego had not considered the fact that you might not love me back or even want to consider the possibility."

She had the audacity to laugh. That stung. He wasn't used to being out of his depth, to laying himself open and making himself vulnerable. He'd just done that, and here she was laughing at him! He turned his head and looked away.

She cupped his face between her hands and made him look up at her. "Gabe, you silly man. I do love you. I think I fell in love with you when you walked into the bakery with Ethan. I just didn't think that you would love me. I'll admit, I haven't taken some of the things you've said very seriously. You've told me that you care about me—I took that to mean you care about me as a friend. You told me you're crazy about me. I thought that was because you're finding yourself again here, and I've been a part of that. I didn't think it was about me, at least not just me. I'm just a part of your process of discovering yourself in a new light. I'm happy to be a part of it. I'm grateful that I am, but I'm realistic, too. You want to think about maybe having a life with a woman and that's something that's never crossed your mind before. I'm here and I'm a known quantity, so you're trying it out with me. That doesn't mean I'm the woman you want to have a life with."

"You're unbelievable, do you know this?"

She shrugged.

"I've never considered having a life with a woman before because I wasn't around you. You're not part of this process I'm going though, you're the cause of it. I confess I didn't even realize that at first, it took Michael to spell it out for me, but it's true. I love you, you stubborn woman, whether you want me or not."

"Now who isn't listening? I. Love. You!" She glared at him, then started to laugh. It was so infectious he had to join in. "Are we seriously fighting about being in love with each other?" she asked.

He nodded. "It looks that way. But I don't want to."

She wrapped her arms around his neck and looked deep into his eyes. "I don't want to either, Gabe. I want to make love to you."

He wasn't going to argue with that. She stood and offered him her hand. He took it and led her inside to her bedroom.

Cupping her face between his hands he bit her lips; she clung to his shoulders and kissed him back. There was something so innocent about the way she kissed him, about the way she made love to him. It made him feel protective of her in a way he never had before. Until Renée. Sex for him had been just another encounter where he went in with a goal in mind and came out once he'd accomplished it. His goal had always been his own pleasure. There'd been no shortage of women who had a similar goal and were happy to have Gabe as a means to achieve it. With Renée it was different. Yes, he wanted her, wanted to take his pleasure in her, but his goal wasn't to make himself feel good. It was to make her feel good, to show her with his body what his words hadn't seemed to get through to her. He wanted to give himself to her, and to take her—all of her—as his own.

She looked up at him. "You said you hadn't had your wicked way with me. Gabe, I want you to. Whenever we have sex, you feel as though you're holding back. Please don't."

~ ~ ~

The way he looked at her when she spoke those words made Renée's heart hammer even harder than it already was. It was true though. He was great in bed, better than she'd thought she'd ever experience, but there'd been something missing. She'd thought it must be because, whether he knew it or not, he was just going through the motions with her. He wanted her, she knew that much, but she'd honestly believed that she was just part of whatever process of evolution he was going through right now. She'd thought it wasn't really about her, just that she was a convenient warm body at a time when he needed one. That he could feel good about it and about himself because he knew she wanted him and he was helping her through a hard time.

A shudder ran through her as he removed her top. The way he looked at her—at her breasts—as he freed them from her bra let her know that she was definitely much more than just a convenient warm body. He walked her back toward her bed and pulled her down on top of him, thrusting his hips, pressing that huge bulge of his between her legs as his hands closed around her breasts.

"I don't want to be wicked with you right now, my love. I want to explore you." As he spoke, he unfastened her jeans and slid them down. By the time she'd kicked out of them, he'd stripped down to his boxers and drew her under him. She looked up into his eyes and caught her breath at what she saw in them. Love. There was no denying it. "You're right. I have held back. I've wanted you to feel safe, to feel good. I haven't wanted to just fuck you."

She felt herself get wetter just at the way he said it.

"But that's all I've known how to do, until now." He trailed his fingers down her neck and on over her throat. "Now, I want to make love to you. Make you mine."

"Yours?"

He nodded as his fingers slid down over her belly and between her legs. She couldn't contain the gasp that escaped her lips as he traced her opening. "Mine. I want you to meet me in a place where neither of us have ever been. You've never let go of yourself, let a man take you mind and body. I've never held back with my body or given my mind and myself."

She didn't know if it was his words or the way his thumb was circling her nub that was making her quiver. As a girl she'd used to wonder about what it would be like to make love to a man. Then she'd met Eric and gotten married—and she'd decided that there was no such thing. Men and women had sex. If they were lucky there were a few fleeting moments of physical pleasure and that was as good as it got. Now it seemed Gabe was asking her to reconsider her beliefs. He wanted to make love to her. She was hardly going to say no!

"I'm not sure I know how to let go." Why was she still talking? Why couldn't she keep her mouth shut and just do what he said? Surrender to his talented fingers and let him take her?

"Trust me?" He dipped a finger inside her as he asked.

This time she had no words; she nodded dumbly and surrendered. He kissed her neck and slid his finger deeper making her hips rise up to meet him. As his mouth worked its way down to her breast, he pressed his palm against her nub, setting up a rhythm of pulsating pressure as he slid his finger in and out. She moaned when his lips closed around her nipple in the same moment that he added a second finger and thrust them deep. She tensed.

"Gabe!"

"Mmm?" He didn't lift his head, but instead grazed her nipple with his teeth sending shockwaves racing through her.

"Gabe, stop! You're going to make me..." She grabbed a fistful of sheet as he added a third finger and plunged them deep inside her. She felt herself stretching around him, the bundle of nerves between her legs pulsating as his thumb kept up the rhythmic pressure against it. She was right on the edge, but she wanted to feel him inside her when she came. She wanted this to be about them, not just her. "You're going to make me come!" she gasped.

This time he did lift his head. "I am. And you're going to let go and give yourself up to me." It was a command. For a moment she tensed, she wanted to fight it. She wanted to be in charge of her own body, not at his mercy. He raised an eyebrow and held her gaze as he thrust his fingers deeper and harder. "Come for me."

Part of her wanted to look away, wanted to resist somehow, but she couldn't. A bigger part of her wanted to do exactly what he said, give herself up to him. And she did. Her hips moved in time with his thrusting fingers. She buried her own fingers in two fistfuls of sheets and moaned as he took her over the edge. Waves of pleasure crashed through her, and she gasped and moaned as he kept working her. He held her gaze the whole time and—though her body writhed and her head thrashed around as he carried her through wave after wave—she never looked away.

When she finally lay still he placed a gentle kiss on her lips. Something had changed, and they both knew it. She wrapped both arms around his neck and looked up into his eyes. She didn't know what to say. She was too full of feelings for words to matter much. It seemed he felt the same way. She quivered as his hot hard shaft brushed against her belly. It would be a while before she'd be ready to help him out with that! It seemed he had other ideas though. He was rolling her onto her back, spreading her legs.

"Gabe, I can't yet. I'm sorry."

He smiled down at her. "You can, my love. Right now, when you think you have nothing left to give."

He thrust his hips and plunged deep inside her, making her moan at the sheer size of him. The last traces of her orgasm raced through her, taken by surprise at this new assault. He moved slowly inside her. Despite her protests to the contrary, her body agreed with him and moved with him—slowly, sensuously—in a rhythm that was new to her.

He held her gaze. "You think you have nothing left. I know this is where I get to the part of you that really matters. The part you've never given to anyone before me."

She had no words as he moved slowly, deliberately, thrusting deep and hard each time. She could feel the tension building low in her belly, and she had no resistance to offer. She moved with him, carried along by his determination and by the pleasure building inside her. Each time he thrust his hips, ripples of pleasures ran through her, surging away from the place where they joined and rushing back there to build in intensity each time. She was gasping now, almost overcome by the intensity, of the sensations, of her own emotions and most of all of the look in his eyes. He was getting close, it was on his face and in his movements as he grew harder still. Every thrust was a mini orgasm she was panting and clinging to him as he drove his way to the inevitable conclusion.

He lowered his head and nibbled her neck, taking her to the very edge, making her legs and stomach tighten in anticipation. "I love you, Renée."

That took her over the edge. "I love you, Gabe," she gasped as she let herself go. She felt as though she was falling through space and time, her body wracked with pleasure like she'd never known. He thrust his hips wildly and she felt him tense. His own release deep inside her was her only point of reference in a swirling galaxy of exploding stars. He was her anchor to space and time as his thrusts spilled his need into the deepest part of her. All she could do was cling to him as he took her on a journey to the place where neither of them had ever been. The place she knew in that moment she'd never go without him.

# Chapter Thirteen

Gabe opened his eyes and smiled at the sight of Renée sleeping on beside him. She slept heavily yet woke immediately at the sound of her alarm. Gabe, on the other hand, had an internal alarm that had his eyes open five minutes before the buzzer went off. He stroked her hair where it tumbled over the pillow, she was so damned beautiful. She really had given herself to him last night, he knew in his heart there was no going back. He'd given himself to her in the same way, in a way he'd never thought he would give himself to a woman. She owned him now, whether she knew it or not. That scared the shit out of him. For a guy who had always liked to maintain a tight hold over his own destiny, he'd willingly given up the controls to a woman—an unpredictable woman at that. He smiled, she'd be no fun if she were predictable.

He was supposed to be leaving this evening, but he really didn't want to. He wanted to stay here, spend more time with her. He didn't have to be back in the office until Monday, though he had planned to spend the weekend in there catching up after his week away, clearing the decks in order to bow out. He'd talked to his partners, Wade and Dane, yesterday after talking to Ben. They hadn't been too surprised to learn that he was planning to take a sabbatical. He'd told them he wanted at least a year, though at this point he didn't think he'd ever want to go back. The Economic Development Manager position was annually funded, and, as he'd told Renée, he was a realist at heart. He needed to cover his bases—for everyone else's sake as much as his own. He was meeting with the guys on Sunday afternoon, so realistically he didn't to have leave here until Sunday morning, if he could find a flight—or Rosemary could. He'd call her once Renée was awake and in the shower. He didn't even think she'd be too surprised. She'd noticed something was up with him this week and he knew he'd be in for a full inquisition from her once he got back.

He smiled as the alarm went off and Renée opened her eyes. "Good morning."

"Mmm," she mumbled. "It will be when I get some caffeine into me; you know I don't like to talk before that happens."

Gabe grinned and drew her to him. She snuggled in close and closed her eyes again. "Don't do it, sleepy head. You need to get up and moving while you can."

She snuggled closer. "It's not my fault. There's this man in my bed; I can't leave while he's here."

"You can't? Why not?"

She opened her eyes again and her sleepy smile made him as happy as her words. "Because I love him, and I don't want to leave him."

He planted a kiss on her full soft lips, wishing he could keep her in bed for a while, but he knew she had to get up for work. "Well, he loves you, and he doesn't want to leave you either."

"But just like I have to go to work, he has to go to New York."

"He does, but not until Sunday."

"Ooh!" She sat up with a big grin on her face. "Really?"

"Well, I hope so. I have to be there on Sunday afternoon, so I'm hoping I'll be able to get a flight early Sunday morning." As he spoke, a thought occurred to him. "Either way, I'll have to get ready to leave for the airport tomorrow afternoon. Do you want to come?"

"I can't. I have to work. I can't just go jetting off to New York."

"I know that. I meant do you want to come to the airport with me?"

She made a face at him. "I'd love to, but I don't think my trusty steed would get me back here in time for work."

Gabe laughed. It was a four-hour drive to the airport, he was hardly expecting her to bicycle back. "Well, I was thinking you could keep the rental car. I'll be coming back as soon as I can, and I'll need it again when I do. You could come pick me up?"

"You mean you want to donate the use of a car, and making it look like I'm the one doing you a favor will make that more acceptable?"

He shrugged. There was no point denying it.

She thought about it. "Let's see when you can get a flight for, shall we?"

It was better than he'd hoped for. He'd been afraid her pride would make her turn him down flat. "Sure, I'll let you know as soon as Rosemary can get something booked. I'll make coffee and give her a call while you're in the shower."

"Thanks." She wrapped her arms around his neck and planted a kiss on his lips before scrambling out of bed.

~ ~ ~

Renée wiped down the counters. She was tired. It would be good to get April in here and be able to share the load. She might even get to sleep in a little longer some days once April knew the ropes. That was how she and Shelly had worked things; they each came in an hour late and left an hour early two days a week. Since Shelly had been gone, there'd been nothing but long shifts and no breaks. She smiled to herself. She hadn't really noticed too much though, her mind had been too full of Gabe. She paused and stared out the window. Gabe, the guy who was in love with her. She didn't think it had sunk in yet. He loved her! She loved him! It was all just a little surreal. But wonderful. She just hoped it wouldn't all come crashing down around her ears. Her life wasn't exactly plain sailing at the moment. Still. There was hope. Hope for a new life, a good life, a life with Gabe in it!

Ben waved at her through the window and came in. "Now that's a smile and a half! Dare I ask what that's all about?"

She shook her head. "Just thinking that maybe things are starting to look up for me, that's all."

"I hope so. It's about time, isn't it?"

"Way past time if you ask me. Anyway, to what do I owe the pleasure? You haven't been in here in ages, and I don't believe you're just after a doughnut."

"Nope, no doughnuts for me. I have to watch my figure."

Renée laughed and looked him over. "You do not. There are plenty of women around here who'd happily watch your figure if you'd just move it in their direction."

"Don't you start on me as well!" Ben grinned at her. "Why's everyone so eager to get me paired off?"

"Because you're a good-looking guy with a heart of gold. You deserve to be happy and we all think that finding the right woman will make you happy."

As she watched the smile fade from his face, Renée could have kicked herself. "Sorry."

"It's okay." For a moment he looked defeated, sad, and so much older. "I don't normally say anything, but sometimes—just sometimes—it gets to me."

He looked so sad she wanted to wrap him up in a hug. "What gets to you, Ben?"

"The way no one gets it. Everyone's moving back here, coming home and finding the love of their life. They all want me to do the same, except it's different for me."

"I can see that, but tell me why. What is it that's so different for you than it is for the rest of us?"

He gave a short, bitter laugh. "Well, for starters I'm not coming home. Apart from going to college, I never left. And I'm not about to find the love of my life." She hated to see the pain and sadness in his eyes as he added, "I lost her years ago."

"I'm sorry, Ben."

He shrugged. "No, I'm sorry. I don't normally say a word, and I shouldn't be dumping on you. I think seeing you and Gabe together brings it home a bit more though."

That surprised her. "How so?"

"Well, you two were friends back then. All these years later, you're finally getting it together."

She had to ask. "You're talking about back then. Does that mean you're talking about Charlotte?"

He nodded sadly.

"I never knew what happened between the two of you."

He met her gaze and for a moment she thought he was going to tell her. Then he changed his mind and shrugged again. "I fucked up. That's what happened. Anyway. Sorry. I didn't come to dump my sorrows on you. I came to talk to you about April. Are you okay with her starting on Monday?"

"More than okay. I'm looking forward to it. She seems nice."

"She does. It sounds like she's been through a lot, and she has her kid, so I won't be surprised if she doesn't get in on time every day. At least until they get settled in and get used to a new routine."

Renée nodded. She'd been thinking the same thing.

"I know it's been tough on you these last few weeks with no late starts or early finishes. Hopefully, once April gets the hang of things you'll be able to figure out something that works for you both."

"I'm sure we will."

"In the meantime, though, do you want to just close up shop for today? Get out of here an hour early?"

"Let me think about that for a minute…umm, yeah!"

Ben laughed. "Let's close up then. Do you want to come have lunch with me? Or do you want to get home?"

"I'd love to have a quick lunch. Gabe's supposed to pick me up after work. He's gone over to see Pete Hemming this morning."

Ben waited while she collected her things and locked up. Then they set out down the street toward the resort. "Can you imagine Gabe and Pete getting their heads together?" asked Ben. "I'm kind of excited to see what they come up with, but at the same time it's a bit scary, too. They're both a formidable force as individuals, I'm a bit worried that instead of dragging the town into the twenty-first century, they'll be shooting us at warp speed straight into the twenty-second!"

"I know exactly what you mean. I think, at least I hope, that Gabe is chilling out a little. The way he's been talking about this job and everything that goes with it, it sounds as though he really wants to embrace the small town growth concept rather than fall into the traps that come with rapid development."

"You're right. I know he does, and Pete does, too. They both love this place, but when you take their personalities and abilities and then set them to work together, you've got admit it's a bit scary!"

"It is. I'll do what I can to keep Gabe in check."

"And I'll do the same with Pete."

Renée knew it was nosey of her, but she couldn't help asking. "And what about his fiancée? Do you think I should join forces with her? Does she have small-town roots that might help slow him down?"

The look on Ben's face confirmed her suspicions that things weren't great between Pete and Holly. "She grew up in LA, but she loves this place. I don't think she feels as though she could slow Pete down on anything at the moment. It seems that the wedding planning is causing them a bit of tension. Pete's being Pete and Holly's feeling forgotten."

Ben's cell rang and he pulled it out of his pocket. "Sorry. I'm going to need to take this. I may be a while. Do you want to grab us a table? Though honestly, depending how this goes, I may not get to join you."

"Let's take a rain check; you can owe me one. You take your call. I've got a couple of things I need to do anyway."

"Okay. Sorry. I'll catch up with you soon."

As Ben answered his call, Renée turned around and headed back to the bakery. It would have been nice to have lunch with Ben, but there was something else she'd been wanting to do. Since she'd been back at the lake she'd been going to the cemetery every couple of days. But with everything that had been going on with Gabe, being by herself in the bakery, and fitting in lunch with the girls, she hadn't been there at all this week. She didn't know why it bothered her so much. She hadn't been for years prior to coming back here, but now she was here something inside her drove her to go visit with Chloe. At least that was what it felt like she was doing. Some part of her mind acknowledged that perhaps she was finally starting to process grief that she'd spent all these years running from. Another part of her mind told her to shut the hell up, get on her bike, and go. She listened to that part and headed out down the old road by the river that led out to the cemetery.

As she neared the gates she saw a big black pickup truck parked outside. It was unusual to see anyone out here during the week. It seemed that most of the town came to visit their dead on Sundays, a day Renée had learned to avoid. As far as she was concerned, she came out here to visit with her sister, not with the rest of Summer Lake. She got off her bike as she passed through the gates, smiling at her own stupidity even as she did it. Just as she wouldn't walk over the graves, she wouldn't ride her bike in here either. It wasn't superstition, at least not in her mind. It was respect. She smiled as the slogan, dismount for the dead crossed her mind. Sometimes she wondered if she was going completely nutso when she came out here. The strangest thoughts occurred to her and she usually found them funny, but she wouldn't share them with anyone else. She was still smiling to herself, as she turned the corner, knowing that she would have shared that with Chloe, and Chloe would have laughed along with her, and no doubt come up with more and weirder little comments of her own.

She stopped abruptly and the smile left her face when she saw him.

Chance was kneeling in the grass in front of Chloe's gravestone. Renée blinked back tears and started to turn the bike around. Chloe may be her sister, but she knew that she was the intruder in this situation.

"Do you still hate me that much?"

She froze at the question. Did she hate him? She mustn't have heard him right. It didn't make sense. He hated her and he had every right to! She couldn't turn around and look him in the eye and she couldn't bring herself to walk away either.

"I'm sorry, Renée. I'm so sorry."

The crack in his voice broke the spell that had been holding her. She lay the bike down and walked toward him. When she stood face-to-face with him she made no attempt to wipe away the tears that were rolling down her face. "Chance, I'm sorry. It was all my fault."

The pain on his face turned to disbelief. "What do you mean?"

"You know damned well what I mean. If I hadn't made you promise not to go after them, Chloe would still be alive. You guys would still be together. And your life wouldn't have been ruined."

Chance's eyes narrowed, his lips pressed together in a thin line. "Your fault? How can you think any of it was your fault, Renée? She went off with Kyle because I was being an asshole. I knew she was mad at me and I let her walk out. If I'd gone straight after her, or if I'd just said sorry before she left, she would never have been out on the lake that night."

"Oh, Chance. That wasn't your fault. You two had a fight, you were kids, you did it all the time, and you made up within minutes. You can't blame yourself for that."

He shook his head sadly. "That's what I've been trying to tell myself all these years. I don't buy it though. I may as well have killed her myself."

Renée couldn't process that. "I've always thought you blamed me. I made you promise not to go after them. If you had, it might all have been so different. I stopped you. I may as well have killed her myself."

"How can you say that? You were right. If I'd found them, I would have killed him. You knew that much. You couldn't have known what was going to happen out in that boat."

They stared at each other for a long moment. Tears running down both their faces.

Eventually, Chance spoke again. "One thing I've come to terms with is that we can't change what happened. All we can do is live with what is."

Renée nodded. That much was true.

"I was hoping I might see you. I wanted to ask if you might find it in your heart to make peace with me?"

Renée wrapped her arms around him and sobbed against his broad chest. "I would love to make peace with you, Chance. But I need you to forgive me."

He shook his head. "There's nothing to forgive."

"There is in my mind."

His light blue eyes brimmed with tears. "Then I forgive you." He hugged her to his chest, and they stood that way for a long time, each softly sobbing on the other's shoulder.

# Chapter Fourteen

Renée dragged the brush though her hair. Her eyes were still red and her face was blotchy. There was no time to fix anything before Gabe arrived though. She heard the doorbell tinkle and gave one last tug before admitting defeat in the fruitless battle to try to tame her hair. She'd come back to the bakery to try to pull herself together after seeing Chance. She hadn't had much success though, she was a mess.
"Are you back there?" called Gabe.
"I'll be right out."
She plastered a smile on her face before going back through to the store.
Gabe's own smile disappeared in a hurry when he saw her. "What's wrong, Renée?"
She sniffed loudly. Why couldn't she be more of a lady and less of a mess? "Nothing. Sorry. Let's get out of here, can we?"
He came and closed his arms around her. "We're not going anywhere until you tell me what's up."
She should have known he wouldn't let it go. She rested her head against his shoulder. "Nothing bad. In fact it's good, but can we please go home and I'll tell you on the way?"
Once they were heading out down Main, he turned to look at her. He didn't need to say anything, she could feel the concern and the impatience he was radiating.

"I saw Chance."

"He came into the bakery?"

"No, Ben came by and said we may as well close up early. I took the opportunity to go out to the cemetery." She checked his face to see what he might make of that; she hadn't mentioned her visits with Chloe to him before.

His eyes were fixed on the road, his face gave nothing away. He just waited for her to continue.

"I've been going out there quite often. Trying to get straight with myself. It seems Chance was doing the same thing."

Gabe nodded, but said nothing.

"You were right. He doesn't hate me. It turns out he thought I hated him. We made our peace, Gabe."

Even though it was sad, there was no question that his smile was genuine. "I'm glad to hear it."

She nodded. "It's still so hard though, you know? There's this sense of relief, a weight lifted. Yet nothing really changes. Chloe's still dead. Chance still lost the life he thought he was going to have."

"And you still lost your sister."

She nodded. She'd never really admitted it before, but her life had changed that night, too. She'd lost her sister, her best friend and her life had been changed. Not as much as Chance's had, but it had shifted course nevertheless. They rode on in silence. Gabe seemed to understand her need to mull it all over.

"Did you get your flight changed?" she asked after a while.

"Yeah, but there was nothing available Sunday morning. I leave at nine tomorrow night. Do you want to come with me? If you drop me off early you could be back here by eleven. I know that's a late night for you though."

She shrugged. "I can catch up on sleep on Sunday afternoon. I'd rather have a few more hours with you."

He smiled. "Good." He was turning into the driveway. "And you're okay with keeping the car?"

"Yes, thank you." Part of her didn't want to, was still struggling with thoughts of charity. The more reasonable part of her accepted that he cared about her and wanted to take care of her. Why should she refuse that? And besides, she really didn't want to go back to riding that bike into town at four o'clock every morning.

He pulled up outside the house and turned to take her face between his hands. "I love you, Renée."

For some reason that set her off again. The tears started to flow. He led her inside and sat on the sofa with her cradled in his lap while she cried, more tears than she would have thought one person could produce. When they eventually dried up, she looked up at him. "Sorry, now your shirt's a soggy mess, and I don't even know what I'm crying about. Things are getting better, so why I am blubbing now?"

"My guess is that it's out of relief. You've carried all that guilt and pain over Chance for all these years. You're not going to just have one conversation with him and be over it all in the blink of an eye. It'll take you time to process it all."

She nodded. He was no doubt right as usual.

"Is he sticking around?"

She shrugged. "He didn't know that himself. We were both a bit emotional as I'm sure you can imagine. It wasn't an in-depth conversation, just all it needed to be. I wish we could have talked more, but it wasn't the time or the place. Hopefully, someday we'll be able to."

"I hope so. For both your sakes."

~ ~ ~

Gabe checked the oven, the lasagna was almost ready. He was surprised at how domesticated he was becoming. Renée had taken a shower, and he'd convinced her to take a nap, too.

She'd been worn out from all her early starts anyway, and he knew the emotional toll of finally talking to Chance would have drained her completely. He'd run back down into town and bought what he needed to make dinner for her. He'd also bought everything he thought she might need to make it through the week until he came back. She refused to talk about money, but the fact that her fridge contained nothing but sandwich meat and peanut butter gave him a clue how tight things really were for her.

He heard her getting up and opened a bottle of wine to let it breathe.

"Hey, sleepy head. Did you get some good rest?"

She nodded and came to wrap her arms around him. "I did, but then I started dreaming about Italian restaurants." She sniffed the air. "What are you making?"

He grinned. "Lasagna."

"Ooh! You can cook, too! You should stick around."

"I wish I could. But you know I'll be back as soon as I can."

She nodded. "I hope so. It's going to be really strange around here without you. I'm going to miss you."

He hugged her closer. "I'm going to miss you, too. I wish you could come with me."

"Nah. You won't give me another thought once that plane takes off."

"Not true. All I'll be thinking about is getting back to you as fast as I can."

The way she smiled back at him made him decide to ask her something that had been playing on his mind. "And when I get back, can we start thinking about where we're going to live?"

She raised an eyebrow. "You don't like it here?"

For once he felt unsure of himself. How to tell her that he hated that she was living like this? He searched for the right words. "I know it's your childhood home and everything, but, well…"

She laughed. "It's not up to the angel Gabriel's standards? Is that what you're trying to say?"

"Come on, Renée. It's not up to livable standards. It'd be condemned in a heartbeat if it were inspected."

She frowned. "But it's not going to be inspected, and it's all I've got."

"It's not though, is it? You've got me now. Don't I count for anything?" It stung a little that she refused to consider that he might be able to contribute something to her situation—hell, to their relationship.

"Of course, you do! You count for everything, Gabe! But I already feel as though I'm leaning on you too much. The one thing I have is a home. All right, it isn't much of a home, but it's where I grew up."

Gabe felt terrible as tears welled up in her eyes again. "It's where I lived with my sister and my dad. And now I've come back to it, I'm not sure I'm ready to just walk away from it. You're going through your process, figuring out what comes next in your life. Well, you know, coming back here has been a journey for me, too. I've come all the way back to my roots, and I don't know that I want to leave them behind, yet. Or ever! Can you understand that?"

He held up a hand. He did understand. "I'm sorry. I wasn't trying to rush you or force you. I just want to live with you. Can you understand that?"

He loved the smile that touched her lips. "I'm not sure I can, no. Why on earth you would want to live with this crazy redhead is beyond me. Especially if it means moving into a rundown shack."

"I want to live with you, you crazy redhead, because I love you. I want you in my life." He looked around. "And I want to be in yours, even if it does mean living in a rundown shack. So what do you say? When I come back, can I move in?"

She studied him for a long moment without replying.

"For Christ's sake, Renée. Would you say something?"

"It's not good enough for you."

"Come here, you stubborn woman. Why won't you get it? I'd live under a bridge with you if that was the only way to be with you. I admit, this wouldn't be my first choice, but it's where you want to be. And wherever you are is where I want to be. So it's quite simple really. Do you want me or not?"

She threw her arms around his neck. "Of course, I want you. I love you. I just don't want you to end up hating me because you have to live like this."

"I don't have to. I'm choosing to. And I'm also telling you it won't be forever." He shook his head at the doubt on her face; he knew what she was thinking—that they wouldn't be together forever. "I'm talking about living here. I'll do it while you get straight with yourself and figure it out. But no, you're right, I couldn't live like this forever. So I'm putting you on notice. As you figure out what you do want your life to look like, you need to think about where you do want to live. Wherever it is, it's going to be with me, okay?"

She swallowed and nodded. "Yes, please."

That made him laugh. "Good. Now, are you hungry? I need to rescue the lasagna from that death trap of an oven."

~ ~ ~

Renée clung to Gabe's hand as he strode through the airport. She didn't want to let go, didn't want to let him go. She wanted nothing more than to beg him to come back to the lake with her. He didn't feel very approachable right now though. His face was set as he marched her toward the coffee shop.

Once they were perched at one of the tables by the window, she sipped her coffee and studied him. "Did I do something wrong?" She felt as though she must have. She hadn't seen him smile since they'd parked the car.

His face softened as he reached out to touch her cheek. "What makes you think that?"

She shrugged. "The scowl fixed on your face maybe? Or perhaps it's the fact that you haven't said a word since we got here?"

"I'm sorry. You haven't done a thing wrong. I feel like I'm doing wrong by leaving you. I don't want to go."

Relief surged through her; she'd been starting to feel like he couldn't wait to leave. She took hold of his hand. "I don't want you to go, either, but you've got a lot to do. You need to wrap things up so you can come back to me. And I've got a lot to do as well. I'm going to have a busy week between training April and going through the papers Paul sent me about getting the divorce started." She smiled at him. "But you haven't gone yet, so can we make the most of the little time we have left? I'd love to see one of your smiles before you go."

There it went. His face really did transform when he smiled, and there was no question that this one was genuine. "Better?" he asked.

"Much. Thank you."

"You know, I think I've smiled more in the last week than I have in the last ten years. And that's all down to you."

"Well, stick around, counselor. That's what happens when you spend time with a crazy redhead."

"I want to spend all my time with you." His frown returned. "What's this Paul guy saying about the divorce, anyway? Has he given you any indication how long it might take?"

"He can't yet. We still don't really know what's going to be involved; it's an unusual situation. He's been asking around, but he hasn't found anyone with a good handle on how best to proceed." She didn't like to ask whether Gabe had put out any feelers. She still felt as though she'd creeped him out when she'd first talked to him about her divorce. In fact, she was a little surprised that he'd brought it up now.

He seemed to read her thoughts. "I haven't forgotten. I've got some calls in to a couple of contacts here in the Bay Area and another down in LA. It may take a while though."

She nodded, not knowing what to say.

It seemed Gabe didn't know what to say either. They sat quietly, each sipping their coffee, lost in their own thoughts.

Eventually he took hold of her hand. "Do you want to get going? I'm already feeling guilty about making you drive back alone in the dark. The longer you stay the later it will be when you finally get home to bed."

She smiled. "I don't mind. It's worth it."

"It is, but I think you should get going. I'm going to have to go through security soon anyway."

"Okay." She stood up. "I guess I'll leave you to it then."

He took her hand and led her to the doors. "You drive safely, okay? Text me and let me know you made it?"

She nodded. "You do the same when you land?"

"I will." He closed his arms around her. "I'll be back as soon as I can."

"I know, just hurry up about it will you?"

He lowered his lips to hers and kissed her. This was different from the usual crushing, demanding Gabe kisses. It was soft and sweet and oh so tender. She held him tight as she felt tears prick her eyes.

"I love you, Renée," he said when he finally lifted his head. "And now I'm going to leave while I still can."

She nodded. She was getting used to his abrupt departures. "Take care."

He nodded and reached out to touch her cheek. "Be safe."

She could feel the tears stinging behind her eyes again. She swallowed. "Keep smiling."

His own eyes were glistening as he replied. "Always."

She reached up and pecked his lips. "I love you, Gabe. I've got to go." She turned and hurried back to the parking lot as the first few tears escaped and rolled down her cheeks.

She got in the car and leaned on the steering wheel for a few moments before straightening up and drying her eyes. This was ridiculous. She was a grown woman, not a teenage girl. Gabe would be gone for a week at the most, so why was she carrying on as though she might never see him again? She pulled herself together. She knew why. It was because she was in love with him. She'd never felt this way before. She wanted to be around him, every minute of every day—and every night, too. She didn't want him to fly away and leave her, and she was dreading the thought of waking up without him in the morning. But, that was the reality. That was how it was going to be, and she was just going to have to deal with it. In the grand scheme of things, she'd dealt with so much worse lately. She just needed to get a grip. That was all. She put the car in gear and headed toward the exit and the long drive home.

# Chapter Fifteen

Gabe grinned as Rosemary peeked her head around his office door.

"Oh my God! Who are you and what have you done with Gabe Morgan?"

He raised an eyebrow. "Want to give me a clue what you're talking about?"

She came in and took a seat, pulling out her tablet as if she were about to start taking notes. "Okay… Well a week ago, my long-time employer, Mr. Gabriel Morgan, Esquire, left this office on a Friday afternoon. The gentleman in question is known to be a hardworking, serious, extremely focused…" She hesitated and smiled at him. "Uptight, slave driver, seriously lacking in the sense of humor department."

Gabe smiled through pursed lips.

"Over the course of the last week, said gentleman has apparently transformed, into a carefree, laughing, joking shadow of his former self, who apparently wants to leave the big city and return to his roots in small town California. Forgive me, but I've been finding this rather hard to believe. This morning I walk in here to find someone who looks like Gabe and sounds like Gabe, but is giving himself away by grinning like an idiot. Something my esteemed colleague would never stoop to. So you see, I'm onto you. You are an imposter!

And I want to know what you've done with my grumpy, overly serious, but much loved boss!"

Gabe had to laugh. "It's all your fault, Rosemary. You were the one who told me to lighten up. To go have some fun. So I took your advice to heart and did just that." He could tell she was brimming with questions, and much as she might tease him, she wouldn't cross the line so far as to pry. "And by the way?"

"What?"

"Thank you."

"You are most welcome. I don't really know what for, but if my ragging you helped you make this transformation, then I am one happy little lady." She raised her eyebrows but still didn't ask any questions.

He had to put her out of her misery. "You told me to try smiling more and to have some fun. I did just that and it snowballed. I met a woman…"

"Yay!!!!"

Gabe laughed. She just couldn't contain herself any longer.

"I'm sorry, but I think having given you the last ten years of my life entitles me to ask."

"Ask what?"

"Everything! Who is she? How did you meet her? What's she like? What kind of spell has she cast on you that within the space of a week you've decided to leave New York and take a sabbatical?"

She was right. She did deserve to know, and, more surprisingly, Gabe wanted to tell. What he really wanted was to talk about Renée. "Hmm. Her name is Renée Nichols. We grew up together. We were friends…" Remembering Renée's own words, he corrected himself. "We were in the same group of friends from Kindergarten through high school. We hadn't seen each other since then, but right around the time I started going back home to visit, she moved back to the lake and we bumped into each other."

"Aha! Is she the reason you've been going back there so much?"

Gabe nodded. "Apparently. Although I'm not sure I was even aware of that myself until my brother pointed it out to me."

"So come on, what does she look like? What does she do?"

Gabe smiled as he pictured her. "If I had to describe her in one word. She's a mess! A beautiful, wild, messy mess!"

Rosemary looked stunned. "I was picturing a perfectly groomed California bleached blonde."

"She's a redhead. A crazy little redhead at that. She has pale skin and the cutest freckles, green eyes, and she's stubborn as a mule!"

Rosemary was staring at him wide-eyed. "And you my friend, are in love!"

He grinned sheepishly at her. "Guilty as charged."

Rosemary's hand flew to her mouth. "I'm so happy for you, Gabe!" She came around the desk and hugged him before stepping back looking a little embarrassed.

"Thanks. I am, too. I want you to meet her. I think the two of you would get along like a house on fire."

"I'd love to." Rosemary's smile faded a little. "Does she have any plans to come to New York? From what I understand you're just here to tie up loose ends and then bug out on me. Right?"

Gabe nodded. "I am. I was hoping you might come out to California?"

"What, since I'm going to be unemployed?"

"Don't be ridiculous. You've got a job for life here, if you want it."

She smiled. "Doing what? I'm a Personal Assistant, and the guy I personally assist is leaving."

"Well, you have a couple of options. I spent a few hours with Wade and Dane yesterday. One of the first questions they had was what you would do. Apparently, they're going to fight over you if you want to work for either of them."

"Really?"

"Yep. You've been with the firm since the beginning. You could run it better than either of them could, and they know it." He grinned, "They wouldn't be as good to work for as I am though."

"Of course they wouldn't," she replied with a laugh. "But you're leaving me. What can I do?"

He shrugged, "Maybe down the line you could come work for me out there. I want to talk to you about this job I'm going to be taking."

Rosemary shuddered. "Leave the city for California? Live in a small town? Sorry, Gabe, but not even for you."

Gabe nodded. He'd known that would be her answer, but he'd had to ask. He hated to leave her. Now he thought about it she was the person he'd been closest to for the last ten years. But his personal life—now that he had one—was so much more important than his professional one. He felt as though he should feel more…something, he didn't know what. More regret maybe, more anxious certainly about upping and leaving the life he'd spent the last ten years building, but he didn't. He was concerned that whatever Rosemary decided to do should work out well for her, but other than that, all he wanted to do was wrap things up and go. Get back to Renée, back to the lake, and get started on his new life—his new adventure.

"Well, you're going to have two of the city's best trial attorneys vying for your services." He grinned when he saw Dane's head appear around the door. "And make sure you squeeze them for a raise; in fact, if I were you I'd play them against each other. See who's willing to give you the best package."

Wade pushed his way past Dane to come in and fixed Rosemary with a very suggestive smile. "There's no competition, Rosemary darling. You'll love my package. In fact, why don't you have dinner with me tonight to discuss it, and then drinks, and then..."

Rosemary shook her head at him with a laugh. "I've been telling you for ten years, Wade. I have no interest in that package of yours. And besides, I'm sure it must be almost worn out from overuse by now."

Gabe laughed. Wade was nothing if not a ladies man. He'd had the same banter going with Rosemary for years; she wouldn't have any of it.

Dane pushed his partner out of the way. "Come on, Rosemary, you may as well face the inevitable. You and I are the ones who've made this firm what it is. Now that Gabe's cracked under the pressure and is running back to the beach or whatever part of California it is he comes from, you know you have to work with me. With you by my side, we can conquer the world."

Gabe watched Rosemary's reaction with interest. She smiled and brushed Dane off, but there was something about the way she spoke to him that made Gabe wonder if she wasn't perhaps leaning toward working with Dane. It'd be quite something if the two of them were to develop a personal relationship out of a professional one. Now he thought about it, they were very well suited. He had to wonder again what on earth Renée had done to him. He'd worked with these three for ten years, known the guys for even longer, and it had never before occurred to him to wonder about their personal lives.

"What are you still doing here, anyway?" Wade turned to him. "I thought you'd be packed up and gone by now."

"Just like that. After everything we've been through together? I say I want to take some time, and you're shoving me out the door?"

Wade nodded. "That's about right. You want out, get gone." He tried to keep a straight face, but he couldn't manage it. "I just can't believe you're really going. I want you out of here before I break down and beg you to reconsider."

Dane rolled his eyes. "I feel the same way, but I'm happy for you. Just don't disappear completely? I have to get to court, and I'm not sure how much I'm going to be around this week. So I guess this is it for me."

As he stepped forward with his hand held out, Gabe felt all the emotion swell up in his chest. He swallowed, hard. He hadn't expected to feel like this. He shook Dane's hand and pulled him into a man hug. "Call me when you get a minute? I want to ask you a few questions."

Dane nodded, his eyes were bright. "Sure thing. Gotta go."

He turned on his heel and left.

Wade watched him go then met Gabe's gaze. "I'm not even that brave. I'm heading down to Miami to take depositions. So, like err, you know." He held his hand up next to his ear as if he were on the phone. "Call me."

Once he'd gone, Rosemary stood up. "They're going to miss you."

Gabe nodded. He didn't trust himself to speak.

Rosemary shook her head. "Why are you men so afraid of showing any emotion?"

He stared at her for a moment. "I know the answer to that one. I discovered it last week. It's because when we try, we discover just how hopeless we really are. We don't like to feel that way, so we avoid it."

"Interesting," said Rosemary. "And you're all supposed to be so smart."

Gabe pursed his lips. "And what's that supposed to mean?"

"That you're dumb when it comes to emotions. Any other skill you're lacking you go out and practice it until you get good. But when it comes to feelings, you avoid them so you don't look like fools—which by the way—just makes you look like bigger fools."

Gabe laughed. "Wow. Good point, well taken."

She smiled as she headed for the door. "I hope so. You're going to need to think long and hard on it if you're about to embark on a relationship with a woman. You have to admit you're late to the game and you really are more hopeless than most."

Gabe stared after her as she closed the door behind her. "Huh. Thanks!" He stared at the door for a long time after she'd gone, considering her words. He didn't think he'd been avoiding his feelings with Renée, had he? No. He'd come straight out and told her that he loved her. Well, after he realized that he hadn't actually mentioned it up to that point. He'd told her that he wanted to explore the possibility of them having a life together. Except that he'd somehow not gotten his point across, and she'd thought he was just exploring the possibility of being able to have a life with a woman in it. Hmm. Maybe it was a skill he needed to practice in order to get good at it. He smiled and reached for his phone. It wouldn't hurt to express his feelings right now.

~ ~ ~

Renée handed the change to the last customer in what had been a long line. It had been crazy for the last hour, and it was only seven o'clock. She smiled at April. "It isn't always like this, I promise. That's just the Monday morning rush." She turned at the sound of the phone ringing in the back. Oh no, that was more than likely a large order being called in ahead for lunchtime. "Come on," she said to April. "You should probably hear this to get the hang of the order slips."

She rushed into the back with April on her heels and pulled the order pad toward her as she put the phone on speaker and hit answer. "Good morning, Summer Lake Bakery, how can I help you?"

"Good morning, beautiful lady. I just needed to call to tell you that I love you, and I miss you so much it hurts. Especially in my pants."

Renée laughed out loud and looked at April who was already heading for the door. "Sorry. I guess this is one order you don't need to listen in on."

Once April had closed the door behind her, Renée turned back to the phone. "Good morning, angel Gabriel. You just introduced yourself to my new coworker."

She had to laugh at Gabe's groan. "Ugh. Sorry."

"No problem. You brightened my morning, but I'm not sure what you did for April's. I just told her to be ready to take notes so we could get the order ready."

Gabe laughed. "If I give you an order, will you take down everything I say?"

Renée laughed with him. He was in a playful mood this morning, it seemed. "I will. What do you want?"

"You."

She picked up the handset. "And what do you want me to take down?"

"Panties?"

She laughed. "I'd have a cold ass by the time you got here to do anything about it."

"Not too cold. I'm almost done here. I reckon I can get back Wednesday night. Would you be able to come get me from the airport? Or should I pick up another car?"

"I thought the point of you leaving the car with me was so that I can come get you."

"It was, but those flights usually don't get in until late. I don't want to make you miss out on a night's sleep."

"Gabe, I can catch up on sleep in the afternoon. I want to see you as soon as you can get here."

April popped her head around the door with an apologetic smile. "I'm sorry. I mashed up the cash register again and I can't give the customer his change."

Renée nodded. "I'll be right out. Gabe, I have to go."

"Okay, I just wanted to hear your voice. I'll call you as soon as I get a flight booked. I love you."

"Love you too, bye."

Renée hurried back out into the store and started jabbing at the temperamental cash register. Once the customer had gone she turned to April, feeling a little embarrassed now. "Sorry about that. Gabe's never called on the bakery line before."

April smiled. "You don't have a thing to be sorry for. In fact I'd think you should be very happy. I can't imagine what it would be like to have a guy call you like that. It's so romantic!"

Renée laughed. "I'd hardly call Gabe a romantic."

"Really? How many women do you think have ever gotten a phone call like that? I know I never have."

"Oh." Now she thought about it, Renée never had either, until she met Gabe. "I guess you're right. It's just I don't think of him that way."

April gave her a puzzled look. "Well, forgive me for saying, but I'd start thinking about him that way if I were you. You have no idea how lucky you are. Most women, me included, would give anything for a man to love her like he obviously loves you. I was married for ten years and it was horrible. I used to read romance novels and dream about what it would be like to be with a man like that. Only I thought that kind of love only happened in novels. It seems like it happens in real life around here, from the stories I've heard, so make the most of it."

Renée nodded. "I will. Thank you. I was married for a long time, too. It was..." she thought about it. It wasn't as horrible as she thought April was talking about, or at least she hadn't known it was for the longest time. "It wasn't good, let's put it that way."

April smiled at her. "And now you've found something great, so make the most of it. Appreciate it and live it well. Give me some hope that I might follow in your footsteps and by some miracle find something good of my own someday."

"Oh, you will. I know you will."

"I doubt it, but by the looks of it at least I'll be able to live vicariously through you and your Gabe."

Renée smiled. "That may be giving me more responsibility for your happiness than I'm comfortable with. I think I'd sooner help you find a man of your own and put you in charge of your own destiny."

April shook her head. "No, thanks. I'm nowhere near ready to even start looking. And honestly, I've never been in charge of my own destiny in my entire adult life. I think that's enough to deal with for now without trying to add a man into the mix."

"I can see that, but give it time."

"I intend to."

"Do you mind if I ask what happened with you?"

April shrugged. "I don't mind, but I don't know where to start either. I reckon it'll all come out over time since we're working together."

"That's true." Renée looked up at the sound of doorbell and caught her breath at the sight of Chance.

"Hi," said April.

"Hey, I wanted to see how you're doing."

She smiled. "I'm getting the hang of it. Renée's teaching me well."

He turned his gaze on Renée and nodded at her. She nodded back, feeling slightly ridiculous, as if they were a pair of cowboys in some old saloon. She didn't feel as though they were squaring up for a shootout though. Their encounter at the cemetery had changed everything between them.

"I wanted to see how you're doing, too."

Wow! "I'm okay. Thank you. How about you?"

He nodded. "Better than I've been in a long time. Thank you." This was weird. They were doing so much more than just exchanging pleasantries. They'd crossed a pretty big bridge out at the cemetery, and Chance's presence here suggested that he now wanted to do some rebuilding, too. "Do you know how long you're going to be staying?"

He shrugged. "I might stick around a while."

Renée took a deep breath and decided to risk it. "Gabe's due back Wednesday night. I know he'd love to see you."

Chance nodded. "It'd be good to see him, too."

Well, that was a start. "Do you want to maybe get together on Thursday after I get done here?"

He nodded slowly. "I don't want to come out to your place though."

"God, no! I mean, I get that." She didn't want him to come out there either. For so many reasons. She wouldn't want to inflict all those memories on him, nor did she want him to see how rundown the place was.

"How about I meet you both here? What time do you close up?"

"Two thirty."

"I guess I'll see you then." He turned and left. Leaving Renée staring after him and April staring at her.

"I gathered at lunch the other day that there was some history between the two of you that wasn't public knowledge. Forgive me, but now I'm even more intrigued."

Renée nodded. "The history between us is pretty much the story of both our lives. I wouldn't know where or how to start."

"And you don't have to, but if you want to...well," she looked around, "I'm here."

"I think, as you said, since you're working here, it'll all come out over time."

# Chapter Sixteen

Renée had to admit that she was grateful for the use of the rental car when she pulled up behind the bakery the next morning. As the week had worn on she was finding it more and more difficult to drag herself out of bed when the alarm went off. She couldn't wait to pick Gabe up from the airport tonight, but she was concerned she might struggle even more tomorrow. This morning she'd gone so far as to hit the snooze button. Those extra few minutes had been wonderful, but nowhere near enough. And it had left her rushing madly to make it down here on time. As it was, April was already here.

"Good morning," she called as Renée let herself in through the back door. "I let myself in and I've got the ovens warming."

"Thanks. I'm sorry I'm late."

"You're on time, not late. I arrived a couple of minutes early. And besides, I need to get the hang of things so I'm ready to do it by myself. You must be desperate for a lie in. The sooner you can turn me loose to open up and take the early shift, the better."

Renée stifled a yawn. "I must admit, it'll be nice to have a couple of mornings a week when I can sleep in a little. I don't know what's wrong with me lately, but I feel wiped out all the time."

"It's hardly surprising. I'm exhausted, and I've only been doing this a week."

"Well, it'll get better for both of us once we can work out a roster. We can't do that until you know the ropes though, so come on. We'd best get to it."

By eleven o'clock it seemed the mid-morning lull had finally arrived. Renée went in the back to make them both coffee.

"Thanks," said April, when she handed her one. She took a sip and then smiled as she stared out the window. Renée was pleased that she was already looking more relaxed than she had when they'd first met at the Boathouse last week.

"How's your son settling in?" she asked. "It's Marcus, isn't it?"

April nodded. "He's doing really well, thanks. I was so scared when we left. I didn't know if his father would try to find us, come after us, or what Marcus would make of it all, how he'd cope. The other night, when I put him to bed, he thanked me for moving him away from there." She smiled. "It was just what I needed to hear, to know that I'd done the right thing for him, as well as for me."

Renée had to wonder how taking a child away from his father without telling him where you were going could be the right thing.

April sighed and met her gaze. "That must sound horrible, but if you knew Guy, you'd understand. He made my life hell—and Marcus's, too." She hesitated, obviously battling with herself over how much to say. "When I married him, I gave up my independence, my freedom, and any say I might have had over my own life."

Renée thought about that. "You know, much as I didn't recognize it at the time, it was the same for me with Eric. He made all our decisions, talked me out of any ideas he didn't agree with. I guess he was very good at manipulating. I had no clue what he was up to for years. If it was left to me, I probably still wouldn't know to this day what he was really up to, what he was really like."

"How did it all come out?"

"The first thing I knew was when investigators turned up at the office. They seized all the computers and carted Eric away. I was in a state of shock for the first few weeks. I had no idea what to do. I thought it must all be a big a mistake. But learning what he'd been up to, what he'd bought, the places he'd traveled to, the gifts he'd bought for women…" She shook her head to clear it of the memories. "I had to accept it. And then, when they did the Forfeiture of Assets thing, I had no choice but to figure out what to do. I needed a place to live and an income."

"That must have been so tough."

She looked at April. "It sounds like you've been through tougher times yourself."

April shrugged. "What matters is that we lived to tell the tale. We both came out stronger and wiser and we will never ever let a man take control over our lives again, right?"

Renée nodded. "Right." She was glad that April had a positive outlook. It was good to hear her sound strong and decisive. She just hoped she herself wasn't missing something when it came to her and Gabe. He was great, he couldn't be more different from Eric, he was a straight shooter, and honest to a fault. But he did like to be in control. Wherever their relationship was going, she wanted to make sure that she didn't somehow lose her independence and freedom in the process. Her biggest concern was that she didn't know what her life would look like yet, and she wanted to be able to figure that out independently and not mold it around what might suit Gabe.

She smiled when she realized April was watching her closely.

"Your Gabe isn't like that."

She laughed it off. "Oh, I know." He wasn't. It wasn't Gabe she was worried about, it was herself. She realized now that she'd spent her life downplaying what she wanted in order to do what she thought was best for other people, what she thought they needed. She couldn't do that with Gabe—not if she wanted their relationship to work.

~ ~ ~

Gabe grinned to himself as he parked a block down from the bakery. He'd told Renée that he'd be back tonight, and she was planning to come pick him up. But he'd had a stroke of luck last night when he'd been talking to one of his long-time clients. The guy had been heading out to his LA office this morning and had offered Gabe a ride in his company jet. It had been a much quicker and more comfortable journey than a commercial flight would have been and had given Gabe time to do something he'd been thinking about doing. He'd taken a taxi from the airport straight to the Auto-Mall and bought himself a brand new Range Rover. Even having done that, he'd made it back to the lake just in time to catch Renée as she finished work.

He peered in through the window; she was chatting with April as they wiped down the counters. She was so beautiful. It'd only been a few days since he left, but he'd missed her so much. April spotted him and smiled. Renée turned to follow her gaze. Her eyes lit up when she saw him, and she ran to the door.

Coming outside she threw her arms around his neck and kissed him. He pulled her against him and kissed her back. He only lifted his head when he heard the doorbell tinkle. April looked a little embarrassed as she smiled at them.

"I'll see you tomorrow."

Renée pulled away from him. "Sorry, April. I…"

"Sorry nothing! I'll see you in the morning." She hurried off down the street.

Gabe pulled Renée back to him.

"What the hell are you doing here?" she asked. "I was about to set off to pick you up."

"I couldn't stay away any longer, I got lucky and managed to hitch a ride this morning."

"Hitch a ride?" She raised an inquiring eyebrow.

He shrugged. "A friend's plane."

"Ah." She looked put out somehow.

"What's up? I thought you'd be happy to see me."

"Oh, Gabe I am. Just a bit surprised." She looked around. "And how did you get from the airport?"

He grinned and dangled the keys in front of her face. "Lock up and come with me, there's something I want to show you."

Her reaction wasn't exactly what he'd hoped for when she saw the Range Rover. "So you just bought yourself a new one, huh?"

He nodded. "Yep, I thought you might like it."

"I do." She turned to look at him. "How do we return the rental car?"

"We'll figure it out."

She scowled at him. "I'm not a charity case, Gabe."

He slid his arms around her middle and planted a peck on her lips. "I know. You tell me often enough. Do you think you can maybe try to accept that I love you? And that I want to take care of you?"

Her face relaxed, and she smiled up at him. "I'm sorry. I love you, too. I'm so glad you're back, and I do like your new car. I think I'm just a bit worn out."

He nodded. She did look tired. "Then let's just go home and relax. And knowing how beat you are, I'm really glad I didn't make you come to the airport to get me."

She nodded. "Me, too. Just let me lock up; you can go ahead if you want. I'll bring your rental car."

The way she phrased it bothered him. *Your* rental car. He let it go. Maybe he was just being too wary, or she was extra sensitive because she was tired. Either way, he didn't question why she phrased it like that. "Okay. I'll see you there."

~ ~ ~

Renée was getting more and more agitated as two thirty approached. Gabe had been pleased to hear that she'd arranged for them to meet Chance for lunch. He was eager to catch up with his old friend, and she knew that it was important to him that she and Chance should come to terms with the past as best they could. She'd thought it was a good idea herself, but now the hour was fast approaching she was starting to wonder why. The three of them had led such very different lives since high school. The more she thought about it now, the more she realized that the only thing they really had in common was Chloe. And Chloe was dead! That hardly made for light lunch conversation, did it?

She jumped when April put a hand on her shoulder. "Are you okay?"

"Yeah, sorry. I'm just a little nervous about this lunch with Chance."

"I'm guessing I shouldn't ask why?"

Renée realized that even with all the talking and getting to know each other they'd done as they worked together this last week, April still didn't know her history with Chance. "No, it's fine. You know we all grew up together."

"I gathered that much."

"Well, Chance and my sister dated for years, from middle school all the way through high school."

"I didn't know you had a sister."

Renée nodded sadly. "She's dead."

"Oh. I'm so sorry."

"That's all right. You didn't know. In fact, not many people *do* know, apart from those who grew up here, of course. Chloe died in an accident after she and Chance had had a fight. I've always blamed myself, Chance has always blamed himself. Up until last week neither of us realized that the other didn't see it that way. I wanted Chance to forgive me, he wanted to me to forgive him." She shrugged. "Does that even make any sense?"

April nodded. "Not the why, and I'm not going to ask you why, but if you blamed yourself it's only natural that you would assume Chance blamed you, too. And all the while he was doing the same thing, right?"

Renée sighed, "That's about it. It sounds so simple when you put it like that; I just wish I'd figured it out years ago."

"We only ever figure things out when we're ready to accept them."

"Aren't you the wise one?"

"No," April shrugged. "If I'd been wise my life wouldn't have turned out the way it did. All I'm doing is drawing conclusions and trying to understand the mess I made. So far I've accepted that you can't change the past, but you can learn from it and hope to apply the lessons to the future."

"Then you're definitely wiser than most."

April looked out the window and waved. "Gabe's early again."

Renée smiled when she saw him sitting out there in his Range Rover. Every time she saw him, no matter where she was or what else was on her mind, her heart rate and temperature soared. She loved him with all her heart and soul.

"Why don't you get going? I can close up."

"That's okay. Chance is meeting us here."

"I know, but you can at least go and say hello to your man while you wait."

"Thanks, I'll just grab my things." As she headed across the street to where Gabe was parked, she saw Chance walking down the sidewalk toward them.

She raised a hand in greeting. Chance nodded and quickened his pace. Gabe climbed out of the car and greeted his old friend with an awkward handshake that turned into a very genuine hug.

Chance stood back and smiled at them. "There aren't too many choices when it comes to eateries around here, but how do you feel about Giuseppe's?"

"Fine by me," said Gabe. "Jump in."

Renée pursed her lips as she walked around to the passenger side. She understood that Chance might not want to hold their little reunion at the Boathouse where anyone and everyone might see them—and join them. She was fine with going to Giuseppe's, but a little irked at Gabe that he hadn't even waited for her to speak, just ordered them into the car.

The little courtyard out back was empty, and Gabe led them to a corner table.

Once the server had brought menus and taken their drink orders, Chance smiled at them both. "So, this is…" he chuckled, "well, I guess weird is what it is, no?"

Renée nodded. "It's good though."

"Very good," agreed Gabe. "How are you?"

Chance nodded slowly. "I'm doing okay. I don't mind telling you I'm doing so much better since we talked."

She was glad to hear it. "I am, too."

"It's been a long road." He held her gaze. "I know people think I went off to live in the wilderness in Montana and became some kind of mountain man or recluse or something, but I landed in a good place."

"That's good. What's it like up there?"

"It's a good place to turn your back on the world and try to figure out what's left of yourself and your life. It's harsh country, but there's something about that. You have to face yourself, face your sins and your weaknesses. I don't know. It's unforgiving, but that's a good place to be when you don't want to be forgiven."

She didn't know what to say to that.

He smiled. "Like I said though, I landed in a good place. When I was released I went through a reintegration program. Met a guy," he smiled. "Dave Remington, who saw something in me. He took a chance on me, gave me a job on his ranch, even though I didn't know one end of a cow from another back then. He treated me like a son, and his four sons treated me like a brother. They still do. I've built a life there, such as it is."

Renée was curious what that meant. "What kind of life, Chance? Are you happy?" She so wanted him to be.

He met her gaze. "Happy is a strong word, honey. I do work I enjoy. For all intents and purposes, I'm as much a rancher now as if I'd been born to it. I have the guys, they really are like brothers. That's all I need. Anyway," he smiled, it seemed he'd done enough talking about himself. "What about you?" he looked from her to Gabe and back. "Looks like the two of you are happy."

Gabe reached for her hand and smiled as he took it. "We are."

Renée felt that little prickle of irritation again. He thought it was okay to speak for her? Her life was a shambles, her career had been blown out of the water, and she was broke! Yes, she loved him, and loved being with him, but should that negate everything else that was happening in her life and make her automatically, across the board happy?

She met Chance's gaze; apparently, he'd noticed her reaction, but he didn't comment on it.

"I always thought the two of you would be good together."

That surprised her, but she didn't get a chance to question him as the server returned with their drinks and took their food order.

Once she'd left, Chance turned to Renée again. "Miss told me things had gone bad for you in San Francisco?"

She nodded and gave him a very brief version of having her life turned on its head when she discovered that her husband and business partner had been a lying, cheating, major-league thief.

"Damn!" he said when she'd finished. "So where do you go from here?"

"Good question," she replied. "I can't really go anywhere for a while. Not until I know whether any charges are going to be brought against me."

"And until you get a divorce," added Gabe.

She nodded her agreement. "Then I have to figure out what I *want* to do," she smiled at Gabe, and added, "and then see what's going to be possible. Though I don't think running a charity is going to be on the list of possibilities."

Chance nodded. "Isn't that a good thing though, Renée?"

"How so?"

He shrugged. "You threw your whole life into that charity, but it was never about you and what you wanted, was it?"

"What?" She didn't understand what he meant, or maybe she was just surprised that he could see what she'd only been starting to understand this week.

"Come on. It was always about Chloe, wasn't it? If that bastard hadn't been drunk, she'd probably still be here. And you went on to spend your life educating kids against the dangers of alcohol."

"My dad was an alcoholic, too, remember? Drank himself to death?"

"Yeah, but you feel guilty about that, too, don't you?"

She shook her head. She was shocked that he would call her out on it. She could feel tears pricking behind her eyes. She didn't want to say out loud that, in a way, she'd held herself responsible for her father's death, too. If Chloe hadn't died, he wouldn't have hit the bottle so hard. And if *she* hadn't stopped Chance that night, Chloe might not have died.

"I'm sorry. I really don't mean to upset you. I just see you with this guy," he smiled at Gabe. "I see you at a crossroads in your life, with a chance to be happy. I'd hate to see you choose to

throw it all away in order to keep doing what you *think* is right. I'm hoping you'll wise up and start living your life for you."
She stared at him. "I chose to do what I did. No one made me."
"Yeah, but if you're honest, it was all for Chloe—not for you—wasn't it?"
She couldn't stop the tears from escaping as she nodded.
"And it didn't make a blind bit of difference, did it? I'm sure you helped some kids make better choices, but it didn't bring Chloe back, and it didn't stop you from feeling responsible for her death did it?"
Renée sniffed and shook her head.
Chance sighed. "I not trying to be cruel, Renée. I'm trying to tell you what no one else knows." He looked at Gabe and added, "Or would ever dare to say. You need to live what's left of your life for you."
She nodded. "I know. You're right. Thanks, Chance."
Gabe put a hand on her shoulder as she pulled herself together. His silent support was comforting, even though she knew he didn't—couldn't—understand in the same way Chance did.
"That's why I wanted to see you; I couldn't leave town without saying it. If you like, I'll go now, leave you guys to it."
"No! Don't you dare. We lost all those years, we just got you back." She smiled. "You just kicked my butt with a harsh truth. No way are you leaving now. We've got a lot of catching up to do, the three of us."
Gabe nodded his agreement.
Chance smiled and picked up his sandwich. "In that case, let's eat."
By the time their plates were empty, Renée felt as though the years since high school had never happened. They'd fallen back into old banter as they chatted. She was happy to see

Gabe and Chance reconnect; it seemed to be doing both of them good.

Chance checked his watch. "I'll get the check on the way out. I need to get going. I told Scotty I'd meet him at the library when he gets done."

Renée stood to hug him. "Thanks, Chance. I'm so glad you came."

He hugged her back. "Me too, and thanks for not getting mad at me for speaking my mind."

"It was hard to hear, but you're right. I do have to ask you something though."

"What's that?"

"Are you prepared to do the same thing you told me to? Live the rest of your life for you?"

His eyes narrowed, and he held her gaze for a long moment. "It's easier advice to give than to follow."

She smiled. "Oh, I know. But will you at least try?"

"I'm working on it." He let go of her and jerked his head toward Gabe. "Besides, it's easier for you. You've got this guy. You can just get married, have a couple of kids, and live happily ever after. You don't need to lift a finger."

She knew he was only joking, but it rubbed her the wrong way. She needed to contribute, to find meaning and purpose in whatever she did next, not just become a housewife.

She smiled. "It's not quite that simple."

"I know, but don't let him go. You two are good together." He smiled at Gabe. "And keep in touch, both of you? Miss says you're both invited to the wedding. I hope you're coming?"

Gabe nodded. "We are."

# Chapter Seventeen

Renée slowly opened her eyes. She felt a moment's panic when she realized it was light outside and she was still in bed.

"Relax, enjoy it." She smiled at the sound of Gabe's voice. He swept her hair out of the way and kissed the back of her neck. "For once you get to lie here with me and just be."

"Mm." She snuggled back against him and closed her eyes again. "This is sooo good."

"Isn't it? I wish we could do this every morning."

"Don't get greedy. Three mornings a week is going to be a hell of a lot better than we've been used to."

"Is it so wrong of me to want you every day?" He pulled her closer and she could feel that he really did want her.

She rolled over to face him and kissed his lips. "Not at all. But I'm afraid this job is my only option at the moment, so we'll just have to make the most of the mornings we do get." She slid her hand inside his boxers and closed her fingers around him, loving the way he closed his eyes and sighed.

He removed her hand long enough to get rid of his shorts and roll onto his back. "Go ahead then, make the most of me."

She slid on top of him and kissed the tip of his nose. "I love you, Gabe."

His hands closed around her hips. "Want to show me how much while you're up there?"

She smiled and pushed herself up on her hands. "I can do that." She lifted herself up so that she was positioned just above him, and moaned as his fingers found her heat. She lowered herself slowly. It seemed she was always wet for him whenever he was close, but the sheer size of him made her take her time savoring the feel of him as he slid deeper and deeper.

He grasped her hips and pulled her down, burying himself to the hilt and making her gasp. "Patience, Gabriel," she murmured.

He shook his head as he thrust his hips, setting up a pounding rhythm that she knew she wouldn't survive for long. "I don't have any when it comes to you, my love."

All she could do was ride the wave of his urgency. He carried her along with him as he pounded his way to his release. In the moment he quickened, her orgasm took her, and, with the next thrust of his hips, he joined her. Gasping her name as he pulled her down to take him deeper. She knew in that moment, just as she did every time he took her there that this was their place. As stars exploded behind her eyes, she knew they were at the center of their very own universe, and he was all she ever needed or wanted.

She eventually collapsed onto his chest and he closed his arms around her. She'd never felt so at home as she did right there in his arms.

~ ~ ~

Gabe poured her coffee when he heard her come out of the bathroom. He loved the way this morning had started. He wished they could start every day this way.

"Ooh, thank you," she said as she swept into the kitchen. She looked so beautiful without a trace of makeup on, with her hair frizzing wildly around her shoulders. "I need to get going."

"Do you though?" he decided to risk asking.

"Yep, this is April's first morning by herself, and I don't want to leave her too long."

It was best to drop it. He wasn't going to get anywhere asking her to give the job up while she was busy worrying about taking care of April. "Okay. I'll see you back here this afternoon then."

She frowned. "You're not taking me?"

"You've got the car."

"Shouldn't you figure out how to return that thing? It must be costing you a fortune."

He shrugged. "It's not that much, and besides, you need transport."

"I have my trusty steed."

"You need a car."

"I can't afford a car."

"So let me buy you one."

"No!"

Gabe let out an exasperated sigh. Why wouldn't she let him in? Why didn't she want them to be a partnership? "Why not?"

"I don't have time for this. I need to get to work."

"Well, when you can spare me a minute would you explain to me why this relationship has to be so one sided?" The words surprised him, but he was getting tired of bottling up his frustration. Living in this house was driving him nuts. There was no place to put any of his things, the hot water rarely worked, and the washer had already turned his whites an off brown thanks to the all the sediment in the water.

She put her hands on her hips and glared at him. "What the hell are you talking about?"

He shook his head and took a deep breath, his intention was to make things better for both of them, not worse by fighting. "I'm sorry. I'm frustrated. I want good things for you." He looked around the kitchen and added, "For us. But you're so stubborn, you won't let me help. That feels like you won't let me in, as though you don't want us to be partners."

She came to him and wrapped her arms around his neck. "Oh, Gabe. I'm sorry. I'm not trying to shut you out; I'm just trying not to lose me."

"How could you do that?" He didn't understand what she meant by that at all.

"I need to stand on my own two feet. Can you understand that?"

He nodded. He kind of did and he knew it was a bigger conversation than she had time for right now. "I suppose so. I'm sorry."

"Me, too. I really do have to go." She gave him a small smile and pecked his lips. "I'll take the car, okay?"

He nodded. "Thanks."

"Can we talk about it later?"

He nodded, knowing that she'd probably find a way to dodge the conversation later, too. "Sure."

He watched her drive away before going back into the house. He couldn't stand to just hang around at the best of times, and this house was not a place he wanted to spend any more time than he had to, not when Renée wasn't in it. He grabbed his keys and headed for his car.

By lunchtime he was quite pleased with the progress he'd made. He'd decided to introduce himself around town, and figure out the lay of the land in preparation for his role as Development Manager. Everything had fallen into place nicely, with Ted Morris apparently having welcomed the opportunity to stand down early. He was tying up loose ends this week, and, on Monday, Gabe would begin taking over the position. He'd had some interesting conversations with a couple of the town's business leaders, one of whom he already knew very well—Ben. He'd introduced himself to the Head of the Chamber, and for his next stop, he was going to meet Pete for lunch. He'd wanted to stop by the bakery to see Renée, but after this morning he'd decided it'd be best to leave it.

He pulled up in the square at the resort and went into the bar at the Boathouse. Pete was already sitting there, talking on his cell phone. He nodded as Gabe pulled up a seat beside him and ordered a sparkling water.

Pete raised an eyebrow when he saw Gabe's drink appear.

"That's great. Thanks, Judy. If you can take care of it, I can get straight back on with the power company this afternoon. Yeah. Okay, thanks. I'll talk to you later." He hung up and looked at Gabe. "I thought lawyers always drank at lunchtime."

Gabe shook his head. "Not this one. You need a clear, sharp, focused mind, and alcohol is not the way to do it."

Pete nodded and took a slug of his beer. "It helps though."

"Helps what?" This wasn't the Pete Hemming he knew.

Pete gave him a rueful grin. "It doesn't help a damned thing. It's just that sometimes you wish it would and you try it to take the edge off. It's a fool's game, I know."

"It is, and not a road I expect to see you go down."

"Don't worry, I'm not. I'm just under a bit of pressure at the moment."

"I thought you thrived on pressure?"

"In the world of business, I do. Pressure in my personal life is a new development for me. And I'm not handling it too well. Or so I've been told."

Gabe rolled his eyes. "Oh, I see. If you'd told me that to start with, I'd have a beer with you, or a bourbon."

Pete laughed. "You too, huh?"

Gabe shrugged. "Not exactly. It's just, well, the same as you, this is all new territory to me, and I don't seem to be navigating it too well."

"That's because there's no frigging roadmap, my friend."

Gabe had to laugh. "You can say that again."

Pete looked him in the eye. "Want to grab a booth and trade war stories?"

"I'd love to. Maybe we can help each other figure it out."

"Maybe, but I think that's a long shot."

An hour later their plates were cleared and their glasses were empty. They were still sitting in the booth, talking. Ben stopped by. "More drinks, gentlemen?"

Pete looked at Gabe. "What do you think?"

He nodded. "Yeah. Why not."

"So what are you going to do?" asked Pete. "I don't know how you can live in that old place."

Gabe shrugged. "What choice do I have?"

"Go for the big romantic gesture and buy her a wonderful new house?"

"I don't think so. I think that would go down like the proverbial lead balloon."

"Do you?"

He nodded. "She's already told me how she feels about her place, how she doesn't want to rush it. And I do understand that. It's just that I'm going crazy in that old shack while she figures it out."

"So buy a new one. Maybe it'll help her make the decision to move on."

Gabe wasn't so sure about that. "Yeah, and maybe it'll just piss her off. There's nothing around here that I'd want to buy anyway. I'd have to build. Part of me hopes that she'll let me tear her place down and build something new out there. That'd be a win-win."

"Or you could buy her the newest, best, high-end property in the whole county."

Gabe raised an eyebrow. "Are you pitching me, Hemming?"

Pete grinned and nodded. "The first phase is nearing completion out at Four Mile. There's one house down on the lakeshore that would be right up your street. I know it."

"How do you know it?"

"Because we have the same taste. It's the best property in the whole development. I'd love it myself. You should come take a look. I was thinking about using it as a show home, but, if you want it, I'll sell it."

Gabe shook his head. "There's no point looking, she won't go for it."

"You don't know until you try. She might love it, she might love you all the more for it, and, if she doesn't, then you've got a great investment property. Hold onto it for a few years and you'll be laughing. You know that's true, because you're the one in charge of growth around here. Property prices rise proportionately to growth, so you'll determine your own gains."

Gabe thought about it. The investment part made sense, but presenting Renée with a fait accompli on something so big as a house—when she wasn't even comfortable using his rental car? That made a whole lot less sense.

"I don't know, Pete. I really don't want to upset her."

Pete blew out an exasperated sigh. "Yeah, I can understand that. What is it with women? They love it when you take charge, swoon when they consider you to be the alpha male, and then consider you to be complete asshole when you don't do it exactly how they want it?"

Gabe smiled. "I wish I knew. If I figure it out, I'll let you know."

"Thanks." Pete downed the last of his beer. "The way things are going, I don't think I'll ever figure it out."

Gabe checked his watch. "Well, I wish you luck. I wish us both luck, but, for now, I've got to get going."

Pete punched his arm as they stood. "What's up? Afraid to be late getting home?"

"No! It's not like that." It wasn't, was it? It was because he wanted to be home when Renée got there, not because he thought he'd be in trouble if he wasn't. Part of him wanted to rebel against even the possibility. "Email me the details on that house would you?" It wouldn't do any harm to look into it.

Pete grinned. "Sure thing, bro."

# Chapter Eighteen

Renée smiled when she saw Ethan's face pressed against the window. He was adorable. He spotted her and waved, then turned back to call over his shoulder before coming in.

"Hi, Miss Renée."

"Hello, Ethan. How are you?"

He nodded. "I'm okay, thanks. Me and Meggie are taking Ollie for a walk, but Meggie's stopped to yack, so I thought I'd come see you."

Renée laughed as he eyed the cupcakes in the display case. "Come to see me, or come to see the cupcakes?"

He grinned up at her. "Both?"

She nodded. "Do you think Megan would mind if you had one?"

He shook his head. "Not at all."

Renée hoped he was right as she reached him one down and handed it over. "There you go."

"Thanks!" He bit into it and smiled up at her as he munched. "Can I ask you a question?"

"Of course, what would you like to know?"

"Can I call you Auntie Renée?"

That wasn't what she'd been expecting at all. "If you want to, yes." She'd always wanted to be an aunt, but hadn't thought she would since Eric was an only child. If this little guy wanted to call her that, she'd love it.

He grinned. "Good. So when are you and Uncle Gabe getting married?"

Oh good grief! She'd thought he meant call her Auntie Renée in the same way he called her Miss Renée. She hadn't made the connection to marrying his uncle! "Who says we are?"

"Well Uncle Gabe wants to, and that's how you get to be my auntie. Auntie Kenzie is Meggie's sister. Uncle Chase is going to marry her, so he gets to be my uncle-forever. And you're going to be my auntie because you're going to marry Uncle Gabe." He stared at her as if it was all so simple and she must be a little bit slow to not understand.

She didn't know what to say. Gabe had moved in with her, they'd talked about having a life together, she thought of him as her future, but marrying him? Hell, she wasn't even divorced.

April surprised her by coming to the rescue as she emerged from the kitchen. "Ethan, sometimes we grownups take a little longer to figure things out than you do." She smiled at Renée. "We're not as dumb as you think we are; we just have more things to think about so we don't get through them as quickly."

Ethan nodded. "I noticed. But," he turned back to Renée, "what do you have to think about? You love him, he loves you. He's living at your house even though he doesn't like it. So why don't you just get married?"

How the hell did he know Gabe didn't like it at her house? That made her heart hammer in her chest, and for once, it wasn't in a good way. What had Gabe been saying—and to whom—that Ethan would know about it? She recovered quickly. "Well, did you know that I'm already married?"

Ethan's eyes grew wide. "You are? Where's your husband then? Does Uncle Gabe know?"

She couldn't help laughing; the kid was so smart in some ways, but he was just a kid. "Of course he knows. My husband," she hesitated, "isn't around anymore. We haven't been together for quite a long time now." She realized how true that was as she said it. "But legally, we're still married. I have to get a divorce before I could even think about marrying someone else."

"Uncle Gabe's a lawyer. He can figure out the legal stuff for you."

Renée had been hoping that he might at least help out with some connections, but that hadn't happened. "I think I need to figure it out for myself."

"Well can you hurry up about it? I want you to be my auntie."

"I'll do my best," she said with a smile. She looked up as the door opened. "Hi, Megan."

Megan smiled. "Hi." she stood in the doorway with her dog outside pawing at her legs and whining. She looked at Ethan. "What are you up to?"

Ethan gobbled down the last of his cupcake and grinned at her. "I just came to see Auntie Renée."

Megan gave him a stern look, "And to see what goodies you can get?"

He shook his head, feigning innocence. "Nope, not me."

Megan sighed and looked at Renée. "What do I owe you?"

"Nothing."

"See, I told you," said Ethan with a grin. "Thanks, Auntie Renée." He winked at her and headed for the door. "Come on, Ollie. Let's go, boy." Megan handed him the leash and he trotted out.

"He had a cupcake. I hope that's okay?"

"It's fine by me," Megan said. "I just hope he wasn't harassing you? He's fixated on expanding his family at the moment. He's already got Kenzie and Chase down to babysit once a week, and you seem to be next in his sights." She popped her head back out the door to check on him. "The poor little guy missed out on having family around until he came to live here, and now he's trying to make up for it." She gave Renée an apologetic smile. "He just doesn't realize that it's not as simple as he thinks it should be."

"It's not a problem. He's great." Renée thought about it for a minute. "And I wonder if it's not really as simple as Ethan thinks it is. As grownups we let all kinds of stuff get in the way. Maybe he's got the right idea, and we just make it too complicated?"

Megan smiled. "Maybe. Anyway, he's off. I'd better catch up with him."

"Bye," Renée called after her.

The sound of the buzzer on the oven had her hurrying into the back to get the bread out. Ethan had given her a lot to think about. Gabe wanted to marry her? Was that something Ethan had heard him say? Or just an assumption on the kid's part? And he also knew that Gabe didn't like living at her house? She fumed quietly over that one for a minute. That could hardly be Ethan making assumptions. Gabe must have said something. She set the bread to cool and pushed her hair out of her eyes. Then she took a deep breath. She didn't even like living there! Why should she be mad at Gabe for it? She had to admit she was hardly being fair. The place was rundown, and she'd bet he was used to living in some luxurious apartment in New York. But what could she do? She felt as though she needed to live there for a while. The last couple of weeks had brought back so much. She felt as though she was making progress—especially after their lunch with Chance. He'd seen what she'd been doing and had laid it all out for her. She was going through a healing process. But she wanted to do it in that house. It felt necessary somehow. She shook her head. She'd figure it out. She'd talk to Gabe about it. They needed to clear the air between them, even if he didn't know it yet. She'd been resenting him for things he wasn't aware he was doing. And he'd even said he felt as though she didn't want him as a partner. She did. She just didn't know how to make that work yet. If they were going to be true partners, then they needed to work it out together, talk about it all. Maybe tonight they'd be able to.

~ ~ ~

Gabe smiled when he heard Renée pull up. For all his frustration over living in this house, he'd meant what he'd said—he'd rather be here with her than anywhere else without her. He'd had a busy few days between spending time out in the community, getting familiar with the players, and the issues that were important to them. He'd made time to make a couple of purchases though. The first one he was going to tell her about tonight, and, the second, he was going to work up to slowly. He didn't need to spring it all at once. He wanted her to understand—not get mad with him.

"Hey beautiful," he said as she climbed the porch steps. He loved that smile!

"Hi. You really mean that, don't you?"

"I do."

She laughed. "You have strange taste, but I'm glad you do."

He closed his arms around her. "Strange taste? I have exquisite taste."

She wrapped her arms around his neck and pecked his lips. "Gabe, look at me. I am far from beautiful, and I know it." She ran a hand through her wild hair and made a face at him. "I have a wild mane," she grinned, and arched her body against him, "a fat ass, and a heavy build."

He closed his hands around her ass. "This is not fat," he said, giving it a squeeze. "It's perfect. Just like the rest of you is perfect. You're a natural beauty." He pulled her hips against his. "You're not heavy, you're real, and I love you."

"Real?" She laughed. "A real mess is what I am."

He shook his head. "I'm not arguing about it, you're beautiful. And, my beautiful, how do you feel about going out for a drive this afternoon? We rarely get chance to go out anywhere together. I thought we could head out, circuit the lake, be home in time for dinner." He gave her ass another squeeze. "And an early night."

She smiled up at him. "That sounds like fun. Give me a few minutes to freshen up?"

"Sure. Whenever you're ready."

A few minutes later she came back out. "You know, I haven't done an entire circuit of the lake since I came back."

"Me neither. I thought it'd be fun."

"I haven't even been up to the North end in years. Have you?"

Gabe nodded. He didn't want to admit that he'd been to Four Mile Creek a couple of times in the last few days. "Shall we take your car?"

She made a face. "You mean the rental car that you really need to return?"

He shook his head, hoping this would go well and wouldn't ruin the rest of the day. "No, I mean your car."

He held his breath while she stared at him. He read people well, but he was having a hard time keeping up with the conflicting emotions rapidly crossing her face. After what felt like minutes, she blew out a sigh and then smiled at him. "Thank you. There are so many other things I'd like to say, but we'd just go round and round, rehash the same old stuff and eventually reach this point. So, you stubborn man, for now, I'll just say thank you."

He grinned. That was a whole lot better than he'd hoped for. "You're most welcome. And thank you. For understanding."

"Understanding what?"

"That I love you. That we're starting a life together, and that that means sharing."

She nodded. "We need to talk about a few things though don't we?"

He nodded. "But not right now. Let's get on the road, make the most of what's left of the afternoon?"

"Okay, but at some point we need to talk." She grinned, "And don't worry, some of it is me wanting to apologize for being so stubborn."

"That's okay I…"

She laughed and wagged a finger at him. "Don't get carried away. Some of it is wanting you to apologize for being so stubborn, too!"

He grinned. "Fair enough. We'll get to it, all of it. But for now let's get going, shall we?

She handed him the keys. "Yep, but you're driving. If that's my car, then you're my chauffeur."

Gabe started to question himself as he drove up the Eastern shore. Was he crazy? She'd accepted the car more easily than he'd expected. But the house was a whole different ball game. That wasn't simply about accepting what he could buy and she couldn't; it was all tied up with her leaving her childhood home. He may not be the most sentimental of people, but he could understand how important that was to her.

She reached over and squeezed his hand. "You've gone all serious on me. What's up?"

"Nothing."

She laughed. "Gabriel Morgan! Aren't you the guy who always claims he doesn't say anything he doesn't mean?"

He pursed his lips. "Okay, you got me."

"So, what is it?"

"Do you want to stop at the new Phoenix development?"

She frowned at him, but said nothing.

"They're going to be great investment properties." He smiled. "Especially with the town having a new Development Manager. I hear the guy they hired is pretty awesome."

She gave him a grudging smile. "He is. Let's go take a look if you want to. Honestly though, I don't see why anyone would want to live in a development like that. The beauty of this place is that you don't have to live elbow to elbow with other people, you can find your own little spot and have some peace and privacy."

Okay, she was telling him without telling him, that she wouldn't want to live there, but at least she was open to going to have a look. He shrugged. "Everyone's different, and wants different things at different stages in their lives." He wasn't going to risk overtly stating that when she'd worked through whatever she needed to in her childhood home, she might love the idea of living out here, in a brand new house on the water's edge, with every modern convenience at her fingertips.

She nodded. "And you can make the most of that by buying yourself an investment property, right?"

"Yep." There was no point pushing it. Not for today, anyway. They could just look around, maybe the place would sell itself to her.

~ ~ ~

Renée came out and plopped herself down in the rocker next to Gabe on the front porch. He'd been edgy ever since they'd looked at the house at Four Mile this afternoon. She didn't like that, she wanted things to be good between them, relaxed like they had been before he moved in here. She turned and smiled at him, but his face was tense.

"It really is a beautiful house."

He nodded. "It is. It's the best spot in the whole development. I didn't realize that they were building down on the waterfront like that. I thought that strip was just for the park and community boat launch."

"Well, what were there? Four houses down there?"

He nodded.

"The most expensive ones of all."

He smiled at her. "I only go after the best."

"And you already got me," she said hoping to lighten things up.

He took her hand. "I know, but I want the best for you, too."

She shrugged, hoping he might understand. "The best isn't always defined by cost or even quality." She turned to look at the house, then out at the orchard. "Sometimes value is defined in a different way. It's what means the most. Do you get that?"

He nodded, "Of course I do. I know this place means the world to you. I'm bumbling around here because for once I don't know what to do for the best. This place means so much to you, but it's not a good place to live—at least in practical terms. I'm uncomfortable here. You know that, and when I'm faced with problems I like to solve them as quickly as possible."

"Yes, but Gabe, this is something that can't be rushed. Not for me at least. I know it's not easy for you living here. It's hardly up to the standard you're used to, but I need to be here for a while for all the emotional reasons involved, and from a matter of pride, too."

He raised an eyebrow at her. "Pride?"

She nodded. "I feel as though my entire adult life was tied up with Eric. He dictated our finances, and look what happened to me there. At first when I realized that everything I worked for was gone, I felt so hopeless—and helpless. When I pulled myself together, I had to figure out what I could do for myself. I had nowhere to turn and no one to turn to. This place offered me the only hope I had. I know it's awful—I'm not stupid—but it's my solution." She shrugged, "My independence. Something I can do all by myself to take care of me. I know you want to help, I know you want us to be partners in a relationship. I want that, too, but it's going to take me a while. I need to feel okay with myself, that I'm bringing something to the table to be an equal partner, not just a dependent. I need to have some say over my own life, not just be a passenger in your life."

Gabe pressed his fingers into his temples and stared out at the hills for a few moments before he replied. How she hoped he would understand.

He took a deep breath. "I get that. It makes all kinds of sense. On an emotional level at least." He met her gaze. "I have to be honest with you though."

She nodded and waited, wondering what was coming.

"I find it hard to deal with on the practical level."

"I know, and I'm sorry. But please bear with me?"

He smiled. "You know I will, but will you do something for me?

"Tell me what it is before I agree."

"Fair enough. Can we make a list of everything you need to achieve? Everything you need to have in place before you can feel like an equal partner with something to contribute? I'm goal oriented. Can we set up some goals so that I know we're working toward them—making progress to where we want to be."

She nodded. "That's a good idea. It's not a long list, but it is a big one. I need to figure out what I can do for a living. I need to get a divorce." She stopped when she saw the look on his face. "I don't mean we have to wait until it's all final, but at least get proceedings underway. And I need to figure out my finances. I talked to Paul again this morning and the Asset Forfeiture Hearing is coming up. He's hopeful that I should get something back as an innocent spouse."

Gabe nodded. "You should. And listen, I've stayed the hell away from everything to do with your legal issues." He shrugged. "It seemed the wisest move."

She waited. She was grateful if a little surprised that he'd never asked any of the details of Eric's investigation.

"I do have a number for you though...if you want it. The guy's an old friend of mine down in LA. He'd be happy to talk to you and Paul about divorce proceedings in a case like yours."

"Thank you! I know I've pushed you away on so many things, but that's one area where I really do appreciate your help."

"I haven't wanted to overstep my bounds." He held her gaze for a moment. "Not when I have so much invested in a speedy outcome."

What did that mean? Was it like Ethan had said? That he wanted to marry her? She smiled. "Thank you," seemed like the safest thing to say.

# Chapter Nineteen

Gabe stared out the window of his new office. The view made him smile. Just a few short weeks ago he'd been looking out at the Hudson. Now he saw the beautiful lake sparkling in the sunshine. Things were going well. His first week on the job had been much more enjoyable than he might have hoped. The business community was welcoming, excited about having someone new at the helm, and, for the most part, open to change. He was under no illusions that he'd meet some resistance along the way, but he was off to a much better start than he'd envisioned. He was feeling more comfortable at home, too. He smiled at the thought that he was able to call it home, not just Renée's place. He still had his issues with living in a ramshackle old house, but after the talk they'd had, he felt better able to deal with them. As he'd told her, he was a goal oriented achiever. She now had a list of goals that needed to be achieved before she would feel like she was an equal partner with him, and he was doing everything he could to try to help her achieve them.

She'd filed for divorce after talking to his buddy in LA. It seemed that might go a little faster and a lot more smoothly than she'd originally hoped. Her finances weren't showing any improvement though. The Asset Forfeiture Hearing had revealed that Eric had refinanced or borrowed against everything they owned. Although no charges were going to be brought against her, and she had been found an Innocent Spouse, there was very little left that could be returned to her. She'd taken that well, and Gabe was glad that she was simply using it to fuel her search for whatever she might do next career-wise. She'd talked to a couple of the big non-profits in the Bay Area—though she'd assured him she had no intentions of moving back there. As it turned out, there wasn't much hope for her to do so anyway, at least not to work for them. Her reputation as a capable fundraiser was still intact, but none of the agencies would take the risk of being associated with her. The non-profit world wasn't one Gabe was too familiar with, but it made sense that no charity would risk their donor's trust and faith in them in any way.

He'd been keeping his ear to the ground for anything that might be suitable for her here in town. It was hard though. She wanted to find meaning and purpose in whatever she did, while most of the local businesses had the sole purpose of simply surviving. Unemployment levels were high, the county wasn't exactly thriving. Gabe thought he could turn that around, but he didn't see how he could help Renée, and part of him felt as though he shouldn't even be trying to. She wanted—and needed—to figure it out for herself.

He hoped she'd figure something out soon. It seemed as though it was the last piece of the puzzle that needed to slot into place. A knock on his door brought him back to the present.

"Come on in." It was strange not to know who he would see when the door opened. For the last ten years Rosemary had managed his schedule and announced his visitors on the intercom. Here he had to fend for himself, and his schedule was subject to the whims of whoever cared to stop by. He smiled when he saw Max Douglas.

"Gramps! How the devil are you?"

The old guy took his hat off as he came in. "Just wanted to stop by and see how you're settling in. I didn't want to be interfering before you had your feet under the table. From all accounts it sounds like you hit the ground running."

Gabe smiled. "I'm off to a good start, thank you. And it's all thanks to you."

Gramps held up a hand. "I'd been hoping with all you young 'uns finally seeing sense and coming home, that it might be time for the town to turn a corner. You're the man we needed. I should be thanking you."

"I think it's going to work out great," said Gabe. "It's a win-win for everyone."

Gramps surprised him, by shrugging. "Is it though?"

Gabe raised an eyebrow. "What am I missing? Who's losing out?"

"She's not losing, but where's young Renée's win in all of this?"

Gabe shook his head. "I don't know, Gramps. I wish I did. She's trying to figure it out, but it's not easy."

"Nothing good is ever easy, is it, Gabe?"

He had to smile at the way the old guy's eyes twinkled. "But you've come up with something, haven't you?"

Gramps stroked his chin. "Let's just say, I see a gap that she might fill. A win-win for her and the town."

"I'm all ears! What have you got in mind?"

"Nothing, in particular. Just an idea. She's spent years doing fundraising, charity work, helping people. I think there's a need for that in this town. Too many folks have nowhere to turn. You can't have economic development without social development, can you?"

Gabe shook his head.

"So you think maybe there's something in the budget that might fund, I don't know, some kind of social fund?"

Gramps shrugged. "I'm too old to know how these things work, what the details might be, and besides you're meant to be the one in charge around here. I just wanted to plant the seed."

Gabe pressed his fingers into his temple while he thought about it. "I like the idea, Gramps—for both Renée and the town—but I'm not sure how well it would go down with her. Not if I suggest it. She…"

Gramps chuckled. "She needs to stand on her own two feet and doesn't want to be the little woman who relies on you, right?"

Gabe sighed and nodded. "That's about it."

"So do what I just did. Plant the seed. And know that if you present a case to the Committee, you shouldn't have any problems with the budget for it." He pushed his chair back. "Anyways. I need to be getting on. I can hear them fishies calling my name. I just wanted to visit with you while I was in town. Oh, and to tell you to call me if I can be of any help. I'm just a feeble old-timer, but I'm happy to serve if ever you need me."

Gabe watched him leave with a wry smile. Feeble old-timer? Ha! Gramps was sharp as a tack, and much as he claimed he wanted new blood leading the town into the future, it seemed he was still happy to nudge them in the direction he thought they should go. His suggestion made a lot of sense. Gabe was a little irritated that he hadn't thought of it himself. He was pretty sure he would have gotten around to addressing social issues the community was facing—just not as quickly as Gramps had. His problem now though was how he might plant the seed of an idea with Renée without her feeling he was directing or—worse—controlling her in some way.

~ ~ ~

Renée hugged April before she left the bakery. Now they had a roster figured out, life was getting a little easier for both of them. They each had a couple of late starts and a couple of early finishes each week. Today Renée was meeting Laura for lunch. She'd been looking forward to it. "Stop by and join us when you get finished if you want to," she told April.

"Thanks, I might just do that. Marcus is going home with Ethan after school today, so I'm going to be a bit lost. I might come and hang with you for a while if you really don't mind."

"I'd love it. You need to take five minutes for yourself when you can." She'd noticed that April rarely went anywhere other than coming to work, and it seemed she never did anything without Marcus. She was still finding her feet, but Renée was hoping that encouraging her to come out and join the girls when she could would help.

She found Laura already seated out on the deck. "Hey, girlfriend. I was starting to think I might need to come find you."

"Sorry I'm late."

"No problem, I'm just glad you're here."

"Me, too. I've been looking forward to this."

Laura smiled. "Good. I was a little worried that you might be dreading it. I won't really interrogate you about your love life if you don't want me to."

Renée laughed. "Actually, I've been hoping I can interrogate you."

Laura gave her a raunchy grin. "You think you can handle the details?"

"Not about your love life! About your life life. I mean, you live here, but you still have a life."

Laura nodded. "Ah, the serious stuff then? You've reached the point where you want to stay, but you don't see how to make it work?"

"Pretty much."

"Well, I'm not sure my solution will translate to you. You see, I work from home, in that I can do all my design work in my little workshop out back. Then I travel a lot, meet with clients to discuss what they want, and usually to deliver the end product." She smiled. "And I'm lucky to have my very own private pilot for a fiancé. He's not exactly at my beck and call whenever I need to go, but it usually works out that he can at least get me to San Francisco or LA." She looked at Renée. "But they're the details of my life as a jewelry designer. If we're going to try to figure out your details, you need to tell me what you are. Or at least what you want to be? The bakery must be driving you nutty by now."

"I'm grateful for it…"

Laura held up a hand. "Stop it, would you?"

"What do you mean? I am!"

"Yeah, I know. It's been a life saver and all the rest of it, but it still has to be driving you nuts. You're used to running a non-profit, it's hardly the same is it?"

Renée nodded sadly. "Beggars can't be choosers."

"You're not a beggar! What you need to figure out is what you are."

"I don't know what I can be."

"Well then it's time we figure it out." Laura beckoned the server over. "Can we get two burgers and fries and two Diet Cokes, please."

Renée watched her reach into her purse and pull out a large sketch pad and pencil. She smiled. "We don't have all day. You ate it when Ben ordered it, I figured I'd do the same to save time. Now. Let's start making some lists, shall we?"

"Okay."

"First, if you could have any career in the world, what would you do?"

Renée shook her head. "I can't though, can I? I have to see what's available and pick something."

Laura put the pen down and looked at her. "Good luck at the bakery then."

"Ouch!"

"That's what's available around here. Come on. Dream a little. Let's figure out what you want and then we can try to cobble some of the elements together to come up with something you'll enjoy."

Renée sighed. "Okay then. If I could do anything at all, I'd go back to my office and go back to work, just as I was before the truth came out about Eric." Even as she said it, she wondered if it was true. Chance's word's echoed in her mind if you're honest it was all for Chloe, not for you. He was right.

Laura watched her face. "Would you?"

"No. But I don't know where that leaves me. First, non-profit work isn't going to be an option anymore. No one can afford to risk hiring me. Eric and I were known as a team. My name is tarnished, to say the least."

"Unfair as it is, I can see that. But what was it you loved so much about that work?"

That was a tough question. She'd always said she loved making a difference. Raising awareness about the dangers of alcohol abuse, but had she really just been wrestling with her own demons, as Chance had said. She shrugged. "I like to help people?"

Laura laughed. "You're not auditioning for Miss World here. We're talking about you. What do you get out of it?"

Renée was starting to wonder. All those years, she'd put herself aside in order to do what she thought was right, what would help others. Yet she had longed for more personal fulfilment. She just didn't know where she might find it. She tried to boil it down to the nuts and bolts of the work she'd done. What did she enjoy about that, rather than what was that elusive, meaning and purpose that she kept talking about?

Laura watched her as she thought. "I'll tell you what. Think in broad terms. What were the responsibilities of your job, and which ones did you look forward to?"

"Umm. I liked running a staff of enthusiastic volunteers. It was fun to organize a team. Strange as it seems to most folk, I enjoy public speaking. I also like leading small group sessions and working one-on-one with people with specific needs." She paused. "That's all way too generic though, isn't it?"

"Not at all. Have you thought about retraining as a counselor or coach or therapist of some kind? One of my friends back in San Francisco trained as a life coach. I thought it was crazy when she started out, but she's doing fabulously—she has a waiting list of clients, and she makes boatloads of money."

"Hmm, that sounds interesting. But what does she coach people about? I mean isn't that for stressed executives who need to find work-life balance or whatever?"

Laura laughed. "That's what I thought, too, but Sally is a—get this—a Women's Empowerment Coach."

Renée raised an eyebrow. "What does that even mean?"

Laura shrugged. "From what she told me, she works with women who are burned out from trying to do too much in their career, their home, or most commonly both. Women come to her when they know they aren't taking care of themselves through the middle of it all, but have no clue how to either. She helps them empower themselves, put themselves back in the driving seat of their own life, in a way that works for them."

Renée let out a short laugh, thinking how she'd told Gabe she wanted to be more than just a passenger in his life. "It sounds interesting, but I have no idea what I could coach people about, and I don't think I'd like just working one-on-one with people. I like leading a team who are all working toward a common goal, and I like helping whole groups of people."

Laura smiled. "See, we're narrowing it down already."

"Hi, Renée!"

She waved when she recognized the woman who had just called her name. "Lily! I've been meaning to call you."

She stood to give the petite woman, who'd approached their table, a hug.

"You keep saying that, but I'm starting to think you're avoiding me."

"I am not. I just haven't figured out how to get out there and come riding with you yet. I really do want to." She turned to Laura. "Sorry, Laura. This is Lily Wells; we went to school together, and now Lily's back here, too, running the riding stables."

Laura smiled and shook hands. "Nice to meet you. I've been wondering about coming out to see you for lessons. I used to ride as a kid back in Texas. I'd love to start again now I'm living here."

"Anytime you want," said Lily. "Just give me a call." She handed Laura her card and then turned back to Renée. "We should see if there aren't a few more ladies interested and start up a class."

"That'd be great. I'll ask around."

"Hi, ladies."

Renée smiled at April who was now also standing beside their table. This was turning into quite a gathering!

"Hey, April. Meet Lily. I don't suppose you have any interest in learning to ride do you?"

April laughed. "Ride horses? You're asking a girl who grew up on a ranch, remember? I'd love to find somewhere to ride here though."

Lily smiled and handed her a card. "Then come see me. I run the stables."

"Great, I will!" That was the first time Renée had seen April look truly enthusiastic about anything since she'd met her.

"Look," said Laura. "Holly's here, too. I told her she should join us if she got done with her conference call in time."

Renée laughed. "The more the merrier."

Holly came and plonked herself down next to Laura. "Hey, ladies."

Renée looked around at them all as they chatted. They were all so different and yet they got along well enough. She knew each of them had their own struggles, except maybe Laura, she took everything in her stride and seemed to live a blessed life. Each of the others was going through a tough time in one way or another. She thought about Laura's friend the life coach, would something like that be of any use to this bunch? She doubted it.

"Well, I need to get back to work," said Lily. "It was nice meeting all of you. I hope you'll come out to the stables. And if you don't, I hope you'll at least invite me to lunch sometime. It's good to be back here, but I'm feeling a bit isolated."

Renée immediately felt bad. She'd been too concerned with her own problems to think about checking whether her old friend was doing okay. "I'm sorry, Lily. I'll call you. We'll have lunch soon."

Lily smiled. "Don't worry. You don't need to make it your personal responsibility. It's just hard being kind of new in town and not having any connections or a network to turn to."

Renée had to wonder what was going on with Lily that she felt the need for a support network. The Lily she knew wouldn't ask for help. At least the Lily she had known, but that was a long time ago—they'd all been through so much and changed so much since then.

April nodded. "It would be nice if there were some organization or something to help newcomers find their feet."

Laura turned and smiled at Renée. Renée knew what she meant. That would be right up her alley, but it could hardly constitute a new career. The town probably had less than a dozen newcomers a year! After Lily had left, she turned to Laura. "So tell me how?"

April and Holly stared at her, not knowing what she was talking about.

Laura shrugged. "I don't know, but it's your kind of thing. You just heard from two people at the same time that it's hard being a newcomer around here." She turned to the others. "We're trying to come up with something Renée can do that will satisfy her need to be a useful member of society—and make her a living."

Holly rested her chin on her hands. "I'd say there are enough women with problems around here that you could probably set up a women's center."

April nodded. "I'd have to agree with that. I was talking about being new, but…" she looked around at them. "There are other issues I need to deal with, and I have no clue where to turn for help or advice."

Renée nodded. "You've probably got a point, but something like that would normally be funded by the town or the county. Helping people tends to take money, not make money. It's a cool idea, but I think it would have to be a part-time, volunteer situation. Not a career move."

Laura chewed her bottom lip. "Maybe, maybe not. You'd have to see what other angles there might be. If you can help women back into the workforce, or help with…I don't know what. Then you might get local businesses interested in funding it."

"I doubt it."

Holly grinned at her. "Well, hell girl. Isn't your man going to be in charge of the town's budget? Surely he could help you set something up. I mean damn, he already bought you that gorgeous house over at Four Mile; I'm sure he'd do whatever he can to help you."

Renée's heart pounded to a halt. Gabe had bought the house? And Holly thought that he'd just allocate town funds to allow her to do what she wanted? She didn't know which of those made her feel more nauseous. She hadn't even considered applying for local funding for anything, because of the shadow Eric's crime cast on her. No way did she want to cast that shadow onto Gabe, create any doubt that he was using town funds improperly.

She couldn't think straight, could hardly breathe. She checked her watch and stood. "I'm sorry. I've got to go." She made her way blindly across the deck and then ran across the square back to her car. Gabe's car! She corrected herself as she unlocked it.

# Chapter Twenty

Gabe sat in the car for a long moment when he got home. He wanted to talk to Renée about the possibilities Gramps had raised with him earlier, but he just didn't know how. He should probably talk to her about the house over at Four Mile, too. He wasn't hiding it from her—it was just that the right moment hadn't come up yet.

He got out of the car when he saw her come out the front door and stand on the porch. Something was wrong. Very wrong, by the look on her face. She didn't say anything, just watched him climb the steps. She looked as though she'd been crying.

"What's wrong?"

She shook her head, sadly. "What's right, Gabe?"

"What do you mean?"

"I mean, I don't think I'm going to be able to make it work here."

He felt as though he'd been punched in the stomach. "Why? What's going on?"

"All I know how to do, all I really want to do is charity work. I'm not going to be able to do that in this town."

"Why not?"

"Because it would involve public funding, which would in some way involve you. I have no intention of casting any shadows on you. If you allocate funds to anything I'm in charge of it'd raise questions, and rightfully so."

Gabe's mind was racing. She had a point, but it wasn't really a valid one. No one here believed she'd had anything to do with Eric's crime. Everyone in Summer Lake who knew her—which was most of the town—knew her character and knew her intentions. "Renée, you're talking about a small town, where people know you, like you, and trust you. I think it's time you accept that it's not the same here. What's got you like this? Has someone said something?"

She took a deep breath and met his gaze. "Actually, yes. Holly mentioned that if I wanted to get funding for a Women's Center it would be easy. Since you're in control of the town's budget and…"

"And what?"

"And apparently you already bought that house at Four Mile for me! People think you're happy to spend for whatever I want—whether it's your money or the town's. I can't live with that. And by the way? I hope you'll be very happy in your new home!" She turned and went back inside, slamming the door behind her.

"Renée!" He strode after her. "Maybe I should have told you I bought the house, but I wanted it either way. If at some point you decide you want to live there, great. If you don't, we have an investment property. Be fair. We're taking the time so you can figure out what you want to do. I don't see why I should have to refrain from doing the things I want to do in the meantime. I'd been considering buying a house out there since I first heard about the development. It had nothing to do with you."

She turned and glared at him. "You're right. It has nothing at all to do with me."

He shook his head and walked toward her. She was hurt and angry and frustrated—all with good reason. He held his arms out to her. "I love you. I'm sorry I didn't tell you. I was worried about how you might react." He stepped closer, wanting to hold her, to calm her down so they could work things out together. She continued to glare at him. He closed his arms around her and held her to his chest. For a moment she was rigid, unyielding.

"I'm sorry."

That made her relax. "I'm sorry, too, Gabe." She rested her head against his chest and tightened her arms around his waist. "I'm really, really sorry. I love you, but I need you to leave."

It took him a couple of seconds to process the words. She couldn't mean them? She stepped away from him with tears rolling down her cheeks. "Please, just go."

"No! Renée, that's crazy. I'm not going anywhere."

"Yes, you are. I want you to leave. We're not going to work out Gabe; we may as well face it now. You go live in your new house, start your new job and your new life. I'm not going to be part of it." She turned and went into the bedroom.

Gabe was stunned. He shook his head to clear it, then started after her. She'd locked the door! "Renée!"

"Go away, Gabe!"

Damn, she was stubborn! "Let me in, and let's talk about it."

"No."

He let out an exasperated sigh. "Fair enough!" He wasn't going to stand here begging her to talk to him. It was pointless and he knew it. He'd wait until she calmed down. Right now she was upset, upset about him buying the house. He should have told her before someone else did, he'd give her that. On top of her frustration about what she might do for a career, it was just too much. He'd give her a chance to cool off, then call her later. Maybe she'd even call him—he could hope.

~ ~ ~

Renée listened to the car pull away with tears streaming down her face. What had she done? She blew her nose. The only thing she could do. She wasn't going to let Gabe risk his reputation or his job by funding a project that she was responsible for. And she wasn't going to go and live in that house with him. This was her home. She looked around and a fresh wave of tears came. She shook her head sadly. She was in a no-win situation. She loved Gabe, but she couldn't just give up everything she was to be with him. And she couldn't allow him to risk his own career so that she could have hers.

~ ~ ~

Gabe pulled into the square at the resort. She couldn't mean it. He could understand her being pissed at hearing from someone else about him buying the house at Four Mile. He could understand her frustration about not wanting to apply for funding because of any doubts it might cast on him. But, damn! He couldn't understand that she didn't want to be with him anymore. That she thought they weren't going to work out.

He got out of the Range Rover and headed for the bar. He needed a drink. Once he was settled at the bar, he sent her a text.

*Please call me when you've calmed down.*

He stared at his phone for a few moments, then put it away as Kenzie approached.

"Hi. Where's Renée?"

He didn't want to get into explaining what was going on. "She's at home." It was true.

Kenzie made a face at him. "Did you leave your smile at home, too?"

Gabe nodded. He hardly felt like smiling right now.

"Oookay. What can I get you?"

"Bourbon."

He watched as she turned away to fix his drink. His mind was racing. He was a problem solver, but he had no idea how he could solve Renée's problems. Well, that wasn't true. He could solve them no problem, if she'd let him. She wanted to start a Women's Center? He could set that up for her. He could lease her a space and let her do her thing. No public funds needed. He could support her, too, if she'd let him. But she wouldn't, and he did understand why. He understood, but it frustrated the hell out of him. He checked his phone again. Still no reply from her. Did she really expect him to go spend the night at Four Mile?

Kenzie put his drink in front of him with a smile. "Want to talk about it?"

He shook his head.

She frowned. "Is Renée all right?"

Gabe met her gaze. "She's pissed at me."

"And you're going to fix that by sitting here drinking bourbon?"

"Stay out of it, Kenzie. She doesn't want to talk to me right now, so I'm giving her some space."

Kenzie put her hands on her hips and scowled at him. Ben appeared behind her and tapped her on the shoulder. "Why don't you go take a break?"

She turned the scowl on him then back at Gabe.

Gabe shrugged.

Ben laughed. "Go on. I'll take care of things here."

Kenzie pushed her way out of the bar, shooting Gabe an evil look as she went.

Gabe rolled his eyes at Ben. "I'm the one in the doghouse, but you can bet Kenzie isn't going to listen to my side."

Ben nodded. "Women stick together."

"So I noticed."

"Want to talk about it?"

Gabe shrugged. "I don't see that it'd do any good."

Ben smiled. "Try me. I've been known to help solve a problem or two. What's going on?"

Gabe downed his bourbon and pushed his glass forward for a refill. "You know I bought the house at Four Mile?"

"Yeah, Pete mentioned it."

"Well, Holly mentioned it to Renée before I had a chance to."

"Ah. And she's not happy about it?"

"Nope. She wants to stay in her own place, and she thinks I bought this one behind her back."

"Well, didn't you?"

"No! It wasn't like that. I've been thinking about buying out there for a while. It's a good investment. Am I supposed to stop doing the things I would do just because I'm with Renée?"

"No, but it might not be a bad idea to tell her about them, especially when your motives are open to interpretation."

"What does that mean?"

Ben smiled. "You've been living out at her place, you don't like it." He held a hand up. "And I understand why. But she wants to stay there. It's a fair assumption that you buying another house is an indication that you want to live in it. Don't you think?"

Gabe nodded. "She sure as hell thinks so. She told me to go live in it and be very happy there."

"Ah."

"Yeah. Ah! I would be very happy in it if she'd move there with me, but she won't hear of it. She's in a tough situation." He sighed. "And now I think about it, I'm her biggest problem."

"How's that?"

"Well, she wants to live in her house—for now at least. Her only problem with that is she knows I hate it. And she came up with the idea of starting a Women's Center, which would be right up her street, but she feels she can't apply for funding because of me."

Ben stared at him for a moment and then moved down the bar to serve a couple who had just arrived. When he returned, he held Gabe's gaze. "She is in a tough spot, isn't she?"

Gabe blew out a sigh. "She doesn't have to be though, she's just stubborn. No one around here would question her trustworthiness or my motivation."

"Come on, Gabe, that's not fair. You're right, as things stand at the moment, there would be no questions or doubts at all, but the minute someone has an axe to grind against you, you'd be laid wide open. She's trying to protect you from that possibility. I'm surprised you can't see it."

"Hmm." If Gabe cared to admit it, he knew Ben was right, and it wasn't that he didn't see it, so much as he refused to think about it. "So what am I supposed to do? I'd stand down if I thought it'd help her, but I know she wouldn't go for it. I'd love to live in the new house, but not without her. At the same time, I couldn't live at her place for much longer anyway. It's driving me insane."

Ben pursed his lips. "Let me think about it."

"Well if you can come up with a solution, I'd love to hear it."

Ben smiled. "There's got to be a way to figure out something that will work for both of you."

"I'd like to think so, but, if there is, I'm not seeing it."

"That's because you're too close. I have an outsider's perspective, which is usually more rational."

Gabe sighed. "Yeah. Thanks, Ben." He checked his phone again. Still nothing. "I guess for now I'm going to head out to Four Mile."

Ben nodded. "Give her some time to calm down. It'll all work out."

"I hope so."

~ ~ ~

Renée picked her phone up then set it down again. She wanted to call Gabe and ask him to come home. But part of her didn't. The longer she thought about it, the more she doubted their future. She was happy for him that he had his new job, but while he was working it, she wouldn't be able to do the kind of work she loved in Summer Lake. She understood his need to buy the house out at Four Mile, but while he was living there they weren't going to be together. This was her home. She also understood that it wasn't fair to ask him to live here. She shook her head. As good as they were together, there were so many conflicting aspects of their circumstances that made a shared future seem impossible.

She took herself outside to sit on the front porch. She and Gabe had sat out here so many times these last few weeks. It felt strange to sit out here without him. More than strange, it felt wrong. She didn't want to be here without him. She heaved a big sigh. What the hell was she going to do? Staring out at the lake, leaving seemed to be the only solution. She didn't want to be here without him, but she didn't want to be here with him if it meant one of them had to give up who they were in order to be together.

Her phone buzzed and she snatched it up. Her heart sank when she saw it wasn't him. It was a text from Ben.

*Can you stop in at the Boathouse before work in the morning?*

She stared at it for a few moments, wondering what was up. Had he talked to Gabe?

*I can. What's the problem?*

*No problem. I want to run a few ideas by you.*

*OK. See you at 7?*

*Great. Thanks.*

She had to wonder what ideas he might be talking about. She shrugged. Maybe he'd be better talking to April. She had the hang of things in the bakery now. She heaved a big sigh, and April was more likely to be around long enough to implement his ideas.

She turned her phone over and over. She should call Gabe. He'd asked her to once she'd calmed down. She didn't want to though, didn't see anything constructive they could say to each other right now. She'd wait until tomorrow, hopefully things would look different in the morning. Maybe she'd see some solution that she wasn't seeing now.

She took herself to bed early and lay there staring at the ceiling, unable to sleep. Things didn't look any better. In fact, the longer she lay there, the worse they looked. Every possibility she came up with led to a dead end. As the night dragged on she reached the conclusion that the only real option was to leave. There were too many reasons she couldn't be with Gabe if she stayed, and too many reasons to leave if she couldn't be with him. Where the hell could she go though? And what could she do? If she left, she'd have no job, no place to live, and no hope of doing the kind of work she loved. She buried her face in the pillow. She'd thought she was going through the worst time of her life when Eric was arrested. But this? This felt a hundred times worse.

She must have finally dozed off. It was still dark when she opened her eyes. She lay there rolling everything around in her head. The only positive she could come up with was that she needed to sell this place. She wouldn't get much for it—she knew that—but she'd get something. The house wasn't worth anything, but the land was. Forty acres had to be worth enough to make a new start somewhere. She felt a tear slide down her cheek as she thought about Gabe. She wasn't completely stupid. She could see the irony of the fact that she would sell this place in order to leave here, and leave him; but, she wouldn't sell it in order to be with him. She had to be true to herself, she couldn't start a life with him on such an unequal footing. It wouldn't work for either of them. She got up and went to make coffee; there was no way she'd be able to get back to sleep. She may as well get started with the day and head down into town to see Ben.

Once she was showered, she took her coffee and her phone outside. She wanted to call Gabe, but it was too early yet. She checked her email and was surprised to see one from Paul. It had come in late last night.

> *Can you call me in the morning? I'll be in the office by 6.30. They've requested a meeting—soon. Can you get down here?*

She checked her watch. It was just gone six thirty. She dialed Paul's number.

"Hi Renée. Can you get down here?"

"When? Why? What's happening?"

"Eric's lawyers have requested a meeting. You need to be here if you can."

"When? What do they want to meet about?"

"I don't know yet, they're being really cagey. He has a hearing coming up. From what they've implied he's ready to clear your name, but he wants to talk to you first. I'd guess that he wants something from you in return."

Renée blew out a sigh. "I'm sure he does. But you have no idea what?"

"Not a clue. Sorry. How soon can you get here?"

"I'm just on my way to work…"

"Can you get time off?"

"Is it that urgent?"

"I wouldn't take any risks if I were you."

"Okay. Let me see what I can do. I'll call you back."

"Good. Don't take too long."

Renée shook her head as she hung up. She was just like a puppet on a string, still dancing to Eric's tune. She had no choice though. She dialed Ben.

"Good morning. Are you running late?" he asked.

"No. I'm calling to ask if I can take some time off?"

"Why? What's wrong?"

"I just spoke to my lawyer and Eric wants to see me. Sounds like he wants to do some bargaining before his hearing. I need to get down there."

"Of course. You go."

"Thanks, Ben."

"Do you want to stop by for a coffee on your way through?"

She thought about it.

"I'll have you a coffee and a sandwich ready. I still want to talk to you."

"Okay, but I can't stop for long."

"It won't take long. See you soon."

"Okay."

# Chapter Twenty-One

Renée pulled up in the square at the resort and spotted Ben sitting out on the deck. He raised a hand as she made her way to him. He pushed a coffee toward her as she sat down.
"Are you okay?"
"I think so. I have no idea what Eric wants, but apparently I need to be there to find out."
Ben nodded. "And what about Gabe?"
She frowned. "What about him?"
"Are you okay there?"
She met his gaze. "I think I'm done there, Ben. I don't see any way the two of us could make it work."
Ben stared back at her. "I don't believe that for a moment."
She shrugged. "Well, if you see a solution, go ahead and let me in on it, would you? His position here makes me finding a position here impossible." She swallowed. "Don't get me wrong, I love him. But I can't stop being me in order to be with him." She decided to tell Ben. That would make it more real. "I've decided I'm going to sell up and leave."
Ben slowly shook his head.
"What? Say something. Don't look at me like that!"
"You've not got time right now, but I wanted to talk to you about leasing the bakery and maybe the space next to it."
"Why?"

"Well, as you know, I've got a lot on my plate. And now the guys are getting close to completion up at Four Mile, I'm going to have even more to deal with, at least until I get a team in place to run the rentals and the retail side of things. I've been thinking about what I can do to lighten my load at the resort. This place is one responsibility I'd be happy to offload. Especially into your capable hands."

"What do you mean? I already run the place."

He nodded. "I know, so how do you feel about leasing the place? Make it your own business."

Renée stared at him. The thought had never even occurred to her. "Ben, you know running a small business isn't what I aspire to."

He smiled. "I know, but if you wanted to set up, say, a Women's Center, I could let you have the space next door for a reasonable rent and you could knock through. You could have your center and have it be self-funding if you turn the bakery into more of a coffee shop, or café type place."

She just kept staring at him. "How do you even know about the Women's Center idea?"

He shrugged. "Laura stuck around for a while after you guys had lunch yesterday."

"Oh." Her mind was racing. It could be a perfect solution. If she could work it. She looked at Ben. Unfortunately, she couldn't work it. She couldn't afford to lease the place from him. She shook her head slowly.

"You don't like the idea?"

"I love it, Ben. But it's hardly realistic is it?"

"Why not?"

"Because I can't afford it, that's why."

"We could work something out."

"I am not charity case!" She pushed her hair out of her eyes. "Sorry. I know you mean well, but I can't do it."

"So, you'd sell your place to leave here, but not to stay here?"

She thought about that. "I don't know, Ben. I'm confused as hell about everything right now."

Ben shrugged. "You don't need to decide now. Think about it, okay? And when you do, just bear in mind that you'd be doing me a favor, too? I really do need to lighten my load somehow." He shrugged. "I don't know, I thought it might be a win-win for both of us."

Renée's mind was racing with possibilities. It really could be a win-win. She smiled at him. "I have to get going, I have a few other things to deal with right now. Let me wrap my head around it?"

"Of course."

"And you're sure about me just taking off like this?"

"You go do what you need to do. April's fine in the bakery, and I'll keep an eye on her. Don't worry about it. Come on, let's get you that sandwich and get you on the road."

~ ~ ~

Gabe held the flowers behind his back and pushed open the bakery door. He felt like a dumb kid. He'd hardly slept all night. Now here he was carrying flowers and prepared to make a public fool of himself by going to see her at work. None of it mattered though. All that mattered was making things right with her. Of course there was a long line waiting to be served. He groaned inwardly, but resisted the urge to turn around and leave. He pursed his lips when he saw his mom in the line. That was all he needed. Oh well. He was here now. April caught his eye and gave him a worried smile.

"Is she in the back?" he asked.

April shook her head. "She's not here."

"Where is she?" Every head in the line was turned toward him now, but he didn't care. He just wanted to see Renée.

"I. Errr…" April looked wary to say the least. What was going on? She busied herself serving the next customer.

Gabe strode to the head of the line. He had a sinking feeling in his stomach. April was hiding something. He knew it. "Where is she?" he demanded.

April looked at him, then over his shoulder. He turned to see his mom standing there smiling. "Why don't you two take this in the back? I can take care of the customers." She winked at April. "It's okay. I worked here for a while, I know the ropes."

Gabe made his way around the counter and grabbed April's arm as he headed for the back room. He let go fast as she jerked her arm back with a little yelp. Jesus, what was he thinking? "I'm sorry, April." He held the door open for her and stood back. "Please?"

She nodded and scurried past him. He closed the door behind them and turned to her, she looked petrified. "I'm sorry. I shouldn't have…"

She shook her head rapidly. "It's okay. It wasn't you I was reacting to. I need to get over that."

Gabe nodded, wondering for a moment what her story might be.

"I just didn't want to get into Renée's business out there in front of everyone. I thought you'd already know. She's not coming to work because she's gone to San Francisco."

Gabe's heart pounded. She'd left town? "Why?"

"All I know is that it's something to do with her ex and the court case. Ben came by early to tell me I'm in here by myself." She shrugged. "She didn't say anything about it yesterday."

Gabe glowered at her. What the hell was going on? She hadn't mentioned it to him yesterday either, but then she'd hardly had a chance, had she? It was obvious that April didn't know any more than he did, but as usual, Ben did. "Thanks, April."

She nodded. "Will you ask her to call me?"

Gabe nodded. He didn't want to say he didn't like his own odds of getting to talk to her at this point. He looked down at the flowers he was still clutching, and smiled. He held them out to April. "Take them, as a thank you?"

He'd always thought of April as a dowdy little mouse, but she looked pretty with a smile lighting up her face like that.

"Thank you!" She clutched them to her chest. "Thank you."

He nodded and went back out into the store. His mom raised an eyebrow at him as she closed the cash register. "Is everything all right, angel?"

He met her gaze. "I don't know, Mom."

She came and gave him a hug. "It will be. I know it will. Do you want to come for a walk with your mom?"

He couldn't help but smile at that. It was her way to help her kids deal with problems, go for a walk and a talk. "I'd love to, but not right now. I need to find Ben."

She nodded. "You do what you need to, but remember where I am if you want me?"

He planted a kiss on top of her head. "Thanks, Mom. I'll call you later." He let himself out of the bakery and headed toward the resort. He needed to find Ben, and find out what was going on. Whatever it was, it bothered him that Renée hadn't wanted to turn to him. She still hadn't called him, hadn't even texted. Did she really mean it, that they were over? He refused to believe that.

~ ~ ~

Renée sat in the waiting area outside Paul's office. She still couldn't figure out what on earth was going on. She'd had no contact with Eric for months, and now he wanted to see her? Paul hadn't been keen to discuss it on the phone while she was driving down here so she still didn't understand what was going on. All she knew was that Eric had a hearing coming up, and he wanted to see her first.

Paul's secretary smiled at her. "He'll see you now."

She let herself in to his office and smiled when he looked up.

"Sorry to drag you down here like this, but I think you'll understand when I explain."

She pushed the hair out of her eyes. "Go ahead, then. Explain."

Paul gestured to the chair across the desk. "Take a seat."

She sat and folded her arms across her chest. Whatever was coming, she didn't feel ready for it.

"Eric wants to see you…"

"I know that much, that's why I'm here."

"Give me chance, will you?"

She nodded, sorry. "I just know this isn't going to be anything good."

"Well, that depends on how you look at it. He's prepared to make a statement that will absolve you of any involvement."

"So why doesn't he just do that? Why do I have to be here?"

"Because, apparently, he has some conditions."

She let out a short laugh. "Of course he does. What does he want?"

"I don't know. He'll only talk to you about that, in private. I was going to ask you if you have any idea what he might want."

"No clue. I don't even feel as though I know the man. The Eric I was married to was just a figment of my imagination, apparently."

Paul nodded. "I thought you might say that. You'll just have to talk to him to find out. But whatever you do, don't agree to anything—anything at all—until you talk to me?"

She nodded. "Of course. And where and when is this meeting supposed to take place?"

"I'm waiting for the call. I let them know that you'd be here this afternoon, and they're supposed to get back to me as soon as they can set it up."

"So I just have to wait?"

Paul nodded. "I'm afraid so."

"Great. I suppose I'd better go find a motel then."

"Okay, I'll call you as soon as I hear anything."

Renée made her way back out onto the street. This all felt so surreal. This city had been her life for years. She'd seen that life crumble around her ears because of Eric. Over the last few months Summer Lake had become her home again and now here she was, yanked out of that life, too. For the first time, she let her mind wander to Ben's offer this morning. Would that really be a way for her to make it at the lake? If she leased the bakery, would she really be able to make a go of it and make enough to fund a Women's Center? She shook her head. How could she lease the bakery? She didn't have the money. In order to get the money she'd have to sell her home. Was that the way to go? Did she need to let go of the past in order to build the future? She just didn't know.

~ ~ ~

Gabe got back in the car and decided to go check in with his mom. His chat with Ben had been very informative. And based on what Ben had told him, he was about to take a huge gamble. He had to believe it would work out. If it didn't...well, he refused to think about that. He drove back out down Main toward his parents place. He still wanted to run the idea by his mom, the thought brought the shadow of a smile to his lips. Not so long ago he would have laughed at the idea of turning to his mom for advice. Now, though, it seemed family was so much more important than he'd understood.

"Want to tell me what's going on, angel?" his mom asked the moment he let himself in the kitchen door.

"I'm not sure I know myself."

She nodded. "I thought as much. Where is Renée?" She took a seat at the table and nodded at the seat opposite for him to join her

"San Francisco, apparently. I had to learn what she's doing from April and Ben though. She's not talking to me."

"And why's that?"

He thought about it, then gave her a brief summary of everything that had happened between them. "So basically. She feels she can't do her work here if I'm doing mine. She's too stubborn to accept my help financially, and she's thinking about selling up and leaving."

His mom rested her chin on her hands and smiled at him. "And you're too stubborn to accept that she might do that, so what are you thinking of doing?"

He stared at her for a long moment, wondering if this was as crazy a move as he feared. He'd find out as soon as he told her, he knew that much. "I'm thinking about buying her place."

"You think she'd sell it to you?"

"Not if she knows it's me, no."

He knew from the way her eyebrows came down, she didn't like the idea. "So you're thinking about deceiving her and hoping that she'll just gratefully accept your charity after you do?"

Hmm. "It's not like that, though."

"Tell me how it is then, Gabe, because that's how it feels to me, and I'm pretty sure that's how it will feel to Renée."

"Then what do I do, Mom? This is frustrating as hell. I don't get what I can do. She doesn't get what she can do. If I buy her place, she can lease the bakery, take me out of the equation in terms of her funding her center. She can be as independent as she needs to be."

His mom let out a little laugh. "How's she supposed to feel independent, if you give her the money for her place, then live there with her, just like you do now?"

Gabe couldn't help his shudder. "I don't even want to live there though. The place is a shack."

"So you want to buy her place and ask her to move out of it, too?"

He pressed his fingers into his temple. "I don't know what I want, other than I want her to live with me, I want her to be happy." He met his mom's eyes. "I want her to marry me."

His mom let out a little squeal and clapped her hands together. "Then we need to come up with a better plan than what you've got going now, because believe me, it wouldn't work."

He couldn't help but smile at his mom's obvious delight and eagerness to help him out. "So what do you suggest?"

"First of all, I need you to tell me everything, then we can decide."

"I have told you everything."

She shook her head grimly. "Why didn't you know where she was this morning?"

He nodded. "Okay, I should probably make us some fresh coffee."

# Chapter Twenty-Two

Renée pushed her hair out of her eyes as she waited. She was nervous. Nervous about seeing him again, nervous about what he might want. She wished she could talk to Gabe. He'd reassure her that she was okay, that everything would be okay. He'd lay out the facts for her, help her see it all objectively. But she couldn't talk to Gabe. She fiddled with her purse. Why was she planning to walk away from him, when he was the one person she wanted to turn to? She didn't have time to ponder that question as she heard her name called. She stood and tried to tame her hair.
"Hi."
Renée couldn't speak for a moment. Eric looked older. Haggard was the word that came to mind. It was hard to process, he's always been so meticulous about his appearance.
"Are you going to sit?" He pointed at the chair across from him, and she sat.
"How are you?" It wasn't what she'd meant to say, but for some reason, she needed to know.
His smile reminded her of what she'd seen in him all those years ago. "As good as can be expected."
She pulled herself together and asked the question she'd intended to. "What do you want?"
He laughed. "That's more like it. That's the Renée I know."

What did he mean by that? She stared at him, wondering what this was all about.

He shook his head and stared off out the window before looking back at her. "I'm going down, Renée." He shrugged. "I've accepted that."

That surprised her, but she nodded and waited to hear more.

"I could make your life very difficult if I wanted to."

She tensed, knowing it was true.

"There are so many ways I could implicate you."

"But you're not going to?"

"Not if you do something for me."

"What's that?"

He smiled. "I want you to admit your responsibility."

She stared at him. "But I'm not responsible for any of it! I didn't even know what you were doing!"

He laughed. "Don't you think a wife who doesn't know what her husband is doing bears some responsibility in that situation? If you'd ever really cared about me, or about us, do you think I would have gotten away with any of it?"

She was dumbfounded.

"Come on. You were always so stubborn in your do-gooding, you refused to see anything you didn't want to see. Good or bad, if it didn't fit with how you wanted to see the world and see yourself, then it just didn't exist."

"I...I don't know what you mean."

He laughed again. "Yes, you do. If you stop and really think about it, you do. Remember the early days? All the vacations I wanted us to go on? The house I wanted us to buy? The way you refused to spend anything on us? You were so focused in on what you wanted to do, you never made room for an us. I made the choices I made, I'm not blaming you for that. I'm just saying, if you hadn't been so damn stubborn we could have had a great life, the two of us."

Renée stared at him. She couldn't quite believe what she was hearing. "So you're saying that it's my fault that you did what you did?"

"No. I'm saying if you hadn't been so damn stubborn we could have done it together."

It was her turn to laugh. "You really think I would have gone along with fraud and embezzlement?"

"No, I think there wouldn't have been any need for it if you'd cared half as much for yourself and your man as you did for your good deeds. You denied yourself a good life out of guilt over your sister, but it never occurred to you that you were denying me a good life, too. I just want you to admit that. Your goddamned meaning and purpose as you call them were so much more important to you than I ever was."

She stared at him. "I...I never knew you felt that way."

"Because you never listened. I tried to tell you often enough in the early days."

"And then you turned to lying and stealing and cheating instead!"

He shrugged. "Yeah, and I had a great few years of it."

"So..." she was struggling to get to grips with what he was saying. Worst of all, a part of her mind was agreeing with him. She couldn't deal with that right now. "What are you saying?"

"I'm saying, I'll make the divorce as easy as possible, and I'll do everything I can to clear your name."

"And what do you want in return?"

He smiled. "Like I said. I want you to admit responsibility."

She shrugged. "Okay. I admit. I was focused on the charity, not on you, not on us. Is that what you want? There. I said it. Can I go now?" She made to stand. She was trembling, shocked at the truth that rang in his words. It didn't excuse or even explain what he'd done, but it had shown her a truth about herself she didn't like.

"Sit down, Renée."

His words were so sharp she sank back into the chair and stared at him. His face was hard now. "I've been with a girl for the last five years."

She felt the air rush out of her lungs. "Oh."

"She knew about you."

Renée was finding this difficult to process.

"I always thought about leaving you for her."

"So why the hell didn't you?"

He shrugged.

Renée understood though. "She didn't run a charity you could dip your fingers into, right?"

He had the nerve to laugh. "Something like that. Anyway. The point is, now she does know about you. She said she'd come visit me, if you got in touch with her. If you confirmed for her that I had my reasons."

She had to laugh; it sounded a little hysterical even to her own ears. "Seriously? You want me to go see the woman who you cheated on me with and reassure her that I'm the villain of the piece and you're a good guy really?"

He nodded. "Pretty much."

Renée pushed the hair out of her eyes. "And what if I don't?"

He shrugged. "Your choice, doll. Quick and easy divorce, having your name cleared, or long drawn-out battles. Which do you want?"

She shook her head. "I want this over with. I want you out of my life."

He pushed a piece of paper across the table to her. "Then here's her number."

She took it and looked up at him. "Is there anything left to fight over in a divorce?"

He smiled. "Nothing that you'd ever get your hands on."

She nodded. She'd suspected as much. He probably still had money, maybe even in this woman's name, but she'd rather walk away than spend any time or energy fighting for it. She stood and looked at the number. "How do I know that you'll keep your word?"

"You don't, do you?" He laughed. "Come on, Renée. I may have been caught, but I'm not stupid. If I don't keep my end of the bargain, there's nothing to stop you from talking to her again, is there?" He held her gaze for a moment. "I just want us both to come out of this with the least damage possible. I did love you for a while, you know."

"You did?"

He nodded and raised his eyebrows in question.

She gave the slightest nod of her head. She had loved him or at least the man she'd thought he was. She couldn't help but wonder now if that wasn't simply the man she'd wanted him to be, and like he'd said, she'd stubbornly refused to see anything else.

"I guess this is goodbye then, huh?"

She nodded, realizing that she'd more than likely never see him again. A wave of sadness swept through her. Something in his words had hit home. She held his gaze for a moment. "I'm sorry, Eric."

He nodded. "Me, too."

~ ~ ~

Gabe stared out at the lake. He did love it up here at Renée's place. The house drove him nuts, no question about it, but the place itself, the orchard, the view of the lake, it was perfect. He was hoping that the plan his mom had helped him come up with would appeal to Renée. He wasn't sure it would, but he had to hope. She was his future, he had no doubt about it. He didn't know what he'd do if she didn't feel the same way. A part of him knew, just knew that she did. What worried him was that her stubbornness might win out. As far as he could see, his mom's idea took into account everything that Renée needed in order to still feel she had her independence and could still do and be what she needed. He pressed his fingers into his temples. He was still worried that as far as he could see might not be far enough. He understood her to a certain extent, but her stubbornness was beyond him. But then he wasn't a woman, and he didn't stand to lose anything by being with her, not in the way she did by being with him.

His phone buzzed, making him jump. He smiled when he saw her name on the display.

"Hey."

"Hi, Gabe. I'm sorry."

"I'm sorry, too, my love. Are you all right?"

There was a long silence before she replied. "I think I'm going to be."

"What does that mean? What did Eric want?"

"I'll tell you all about it when I get back. I'll be home tomorrow."

"Good. Will you have dinner with me?"

"I'd like that. Should I come out to Four Mile?"

"I'd like to make you dinner there, but then can we come home to your place."

"You want to?"

He smiled. "I'd love to. I'm here now. I missed you."

"Aww, Gabe. I miss you, too. I'm really sorry about last night."

"So am I. I want to talk to you. I have an idea I want to run by you."

"What?"

"I think we should wait until you get here. What time do you think you'll be back?"

"I don't know yet. I have to go see someone in the morning."

"The lawyers?" She sounded edgy. He wanted to know why.

She sighed. "Eric has a girlfriend. He wants me to go tell her that he only did all of this because I'm such a stubborn bitch!"

"And you're going to?"

She was quiet for several moments. "I am. But only because, in a way, I think he's right."

"Renée!"

She let out a short bitter laugh. "What, you don't think I'm stubborn?"

He smiled to himself. "No comment, but I don't think anything you did or didn't do made Eric do what he did. That's his responsibility."

"Oh, I know that. I'm going to go talk to her for my sake, not for his. I hate it, but he made me realize something about myself today. I'm hoping that he's done me a huge favor…"

"What's that?"

"He's saved me from making the same mistake with you. I need my independence, I need my meaning and purpose, but they don't mean more to me than you do. I want to find a way for us to work this out together. If you still want me?"

"I do. I'll always want you. I love you."

"I love you, too, Gabe. I'd better go though. I'm meeting Paul later."

"Okay. Call me and let me know when you'll be back?"

"I will. Bye."

Gabe hung up and stared out at the lake again. Wow! He'd hated the thought of her going to see Eric, but it sounded as though the guy had done her some good—maybe even done him a favor, too. He couldn't wait for her to get back. Couldn't wait to tell her his idea. It sounded as though she might be more open to it than he'd dared to hope. He'd find out tomorrow.

~ ~ ~

The next morning Renée pulled up at the address the woman on the phone had given her. Alison. That was her name. This felt so weird. She was going to meet the woman her husband had been seeing, hell sleeping with for the last five years. And going to tell her that she was…what? To blame for what he'd done? No. Partly responsible? She couldn't even buy that. All she could do was admit that which she accepted to be true. She hadn't loved him the way he'd wanted her to. Hadn't made him a priority, because she was too stubborn to see beyond her own priorities. She could admit that, and it would do her good. What this Alison person chose to do with that was none of Renée's business.

She got out of the car and walked up the path to the front door. It opened before she had chance to ring the bell. She hadn't known what to expect, but the woman standing there wasn't what she would have pictured.

"You must be Renée."

She nodded.

"Come on in."

She followed her through to a bright kitchen looking out onto a small, but neat backyard.

"Can I get you a drink or anything?"

"No thanks." Renée had no intention of being here any longer than necessary.

Alison looked decidedly uncomfortable. Renée had to wonder what must be going through her mind.

"So, what do you want to know?"

Alison met her gaze. "I don't know. I think you've answered most of questions just by coming here. He'd always painted you as the mean and nasty unfeeling bitch. He was the poor misunderstood man who just wanted to be loved. I'm not proud of being with a married man, but, in a way, it seemed okay."

Renée's heart was pounding. How could it ever be okay to have a relationship with another woman's husband? She didn't get it. "How was it okay?"

Alison shook her head. "I guess because we were united in the face of adversity. You were the evil oppressor, and he was the good guy who just wanted to be loved and understood."

Renée couldn't help the bitter laugh that escaped. "And all the while I had no clue what was going on. I just wondered why he didn't love me more."

Alison met her gaze. "But you never shared anything with him, never let him in, overrode him on all the decisions. Or is that just what he told me?"

She thought about it, then nodded slowly. "I guess it's all true. I just never saw it. Up until yesterday I would have told you that he never explained to me that he felt that way. Apparently though, he tried, and I just never listened. So, I guess what he told you was the truth. It's just a different truth from mine."

"Thank you."

"What for?"

"For being brave enough to be honest."

Renée smiled. "Strange as it sounds, I'm actually grateful for the chance. If Eric hadn't wanted me to come see you, I would probably never have realized how he saw it. How I was in his eyes. It's tough, but it's going to help me going forward in life." She looked at Alison. "What about you? What are you going to do? He's going to be going to prison for a long time by the looks of it."

Alison smiled back. "I know. Honestly, I don't know what I'm going to do about Eric. I'll go see him, but wanting to meet you was more about making my peace with myself. I needed to know who you are, whether everything he told me about you was a lie."

"It seems as though it wasn't really a lie, but it wasn't really the truth either."

Alison nodded. "That about sums it up. It doesn't change the fact that everything he spent on me was stolen from you."

"Oh, no. Not from me, that'd be bad enough. He stole from the charity. He stole money that people trusted us with, trusted us to do good with."

"I know." She met Renée's gaze. "But I still love him."

Renée found that hard to process. She shrugged. "That's your dilemma. I've got enough problems of my own." Even as they came out, the words surprised her. She didn't want to help, she just wanted to be done with all of this, get back to her own life and get on with it. She stood. "I wish you luck."

"Thank you." Alison followed her to the door. "Thank you for doing this. I have to ask though, did he blackmail you into it?"

Renée smiled. "Let's just say he offered me a trade. He said he'd give me an easy divorce and help clear my name if I came. It was more the fact that he pointed out my shortcomings that made me come though."

Alison nodded. "I'll go see him, tell him you did your best."

"Thanks."

# Chapter Twenty-Three

Gabe paced the kitchen in the Four Mile House. She should be back any time now. He couldn't wait to see her. He wanted to hear about her meeting with Eric—and with his girlfriend. More importantly though, he wanted to put his idea to her.
He heard her car pull up and went to the front door to meet her.

~ ~ ~

Renée pulled up outside the house and looked around. It was beautiful. She wouldn't deny that. As a child she'd dreamed of one day living in one of the big waterfront houses in town. It no longer held the same appeal though. Her house was her home. She'd realized over the last few weeks that it was her one connection with the past. Her last link to Chloe and to her dad, she didn't want to let go, not yet, and the way she felt, maybe never.
Gabe appeared at the front door. He was so handsome. She felt so lucky that for some reason a guy who looked like he did should think that she was beautiful. Standing there on the front steps he looked like a model in a magazine—or a real estate brochure. He certainly looked like he belonged here. This was his style. As she got out of the car and went to meet

him a thought struck her. Maybe by refusing to let go of her house she was clinging to the past? Perhaps what she should be doing was moving here? Accepting this place and this man as her future. She just didn't know.

She wrapped her arms around his neck and planted a kiss on his lips.

He held her to him and smiled down at her. "Hello yourself. I missed you."

"I missed you, too, Gabe. And I'm so sorry. It just all got to be too much, and hearing about you buying this place, well, it was the last straw." She reached up and pecked his lips. "My visit with Eric couldn't have come at a better time though. He really opened my eyes to just how stubborn I can be. I don't want to do that with you. I want to be with you. No matter what it takes." She looked around, wondering if this place could ever feel like home. "If you want us to live here, then I will."

"Don't worry, this isn't a set up. I'm not trying to get you used to the place."

"Are you sure?"

He nodded. "I'd love to do that, but I know better. I just wanted to cook us a nice meal in a real kitchen for once. It's been quite a couple of days, for both of us. I want to hear about Eric." He smiled. "And I do want to talk to you about our housing situation."

She swallowed. She'd known as much, and it was only fair.

"Don't look so scared. We're going to find a solution that works for both of us."

"Do you think we can though?"

He shrugged and led her inside. He poured two glasses of wine and handed her one before raising his own as he said, "Here's hoping."

She raised hers back to him and smiled. "Maybe with a bit more time I'll feel okay leaving my place. I know it's not fair on you the way things are." She looked around her. "This place is gorgeous, even I can see that."

"What do you like about it?"

She laughed. "What's not to like? It's huge. I like the floorplan. This kitchen is amazing. I love everything about the place."

"Can I ask you a question then?"

"What?"

"You love this place, but you don't want to give up your place to move here. I understand it's the memories that you don't want to lose. Are the memories tied up in the house itself, or in the place?"

She raised an eyebrow not understanding the difference.

"The place where the house is, the land, the orchard." He shrugged. "What I'm getting at is, what if we were to build a place like this out there? Would that work?"

She took a sip of her wine while she thought about it. "Maybe. I'd be sad to see the house torn down, but..." she nodded. "That might be our best compromise." She had a huge ball of dread in her stomach. He was doing so much to work with her and she was about to raise another obstacle, but it was too important to her not to.

"But?" asked Gabe.

"But I don't know how comfortable I would be with you doing that. It would have to be you paying for it all. I don't have any money, let alone the kind of money it would take to build a house like this."

Gabe pursed his lips. "That's something I want to talk to you about."

"What?"

"Do you want to sell me half the land?"

That didn't make any sense. "Why would you do that?"

"So that we're equal partners. Equal in owning the place, and I'm guessing it might make you feel more equal in everything else, too. I know it's not easy for you that our financial situations are so different. If you have the proceeds from selling twenty acres of land, you're going to feel a lot more independent."

It was true, but he'd only be doing it to make her feel better. She frowned as she thought about it. "You'd just be doing it for me though. There's no benefit to you in doing that."

He shook his head. "Not true. If you look at it from a cold hard business point of view, why would I build a house on land I don't own? What would happen if you get sick of me and wanted to get rid of me. That would lead to a very messy legal situation." He smiled. "It's not just for you, I'm covering my ass."

"Are you really?" She didn't believe that was his motivation at all, but it was a good point. And she wouldn't deny that the thought of having some money of her own made her feel a lot more comfortable about moving into the future with him.

He took her hand. "Not really, no. But it makes a lot of sense. What do you say, will you at least think about it?" He smiled. "And you know, if you had the money from the land sale you could maybe, lease the bakery, or something?"

She stared at him. "Ben told you about that?"

He nodded. "It'd be perfect for you."

"It would." Her mind raced with possibilities. It all seemed to be coming together. Part of her wanted to refuse his offer to buy the land, to build the house, but another part of her just wanted to accept—graciously for once in her life.

"It looks like things are finally coming together for you, if you'll let them?"

She nodded. "They are. You're the most important though. I couldn't do any of it without you."

He laughed. "You were determined to do all of it without me."

"I know. I'm sorry. But I'm getting there now. I'm learning, I'm letting you in. We're compromising and building together."

"I want to build so much more than a house with you, Renée." His eyes were that intense green as he looked down at her. "I want to build a life, a family, a future. Not just a house."

She felt tears prick her eyes. "That's what I want more than anything, Gabe."

"You told me that love, and family and happiness are the most important things in life."

She nodded. "And they are. I've been searching all the time for this ever elusive meaning and purpose. I get it now, what greater meaning and purpose could there be, than love and family and happiness?"

He smiled, "So what do you say? Will you marry me?"

Her heart felt as though it might explode in her chest, but she couldn't make any words come out.

~ ~ ~

Gabe held his breath. She wasn't answering him. She did have the biggest smile he'd ever seen on her face, but he needed to hear her answer.

Eventually she sputtered, "It's going to take a long while. My divorce isn't going to come through any time soon."

What did that mean? Was she putting him off? He had to ask. "Are you saying you don't want to?"

She threw her arms around his neck "I'm saying I do want to. More than anything in the world. I love you, Gabe. I want nothing more than to marry you. I just hope you'll still want me by the time I can."

"I will. I promise you I will. I want you for the rest of my life, Renée." He was pretty sure his smile matched hers—and he was damned sure that he meant it;

# A Note from SJ

I hope you enjoyed visiting Summer Lake and catching up with the gang. Please let your friends know about the books if you feel they would enjoy them as well. It would be wonderful if you would leave me a review, I'd very much appreciate it.
To come back to the lake and get to know more couples as they each find their happiness, you can check out the rest of the series on my website.

www.SJMcCoy.com

Coming next is a chance to catch up with the whole gang at Missy and Dan's Wedding in "The Wedding Dance"

Additionally, you can take a trip to Montana and meet a whole new group of friends. Take a look at my Remington Ranch series. It focuses on four brothers and the sometimes rocky roads they take on the way to their Happily Ever Afters.

There are a few options to keep up with me and my imaginary friends:

The best way is to Join up on the website for my Newsletter. Don't worry I won't bombard you! I'll let you know about upcoming releases, share a sneak peek or two and keep you in the loop for a couple of fun giveaways I have coming up :0)
You can join my readers group to chat about the books on Facebook or just browse and like my Facebook Page.

I occasionally attempt to say something in 140 characters or less(!) on Twitter

And I'm always in the process of updating my website at www.SJMcCoy.com with new book updates and even some videos. Plus, you'll find the latest news on new releases and giveaways in my blog.

I love to hear from readers, so feel free to email me at AuthorSJMcCoy@gmail.com.. I'm better at that! :0)

I hope our paths will cross again soon. Until then, take care, and thanks for your support—you are the reason I write!
Love
SJ

# PS Project Semicolon

You may have noticed that the final sentence of the story closed with a semi-colon. It isn't a typo. Project Semi Colon is a non-profit movement dedicated to presenting hope and love to those who are struggling with depression, suicide, addiction and self-injury. Project Semicolon exists to encourage, love and inspire. It's a movement I support with all my heart.

*"A semicolon represents a sentence the author could have ended, but chose not to. The sentence is your life and the author is you."*

- Project Semicolon

This author started writing after her son was killed in a car crash. At the time I wanted my own story to be over, instead I chose to honour a promise to my son to write my 'silly stories' someday. I chose to escape into my fictional world. I know for many who struggle with depression, suicide can appear to be the only escape. The semicolon has become a symbol of support, and hopefully a reminder – Your story isn't over yet

;

# Also by SJ McCoy

## Summer Lake Series
Love Like You've Never Been Hurt (FREE in ebook form)
Work Like You Don't Need the Money
Dance Like Nobody's Watching
Fly Like You've Never Been Grounded
Laugh Like You've Never Cried
Sing Like Nobody's Listening
Smile Like You Mean It
The Wedding Dance
Chasing Tomorrow
Dream Like Nothing's Impossible
Ride Like You've Never Fallen

*Coming next*
*Live Like There's No Tomorrow*

## Remington Ranch Series
Mason (FREE in ebook form)
Shane
Carter
Beau
Four Weddings and a Vendetta

*Coming next*
*Chance*

# About the Author

I'm SJ, a coffee addict, lover of chocolate and drinker of good red wines. I'm a lost soul and a hopeless romantic. Reading and writing are necessary parts of who I am. Though perhaps not as necessary as coffee! I can drink coffee without writing, but I can't write without coffee.

I grew up loving romance novels, my first boyfriends were book boyfriends, but life intervened, as it tends to do, and I wandered down the paths of non-fiction for many years. My life changed completely a few years ago and I returned to Romance to find my escape.

I write 'Sweet n Steamy' stories because to me there is enough angst and darkness in real life. My favorite romances are happy escapes with a focus on fun, friendships and happily-ever-afters, just like the ones I write.

These days I live in beautiful Montana, the last best place. If I'm not reading or writing, you'll find me just down the road in the park - Yellowstone. I have deer, eagles and the occasional bear for company, and I like it that way :0)

Made in the USA
San Bernardino, CA
01 June 2018